HC WIFE

BOOKS BY VALERIE KEOGH

Secrets Between Us

VALERIE KEOGH

THE
HOUSE
WIFE

bookouture

Published by Bookouture in 2019

An imprint of StoryFire Ltd.

Carmelite House
50 Victoria Embankment
London EC4Y 0DZ

www.bookouture.com

Copyright © Valerie Keogh, 2019

Valerie Keogh has asserted her right to be identified as the author of this work.

All rights reserved. No part of this publication may be reproduced, stored in any retrieval system, or transmitted, in any form or by any means, electronic, mechanical, photocopying, recording or otherwise, without the prior written permission of the publishers.

ISBN: 978-1-78681-689-4
eBook ISBN: 978-1-78681-688-7

This book is a work of fiction. Names, characters, businesses, organizations, places and events other than those clearly in the public domain, are either the product of the author's imagination or are used fictitiously. Any resemblance to actual persons, living or dead, events or locales is entirely coincidental.

For my husband Robert and my siblings, Patricia, Deirdre, Heather, Geraldine, Declan, Joyce and Brendan.

CHAPTER 1

Diane looked across the dinner table at her husband and knew she wasn't going to like what he said. It was something about his eyes, they looked at everything except her.

Paul's puppy-like brown eyes were the first thing she'd noticed about him when they'd met, that and his towering six-foot-two height. She'd been queuing for coffee in a café near where she worked and was trying to find change for the tip bowl. Fumbling in her purse, she'd dropped a pound coin on the floor and, as she'd stooped to pick it up, so did the man behind, both of them reaching for it at the same time. Her blue eyes had met his brown. He'd laughed, so had she. Moments later, he'd stood beside her table and asked if he could join her. 'All the other seats are taken,' he'd explained.

Looking around the almost-empty café, she had laughed and waved to a chair.

And that was that. Paul had only planned to be in Bristol for the day, but by the time they'd finished coffee they'd arranged to meet for dinner the following Saturday. After that, they'd spent every weekend together; Paul catching the train to Bristol after work every Friday to spend the weekend with her in her tiny rented apartment. At night, the two of them curled up in her small double bed, sometimes staying inside all weekend until he reluctantly dragged himself away on Sunday evening.

Six weeks after meeting, back in the same café, he'd gone down on one knee and asked her to marry him. It was crazy. Way too fast. But when he'd said he couldn't live without her for one more day, she'd found herself agreeing with him; she loved him, her friends loved him and, reluctant to ever drop off the wave of romantic euphoria, she had grinned and said yes.

They didn't wait, marrying as soon as they could arrange it and, a mere two months after meeting, Paul had carried her over the threshold of his London home. 'Welcome home, my darling wife,' he'd announced, setting her down in the hall of the beautiful Victorian house he owned in Copse Hill.

'Wow,' she'd said, her eyes wide. 'When you said you had a house, I wasn't expecting something so grand.'

Visibly pleased with her response, he'd taken her hand and brought her into the family room that stretched across the back of the house. 'When I bought the place, it was falling apart,' he'd explained, 'it was the only reason I could afford it. Back here,' he'd waved his hands around, 'there was a small kitchen, a couple of storage rooms and a dark, dingy sitting room. I had them all knocked into one and extended.'

'It's amazing,' Diane said, trying to take it all in, her eyes sparkling. She moved into the kitchen, fingers trailing along the cool granite of the counters, her eyes taking in the top-of-the-range cooker. She stopped in front of the huge American fridge-freezer. 'I've always wanted one of these,' she said, turning to him with a smile.

He grinned. 'There's not much in it apart from beer.'

Opposite the kitchen, the room spread into a living room where a large comfortable-looking L-shaped sofa faced a huge TV screen. Floor-to-ceiling windows overlooking the garden flooded the room with light and French doors opened onto a patio.

'It's just lovely,' Diane said, seeing his face light up with pleasure at her enthusiasm. 'Maybe we could get a big table for here?' She sketched a space between the kitchen and living area with her hands. 'There's plenty of room.'

'I usually eat in front of the TV,' he'd admitted, 'but I like that idea. We can go shopping at the weekend.' He'd pulled her close. 'We're going to be so happy,' he'd promised, kissing her lightly on the lips. 'Now, why don't I show you the bedroom?'

Diane had laughed and kissed him hard. 'How about,' she'd said, huskily, 'we start down here?'

An hour or so later, smiling as Paul snored softly beside her on the sofa, she'd squeezed out from under his arm, grabbed her clothes and headed off in search of the bathroom, dressing as she walked.

Turning the knob on the only other door in the hall, she found a small sitting room that looked over a pretty front garden. Decorated in dated floral wallpaper and with a clashing carpet, Diane guessed Paul had not got around to redecorating. It would, she'd thought, make a lovely room to sit in to read. She'd stood on the stairway and smiled. The house gave her a good feeling. She was going to be happy here, she thought, hugging herself with the sheer pleasure of life. *They* were going to be happy here.

She'd found a job almost immediately in what was grandly called the IT department of a haulage company, but was disappointed on her first day to discover it was a new department and, for the moment, she'd be working alone. Her office was located down a quiet corridor and, apart from the odd person who rang with queries, she rarely got a chance to speak with anyone.

'I'm not going to make new friends there,' she'd said to Paul after her first day.

He'd smiled at her and pulled her into his arms, whispering. 'You've got me, darling.'

She'd snuggled into him. He was right. She had everything she needed.

When her girlfriends visited from Bristol for a weekend, they oohed and aahed over the house, her happy life and the pubs she took them to where they flirted with the locals and drank too much wine. They'd promised to return, she'd promised to visit them but then she discovered she was pregnant and everything changed.

For a moment, just for an infinitesimal fraction of time, she'd felt terrified of the unstoppable roller coaster her life had become. But Paul's love was an anchor; she'd clung to it and the moment had passed. She'd looked around their great big house and, imagining the sound of children's laughter filling it, rested her hand on her flat belly and knew, despite the timing, that she wanted their baby.

So, it turned out, did Paul, a grin splitting his face almost from ear to ear when she'd told him.

'Seriously?' he'd said. 'I thought you were on the pill.'

She'd held her hands up. 'I am. I mean, I was. But so much has happened in the last few months with the wedding and moving to a new house, maybe I forgot? I've done the test. It's really happening. I—'

'That's fantastic news,' he'd interrupted her when he saw the look of concern on her face. He'd folded her into his arms. 'So, it's a bit sooner than we'd planned. It will be perfect. Don't worry.'

She hadn't worried but, sometimes, she'd felt overwhelmed.

Everything was different now, including, she realised with a quiver of sadness, Paul's eyes. They used to be warm, now they had the cold sheen of amber. Guilt whipped her. It was her fault; she'd put him through so much in the last few months, he'd been so supportive, so understanding no matter how many times she'd whispered, *I don't remember.* There had to be a way to make it up to him, to get them back on track.

She rested her elbows on the dining table they had bought together that first weekend, almost four years ago. Putting her fork down, she laid her hand on it, fingers splaying on the warm oak, trying to connect with times when they'd been happier. It seemed such a long time ago.

'Are you listening to me?'

She heard the touch of impatience in his voice and lifted her eyes to look at him. 'Sorry,' she said with a smile before picking up her fork again. 'What were you saying?'

'That I've read some research,' he said, cutting into his chicken.

She sighed and wished he'd get to the point. He was obviously afraid to upset her; she appreciated his concern, his gentle approach, but sometimes it had the opposite effect to what he'd intended. Like now. She could feel anxiety uncurling.

Oblivious, Paul took another mouthful, chewing and swallowing before he continued. 'It appears that children who mix with others from an early age are more advanced than their peers.'

'Really?' she said carefully, as she tried to read his face. He'd changed his workday smart suit for casual chinos and a T-shirt that emphasised his broad shoulders and athletic build. He seemed relaxed, but he still wasn't looking directly at her.

He pushed a lock of his mousy-brown hair from his face. 'According to the article, they learn better,' he said, 'and find it easier to interact with others. They cited a number of studies. There seems to be no doubt.' He looked across the table at her, finally meeting her eyes. 'I contacted a local nursery, Diane, they invited me to come and look around, so I did. The manager, Susan Power, is a great believer in starting young.' He dropped his gaze to concentrate once more on his dinner. 'We're in luck,' he said, 'they have a place available in one of the classes. I met the teacher, a Miss Rogers. Emma will love her.'

Emma looked up from her plate when she heard her name and grinned. 'Finish your dinner, sweetie,' Diane said, turning her plate around and watching her for a few minutes, smiling at the determination on her little face as she concentrated on getting peas onto her spoon. She wished she could stay looking at her but, from the corner of her eye, she saw Paul wasn't finished. His face still wore a pinched expression.

'She can start on Monday.'

It was a statement, not a suggestion inviting comment.

She let the breath she'd been holding out in a sigh, her fork falling from suddenly limp fingers to clatter noisily onto her plate. 'Monday. That's so soon. Isn't she too young?' Her knuckles whitened on the handle of the knife she still held. 'I feel like I've already missed so much.'

He heaved a sigh, reached across the table and caught her hand. 'It's a month since you came home from the clinic, Diane,' he said gently. 'You're doing fine.' He nodded toward where Emma was still chasing peas with her spoon. 'Mrs Power says she's the perfect age to start.'

'But Monday?' Diane said, looking at her daughter, her face angelic despite the rim of tomato sauce that circled her mouth. 'It's so soon.'

'She's three,' he said quietly. 'You don't remember, but we did discuss this at length before, months ago. You agreed then it was a good idea.'

'I did?' She had no recollection, but she knew that didn't mean anything. It was, after all, just one of hundreds of things she couldn't remember.

He sighed. 'Yes,' he said, squeezing her hand. 'It's even more important that she goes now, Diane, you've become quite clingy. It's not good for her. Or you.'

Too clingy? She let out a tremulous sigh. 'Couldn't we wait a few months?' she tried again, hating the note of desperation that had crept into her voice.

Taking his hand back, he concentrated on his dinner.

She pushed her plate away, waiting for him to say something, to agree to wait, just for a few months, even a few weeks. But she knew when she saw his set face that his mind was made up.

Finally, he put his cutlery down and pushed his plate away. 'These places are like gold dust, Diane,' he said. 'You have to grab them when you can.' He reached for her hand again, moving his thumb over the back of it in a soothing caress. 'It's best for Emma, you know it is.'

There was nothing more to be said.

CHAPTER 2

The next day, Saturday, Paul was up before her and making Emma breakfast when she arrived down. 'Hello, poppet,' she said, bending to give her daughter a kiss on her cheek and running a hand over her blonde curls.

'Hello, Mummy. I'm going to school,' she said, dipping her spoon into her cornflakes.

'I've been telling Emma about the fun she's going to have on Monday,' Paul said, catching her eye. 'She's very excited about meeting other children and making friends.' Diane forced her mouth into a smile. If she'd had the slightest hope that he would change his mind, it faded in the face of his words. Reluctantly, she conceded defeat.

'You'll need a school bag,' she said, when Emma had finished her breakfast. 'Let's go shopping and buy you one.' She lifted her out of her seat and held her tightly for a moment, until she wiggled free.

'You're squashing me, Mummy,' she said.

'Sorry, darling,' Diane said, putting her down and running a hand through her hair. 'I just love you so much.' She looked at Paul and pinned a smile on her face. 'Why don't you come with us? It'll be fun buying stuff.'

He put an arm around her shoulder and pulled her close in a quick hug. 'Impossible, I'm afraid. I know I usually take Emma on Saturdays, but I have so much work to do, sorry.'

Disappointed, she shrugged and reached for Emma's hand. 'Just you and me then, kiddo.'

Her local supermarket was a short ten-minute drive away. As usual, bustling with Saturday shoppers, it was chaotic and noisy. For safety, she'd have preferred to carry Emma, but she had insisted that she wanted to walk. Holding her hand tightly, Diane grabbed a trolley and headed toward the children's section where she picked up a tiny, brightly coloured back-pack. 'See,' she showed her, 'you can carry a drink and a snack in it.'

She added a few coloured markers and a pink jotter and Emma sat in the trolley playing with them while Diane finished the grocery shopping, piling stuff around her.

Back at home, with Emma asleep on the sofa and the groceries unpacked, she made herself a cup of tea and settled down at the table with her laptop to check out the nursery's website. They gave clear directions to it, and she was pleased to see it was only about a fifteen-minute drive away from Copse Hill. Her eyes scanned the rules and regulations. Nothing out of the ordinary, although they appeared quite rigid, especially about time-keeping. That didn't worry her, she was always on time; it's not like she had anywhere else to be these days.

Shutting the laptop, she turned to watch Emma sleep. Paul was right, she was being selfish wanting to keep her home for longer. Pressing her knuckles to her eyes, she swallowed. He seemed to think she was doing fine. She wasn't too sure, but there was really no point in crying.

She'd done too much of that already.

CHAPTER 3

Monday came around too quickly. The nursery didn't start until nine fifteen, but Diane was up and dressed before eight, determined to have everything just right. She wanted to look the part amongst the other parents; efficient, together, in control. She took her time choosing the right clothes, eventually pulling on tailored navy trousers and a pale blue cashmere jumper she rarely wore. She applied a little more make-up than usual and finished with a scarf.

It was all armour, she knew; a thin façade to hide behind so they wouldn't see how nervous she really was. She'd been home a month and Paul said she was doing fine; she just wished she could believe him.

It was stupid to be nervous about meeting the other mothers, but deep down she was desperate to make a good impression and maybe even make some friends. She hadn't made new friends since she'd moved to London, and her plans to return to work after Emma was born had fallen by the wayside when she just couldn't face leaving her with a childminder. 'I'll go back to work when she's older,' she'd said to Paul. 'I don't want to give up permanently.'

She'd settled into being a wife and mother quickly, surprising herself at how content she was. Emma had brought her and Paul closer than ever, but then, just after Emma's first birthday, he was promoted to partner in the accountancy firm he worked for and things changed. It meant more money, but more responsibility.

Even when he was home, at evenings and weekends, he spent hours in the office working.

Proud of her successful husband, she tried not to complain, but found herself feeling increasingly lonely. Her Bristol friends had drifted away into their own busy lives and, without a job, she didn't really get a chance to socialise. Then, almost two months ago now, things really fell apart for her and, so far, despite what Paul said, she'd not managed to put them back together again.

She ran her fingers through blonde hair that was just a few shades darker than Emma's. Sometimes she had highlights done but, lately, she hadn't bothered. She thought about tying it up, but instead brushed it and left it loose.

With a final glance in the mirror, she headed downstairs and found Paul in the kitchen dabbing the crust of his toast with a little extra marmalade. He looked at her carefully and nodded. 'You look very smart,' he said, 'but I'd lose the scarf, it's not really you.' Diane blushed, her hand going to the silk scarf around her neck and pulling it away. 'Better?' she asked.

'Much.' He checked his watch. 'I'd better go,' he said, and reached to give her a kiss on the cheek. 'Don't be nervous. It *is* the best thing for her, Diane.'

'Yes, of course, I know,' she said, trying to sound like she believed it.

At ten to nine, she bundled an excited, babbling Emma into the car, strapped her into her child seat and gave her the backpack to hold.

As soon as the car started to move, Emma began to sing a song Diane had taught her, forgetting most of the words and making them up. Diane smiled, her eyes flicking to the rear-view mirror to admire how much her beautiful daughter had grown over the last few months. There was so much she couldn't remember, so much she'd missed. She could hardly bear to let Emma out of her sight for a minute, how was she going to manage a few hours?

It was tempting to keep driving, to pass the nursery and go somewhere exciting for the day. Maybe to the coast? But as Emma bobbed her head to her own song, curls bouncing, she knew her little girl needed this, as did she.

Pulling into a generous car park at the front of the nursery, she parked beside another car where a heavily pregnant woman was shutting her car door, a small boy hanging from her other hand. Lifting Emma out, she helped her on with the back-pack. 'You look so grown up,' she said, wanting to pull her into her arms and never let her go. Instead, she took her daughter's hand and walked the short distance to the front door, following in the pregnant woman's footsteps, feeling that first-day awkwardness of not knowing where to go or what to do.

Inside the double front doors, there was a large reception area where several adults stood, children close by, collective voices raised in chatter and laughter. Everyone seemed to know one another. It was incredibly noisy and Diane, used to the quiet of home, felt overwhelmed. Tension knotted her stomach. It wasn't too late to change her mind; she could tell Paul she got a bad feeling from the place. She squeezed Emma's hand and looked down at her, searching for a sign of the same anxiety, only to find a look of pure excitement in her eyes as she took in her surroundings. Diane swallowed the lump in her throat, and tried to relax.

On the dot of nine fifteen, a door opened into the reception from a corridor behind and three staff members entered and began huddling their charges together with a nod and a word of reassurance to each parent, before leading them away.

A thin woman in a dark-green shift dress entered and made her way through the group, smiling and chatting to various adults and children before purposefully making her way over to Diane.

'You must be Mrs Andrews,' she said, holding out her hand. 'I'm Susan Power, the manager here.'

She was tall, maybe three inches taller than Diane's five-seven, her hair cut in a tight pixie style that seemed to exaggerate her height. But her eyes were warm and twinkling and Diane liked her immediately. She held out her free hand. It was the wrong one, but Susan took it with a reassuring smile, holding onto it as she turned her attention to Emma. 'And you must be Emma,' she said, stooping down. 'You're very welcome here and I know you're going to be very happy.'

If Diane was worried about any separation issues her daughter might have, they were quickly laid to rest as Emma, with a beaming smile, released her hand to reach for Susan's.

'She's going to be just fine, Mrs Andrews,' she said, looking back to Diane with a wealth of reassurance in her voice. 'We'll see you back here at one,' she added, before concentrating on Emma. Diane didn't know whether to be relieved or heartbroken.

Back in her car, she sat with the window open, listening intently for the merest whisper of a scream, knowing she'd instantly recognise Emma's voice above them all; that deep-seated, motherly instinct that would send her running to the rescue.

She'd heard nothing by the time her mobile rang almost an hour later. It wasn't necessary to look at it to know it was Paul. He rang at around the same time every morning to ask how her day was going. She shut the window before answering, unwilling to explain why she needed to stay outside the nursery; he didn't need to know how much she still worried. 'Everything is okay,' she said as cheerfully as she could. 'No,' she answered when he asked if Emma had been upset, 'she was completely fine.'

Hanging up, she opened the window to listen again. A light breeze had picked up, drifting through the copper beech hedge that surrounded the school, causing the dried old leaves to rustle and whisper. It was a pleasant sound and for a moment she relaxed, her eyes drifting shut. It was seconds before she realised the whisper had changed; now it wasn't quite so pleasant. A shiver ran down her spine and her eyes flew open as it came again, a cry, a child's sad cry. She pushed open the car door and ran towards the school, reaching for the doorbell as her head tilted to listen again. But now, all she could hear was the faint sound of childish laughter. Dropping her hand, she stood a moment before, with a shake of her head, she went back to the car and sat staring at the front door until it opened at twelve forty-five.

Driving home, with Emma happily babbling away in the back, she promised herself that the next day she would go straight home after dropping her off; she'd drink coffee, watch daytime TV, tidy the house – anything to fill the hours until it was pick-up time, anything to stop her going crazy.

Again. She looked at her reflection in the rear-view mirror.

She shook her head, brushing the thought away. Perhaps now she should go back to work? It was what she'd always planned to do once Emma was old enough but now, remembering her last job and the small, isolated office she had worked in, the idea filled her with dread. What if she ended up working somewhere like that again? No, she needed something different, something safe and sociable.

At home, when Emma had settled for her nap, she made herself some coffee, switched on her laptop and spent a couple of hours looking for options, her face gradually losing its tense, worried expression as they opened before her. That evening, over dinner, she mentioned to Paul she was thinking of doing some kind of voluntary work. 'Now that Emma is in nursery,' she said, almost nervously, worried he'd think that it was still too soon.

'What a good idea,' he said, reaching across and squeezing her hand. 'It will be good for you to get out of the house and take more interest in things again.'

She rested her hand on his, grateful he hadn't asked why she didn't consider going back to work. 'I emailed a couple of places today to see if they had anything,' she said. 'I'll send you the links, see what you think.'

By late morning the next day, only one place had replied. A charity shop in a nearby shopping centre was looking for volunteer staff. They'd be delighted if she could do a few hours a week and asked her to drop in and see them.

'I'm going to call in after I drop Emma off tomorrow,' she told Paul that evening. She shrugged. 'I hope they like me.'

Paul laughed. 'You're willing to work for nothing,' he said, 'of course they'll like you!'

She felt energised, better than she had in a while. Perhaps Paul was right, and she *was* doing fine. Okay, it wasn't a high-powered career move, but even a part-time position as a volunteer was a huge step forward for her.

Choosing her clothes with care the next morning, she eventually settled on jeans, a white shirt and a navy jacket. She thought a scarf might look good, but she remembered Paul's comment the last time and decided against it. The shopping centre was only a short drive past the nursery, so she dropped Emma off, took a deep breath and headed off, feeling apprehensive but excited. It felt so good to be doing something normal.

The charity shop was tucked away in a quiet corner of a shopping centre, the small display window crammed with too much stuff, the door almost invisible under layers of posters, stickers and adverts. One large central poster, battling to stand out, indicated that the shop supported a local hospice. *A good cause*, Diane thought, pushing open the door.

Inside, the shop was cramped and jammed with the usual charity shop offerings; racks of clothes, shelves stacked with books and more packed with china and ornaments. A chest-high counter stood in one corner towards the back. From behind it, a plump woman with a mop of tight, old-lady curls raised her hand in greeting. 'You must be Diane,' she said, and then, almost before her nod had finished, she turned and yelled out, 'She's here!'

'Excellent,' replied another woman, entering the shop through a door at the back and approaching Diane with both hands extended and a welcoming smile on her face. Heavy eye make-up accentuated sloe-shaped eyes and her lips were bright glossy red. 'I'm the manager,' she said, taking her hand in both of hers and holding it for a long moment, assessing her without embarrassment.

A rush of anxiety flooded Diane, her breath catching, but she let it out slowly when the manager smiled and dropped her hand. She felt as if she'd passed her first test.

'Call me Red,' the manager said with a smile that seeped into the laughter lines that fanned her eyes as she lifted a lock of her rich red hair. 'I doubt if I'd know how to answer to my real name any more.'

Leading her through the shop into an office at the back, she gestured for Diane to sit on a well-worn chair on one side of a grey metal desk before taking an even more decrepit one on the other side. As she sat, the chair creaked alarmingly. Seeing Diane's eyes widen, she chuckled. 'Don't worry, it always does that.'

The office was small, over-stuffed plastic bin-bags filling what little available space was left. Red didn't make excuses or explain, she sat back, looked at her and said, 'Tell me about yourself.'

If it was an interview, it was the most casual one Diane had ever done. She twisted her hands in her lap and spoke quietly. 'I've worked in a variety of IT roles over the years,' she explained. 'When my daughter was born three years ago, I– I stopped working to look after her.' She waited for a comment and when none came, she continued, 'She's just started in nursery, every morning nine fifteen to one.' Annoyed to hear a quiver of nervousness in her voice, she cleared her throat and finished, 'I'm feeling at a bit of a loose end so thought maybe it would be good to spend my time helping out somewhere.'

'You didn't want to go back to work after your maternity leave was over?' Red asked. Her face was kind, her question was more curious than judgemental, so Diane decided on the truth.

'I wanted to stay at home with Emma for the first couple of years. And then,' she tried to relax her shoulders and took a deep breath. 'I had a bit of a breakdown.' When there was no reaction on the other woman's face, she continued, her voice a little stronger. 'I'm much better now, obviously, but working in IT can be quite stressful and I don't feel able to go back to it just yet.' There was only so much truth she was going to offer for a voluntary position.

'It's more common than people might think,' Red said, tapping her pen on her desk. 'I can do a Disclosure and Barring Service check online now, if you're interested. And if you can give me the name of two referees, I'll follow them up and you can start as soon as they're through.'

Diane stared in surprise. 'I've got it?' The tight knot of tension eased slightly.

Red smiled. 'Once the DBS comes back, yes. How many mornings would you like to come in?'

How many? The knot eased a little more. 'I think I'd like to do three,' she said, pleased when she saw a look of satisfaction on Red's face.

'Great, okay, I just need a few details for the DBS. Current and previous address and your national insurance number.' She scribbled the information down. 'And, finally, two referees?' she said, looking up from the pad she'd been writing on.

Diane hadn't thought this far ahead, surprised it was all happening so quickly. Was this too much, too soon?

Red seemed to sense a change in mood. She sat back in her chair and said nothing for a few minutes. But her calm, unthreatening manner had the required effect and Diane felt herself relax.

'Sorry,' she said, 'it's been a while. Yes, of course, I can provide two referees. Geoff Summerton, he was the CEO of the company I worked for, here in London; and Ralph Barton, he was my manager in the last job I had in Bristol.' She watched as Red wrote down the names and contact details.

Twenty minutes after she'd gone in, she was back out on the street with a bounce in her step. This had been such a good idea. It was time, as Paul had pointed out, that she got out of the house more.

And she hadn't lied. She *was* almost better. Red had no need to know that she'd spent three weeks in a private clinic, nor did she need to know that there was a large part of the last year, weeks and months, that she couldn't remember. And if there were times when Diane was distressed and terrified at the huge absences in her memory, well, she didn't need to know that either.

CHAPTER 4

Everything moved very quickly. Red rang the next day to say her DBS check had come through. 'You mentioned wanting to do three days,' she said, 'would you be happy to do Monday to Wednesday every week?' she asked.

'Perfect,' Diane said and agreed to start the following week. Hanging up, she clasped her hands together in satisfaction. It was a big step in the right direction. And, for the first time in ages, she didn't need Paul to tell her she was doing well, she actually felt it.

The following Monday, she fussed about what to wear, settling in the end for jeans and a long-sleeved T-shirt. She tied her shoulder-length hair back in a ponytail and looked in the mirror, pleased with the young, *fun* woman who looked back.

Paul laughed at her excitement. 'Maybe, you should have got a proper job,' he said. 'It's a shame to waste all that enthusiasm in a volunteer role.'

She looked at him, hurt, but he'd already turned away. 'This is already quite a big step for me, Paul,' she said to his back. 'Maybe, in a few months, I'll be able to go back to what I used to do.'

He might have missed the look on her face, but he couldn't ignore the tone of her voice and he turned to her. 'I was joking,' he said with a smile, reaching for her and pulling her into a hug. 'It's good to see you so enthusiastic. You'll be back to your old self before you know it.'

He gave her a kiss on the cheek, released her and picked up his briefcase. 'Good luck,' he said, and then, 'nice ponytail.'

She watched him go with a lump in her throat. Was that another joke, or a compliment? Pulling the ponytail down, she tried desperately to ignore the anxiety she felt creeping up on her.

Dropping Emma at nursery, she made her way to the charity shop where Red was waiting for her, a smile on her lips that did nothing to dispel Diane's nerves.

The work wasn't difficult and, apart from the dodgy cash register, a reject from a shop that was upgrading, there was nothing complicated about it. Beth, the plump woman she'd seen the first morning, took her under her wing. 'There's a knack to using the till,' she explained kindly, 'once I've shown you a few times, you'll have no problem.'

In fact, Diane had no problem after the first attempt, serving the next few customers under Beth's supervision. She was a pleasant, chatty woman, full of useful information that she delighted in imparting to anyone who would listen. 'Do you know,' she told Diane, with wide eyes, 'that although we're asked to separate bottles for the bottle-bank into clear, brown and green, they are picked up by a single truck and all tossed in together, higgledy-piggledy.'

Diane hadn't known. She shook her head in amazement, and Beth took this as an invitation to continue imparting tit-bits of useful information for the next couple of hours as customers milled in and out of the shop. It had been a long time since Diane had chatted to anyone apart from Paul so she enjoyed the easy conversation, joined in with the occasional comment and began to relax.

After a quick tea break, she was moved over to the task of going through the donated items with one of the other volunteers, Anne, a very thin woman with a mop of curls tied up with a wildly colourful silk scarf. Diane took to her immediately, admiring her exuberance and confidence. Like Beth, she was pleasantly chatty and she felt more tension melt away. She was going to enjoy working here, maybe even make friends.

'Anything not in a saleable condition is packed into black bin-bags,' Anne explained, tearing a bag off a roll and shaking it open. 'Clothes are labelled as *material*, the rest as *junk*. The bags are then stored in Red's office to be picked up at a later date.'

'What happens to them then?' Diane asked, tying a knot in the top of one she'd filled.

'All the material is sold to a firm that recycles it to make paper or card, the other stuff is brought to the recycling centre and it goes into landfill.'

'Some of this stuff is just junk,' Diane said, opening, and then immediately shutting the box she'd just opened. 'Do people just use us as an easy way of getting rid of their rubbish?'

Anne grinned. 'See, you've only been here a couple of hours and you have it sussed.' She pulled Diane's box over, opening it again and rummaging through. 'Sometimes, there's something decent under the rubbish.' Then she started to laugh. 'Look!' she said, holding up a black leather basque with one hand and a riding crop with the other. Diane looked at Anne with wide eyes and then she started to giggle. Before long, they were holding onto each other as tears of laughter ran down their cheeks.

It had been a long time since she'd laughed with such abandonment. It felt so good and washed away the last of the tension, leaving her more relaxed than she'd been since…she couldn't remember when. She was still chuckling when she relieved Beth, who was manning the cash register. 'Time for coffee,' she said with a smile, stepping aside to let her pass.

She settled onto the stool behind the counter and let her eyes sweep around the small shop. A harried-looking woman in the children's section was picking up and putting down game after game with a look of frustration on her face. Just as Diane began to wonder if she should go and offer her some assistance, the woman turned on her heel and left. The only other customer was a well-dressed woman of about her height with a sleek bob that made her automatically smooth a hand over her own hair. She was looking at the books with the air of someone who wasn't in a hurry, so Diane rested herself back on the high stool in the small cluttered space behind the counter and waited. She let her mind wander, as it so often did, to Emma. What was she doing right now? How was she settling in? Was she happy? For those three long weeks at the clinic, thoughts of her precious daughter were all that kept her sane. She shook her head slowly. How often people used the words *crazy* and *sane* without thinking about what they really meant.

Forcing her brain to concentrate on more mundane things, she made a mental list of things she needed to pick up in the supermarket that afternoon. When the door jingled, she looked up just in time to see that a customer she hadn't even noticed enter, was now leaving. She shook herself for being so absent-minded, calling a quick *goodbye, thank you for calling*, as she'd been advised to do by Beth, the door closing before she'd finished the words.

Laughter drifted though from the office. She looked over, wondering if Anne was showing Beth the bondage stuff, smiling as she imagined Beth's look of horror. Distracted, she didn't notice the woman with the bob until she was almost at the counter.

'I'll take these,' she said, putting three paperbacks on the counter and reaching into her bag for her purse.

Diane stood to take the books, checked the price on the easy-peel sticker on the front cover and pressed the relevant keys on the register. 'That's one pound fifty, please. Would you like a bag?' she asked with a smile, reaching down to the plastic bin under the counter.

When she didn't get an answer, she looked up to ask the question again, stopping in surprise when she saw the woman had frozen, staring at her with a look of shocked recognition on her face.

Diane tilted her head, slightly taken aback. 'Do I know you?' The woman was her age, maybe a year or two younger. She was almost sure she'd never met her before. But then again, these days, she never seemed very sure of anything.

The woman's cold grey eyes swept over her, her well-shaped lips turned down in a sneer. She looked as if she wanted to say something but, without a word, she turned and left the shop, leaving Diane stunned and staring after her until she vanished from sight. Perhaps she thought she was someone else? Unsure of what had just happened, and feeling completely on edge, she looked down at the three books still clasped in her hand, and then at the register in bemusement. She'd not been shown how to void a transaction.

In a panic, she fumbled with a few keys, which only served to produce an error message on the screen and a strange sound she'd never heard in her brief training. Frustrated, she pressed another – she had a degree in information technology, for goodness sake, how difficult could it be? But this time, the register emitted a low-pitched whine.

She knew she ought to leave it and explain to Beth when she came back, but would she perhaps quiz her about *why* the woman had changed her mind? Maybe she'd think it was Diane's fault, that she wasn't approachable enough, that she wasn't right for the job. She knew it was an overreaction, but she couldn't ignore the sudden cold quiver of failure.

Picking up the books again, she realised with relief that she hadn't read any of them. The easiest thing to do would be to simply buy them for herself. Reaching down, she pulled her handbag from under the counter and rummaged around inside it for her purse, paid the one pound fifty into the register and put the purse and books into her bag. Job done, no explanations necessary.

Swinging her bag back under the counter, she stared back at the door wondering about the woman's unsettling behaviour. Perhaps she looked like someone the woman knew? But what had this doppelgänger done to deserve such a reaction? The thought sent a shiver down her spine and suddenly, without warning, the room started to spin around her. She tried to find the stool to sit down, stepping back and turning to reach for it, missing and knocking it over instead. As the edges of her vision faded to black, she knew was going to faint. Her hands flailed as she turned again, reaching for the counter, her hands finding the register, holding on to it, steadying herself before her vison faded completely and her legs gave way. She collapsed, pulling the register with her as she fell, grunting with pain as it landed on her before it rolled onto the floor with a loud crash.

The noise brought the other staff running. Beth and Anne crowded around her, squeezing into the small space to loom over her with anxious faces. Red, the last to arrive, took one look, sized up the situation and moved them back. 'Are you okay?' she asked, bending down beside her. 'What on earth happened?'

Diane took a deep breath. It hurt. She held her arm tightly to her side and struggled to sit up. 'I'm okay,' she said, rushing to put their minds at rest. She looked at the register in pieces on the floor beside her. 'I tripped and fell against it,' she lied, hearing the catch in her throat. What had come over her? 'I'm so sorry, it's destroyed.'

'Don't worry about that, for goodness sake,' Red said, 'it's time we got a new one anyway. I'm only concerned about you, you look white as a sheet. Perhaps you should go to hospital?'

Dizzy, confused and mortified, all Diane wanted to do was get out of there. 'No, I'm fine,' she said, feeling another pinch of pain in her ribs as she tried to move. If she'd broken a rib there was no point going to hospital, they'd only suggest painkillers. With Red's help, she managed to get to her feet and leaned against the counter. She still felt uneasy and weak. 'I think I'll go home, if that's okay?'

'Of course, but are you sure you'll be okay to drive? Why don't you wait a bit?' Red said, continuing to be concerned at her pallor.

Diane shook her head and pushed away from the counter. 'Honestly, I'm fine. I'll just get my bag and go.'

'Don't bend down, I'll get it,' Anne said, squeezing past and ducking down to pull the bag from under the counter. The group fell silent as she lifted it up and held it out for Diane. She hadn't closed it properly and the books she'd carelessly tossed in were sticking up, the red easy-peel stickers they used to price them, glaringly obvious.

'I paid for them,' she said, too quickly. Looking around at their wary faces, she felt her face flush with colour. She could have explained about the woman and her strange behaviour, but it was too late, whatever she said now wouldn't matter. Grabbing her bag from Anne, she fled the shop as fast as she could without looking back.

By the time she reached her car, her eyes were brimming with unshed tears. She was good at that, at keeping them in until she was somewhere private. Safely inside the car, she rested her forehead on the steering wheel and let them fall. She cried for a long time, tears of frustration, sadness and disappointment peppering her jeans until each knee was soaked through with her misery. Finally, she sat back and checked the time, swearing softly under her breath when she saw it was almost time to go and collect Emma.

Drying her face with her sleeve, she looked in the rear-view mirror, tears gathering again when she saw the state of her face. Blotchy from crying, streaked with black from the mascara she'd so carefully applied that morning, she was a mess. There wasn't time to go home first; in desperation, she pulled a tissue from her pocket, spat on it and tried to clean up. She'd pass, she guessed looking in the mirror, as long as nobody looked too closely. *The story of my life*, she thought with a sigh as she started the engine and headed from the car park, joining the heavy traffic until she could turn off for the nursery, her heart still thumping in her chest.

Finding some sunglasses in the glovebox, she managed to keep her head down as she collected Emma and if anybody noticed anything amiss, they were too polite to say. Emma was her usual bubbly self, chatting away as she drove the short journey home. Listening to her helped put the morning into perspective. It was a volunteer job; she'd ring them tomorrow and say she wasn't going back. Maybe, in a few months, she'd try something else. Remembering Paul's remark, she shook her head; she was a long way from getting a proper job.

Back at home, she rummaged in a cupboard for painkillers and took two with a mouthful of water. Making a sandwich for Emma, she sat with her while, between mouthfuls, she chatted about her morning and the other children she played with. What Miss Rogers said about this and that played a large part in her anecdotes. Perhaps Paul was right, she thought, watching her animated face; it was good for her to mix with other children rather than being stuck at home with her.

After lunch, she settled Emma down for a nap, pulling a blanket from the back of the sofa and tucking it around her, looking down on the sleeping child and thanking her lucky stars for her. She felt a lump in her throat. Without her, without her and Paul, she wasn't sure what she'd do.

She turned away. Emma would sleep solidly for at least an hour, giving her a chance to relax and get some perspective on her day. She made coffee, making it stronger than usual, feeling the need for the extra boost. With a final glance towards the sofa, she opened the door into the hallway, and, leaving it open behind her, went into the lounge.

The brightly coloured family room that stretched across the back of the house was Paul's favourite space in the house. But the small lounge was *hers*. She'd loved it from the first day she'd seen it and asked Paul to decorate it in soft pastel shades. 'You never use it anyway,' she'd said when he'd argued for brighter colours. 'I'd like it to be a room where I can come to read.' He'd conceded, and for a brief moment she'd felt empowered and the room became her place of comfort, somewhere she could relax and be herself.

She stood at the bay window, the coffee mug cupped between her hands, and looked out across the front garden, wondering what she'd plant in the flower beds this year. Last year, she'd gone with pink and white. Maybe yellow this year, she thought before movement on the pathway across the road caught her attention and she looked over, expecting to see a neighbour or a passer-by. But it was neither.

She squeezed her eyes shut for a moment. This wasn't possible. Opening them, she looked across the road, squinting to make out the details. It was her, the woman from the shop, staring directly at her; the same navy coat, the same sleek bob she had admired. It was definitely her.

Disbelief and a sudden choking fear made her jerk back, the mug falling from her hands, hot coffee spilling as it fell. Ignoring it, and swallowing the lump in her throat, she reached for the blind cord with shaking fingers and closed them with a snap. But she didn't move away. She was imagining it, she had to be. Holding her breath, she lifted one slat and peered through. She was still there.

Backing away, one slow step after another, her foot landed on the handle of the fallen mug and she stumbled, falling back onto the sofa and collapsing into it with a grunt of pain from the jolt to her ribs.

Who on earth was she? What did she want? She felt her stomach lurch and knew she was going to be sick. Stumbling out the open door, she made it to the downstairs toilet just in time, sending all the coffee she'd managed to drink splashing into the toilet bowl.

She stayed a few minutes and then stood and wiped her face with the hand towel, taking it with her as she went back and dropping it onto the puddle of coffee on the floor. The slat she'd raised to look out still sat askew. Stepping closer, she took a steadying breath and squinted through the gap. The woman had gone. She reached out, raised the slat fully and looked up and down the road. Definitely gone. She turned away, heaving a sigh of relief that became a gulp of despair. Everything had gone wrong. Her wonderful new start ruined before it had really begun. And now this. She peered out across the street again. There was nobody there, had there ever been? Fear curled inside. Was this what happened last time? Failure overwhelmed her. She wanted to roll up on the sofa and cry, but a sound from next door told her Emma was awake, she must have disturbed her. 'I'm coming,' she called, wiping her eyes with the sleeve of her T-shirt, taking deep breaths to try and find some sense of calm. With a final look at the mess on the floor, she shut the door and went to see to her daughter, pasting a smile on her face as she moved.

Emma was still curled up on the sofa.

'How about I read you a story?' she asked her, coughing to disguise the thickness in her voice.

'Yes,' the sleep-groggy voice replied.

'Yes, what?'

'Yes, please,' Emma said with a grin, scrambling out from under the blanket and throwing her arms around Diane's legs.

Already choked, she tousled the blond curls. 'Go get your book, darling,' she said. 'Mummy's just going for a wee.'

By the time she came back, a few minutes later, Emma was sitting with her book open beside her. Diane, her face washed, a smile pinned firmly in place, sat beside her and read the tale of Henry the Hedgehog from cover to cover.

When it was finished, she left Emma looking at the pictures while she went to make herself another coffee, her eyes shutting in dismay when she saw the almost empty milk carton. She'd planned to go shopping after the charity shop. Understandably, she'd forgotten. It was the last thing she wanted to do now, but they couldn't do without milk. For a moment, she debated ringing Paul to ask him to pick some up on the way home. But that would entail explanations she didn't want to give. No, she took a deep, shaky breath. She had to go out.

'Let's go shopping,' she said to Emma, who had thrown the book to one side and was sitting on the floor of the family room playing with her toys. She smiled as she dropped her toys and stood without complaint. She was such a well-behaved child; she must be doing something right.

With their coats on and the car keys in her hand, they were ready to go but she hesitated at the front door. 'Just hang on a second,' she said and went into the lounge. She took a deep breath and peeped through the blinds. The road was empty. Of course, it was. But, outside, she couldn't resist a quick look up and down the empty road. Her side ached and she realised lifting Emma into the car was beyond her, so she made a game of it, encouraging her to climb into the car and up into her child seat. Emma, always happy to have a new game to play, was begging to try again as she strapped her in.

As soon as the car started moving and the radio came on, Emma started to sing. Usually, Diane would smile and join in, but today she was too distracted, checking out every woman they drove past, the car slowing and accelerating until, finally, a car that had been behind her for a few minutes honked its horn and overtook. As he passed, he gave her a hand gesture that she had no difficulty in interpreting.

She knew she was being ridiculous. The incident this morning had upset her, but there was nothing more to it. There definitely had been a woman outside her house but she was probably lost or looking to buy one of the houses that were for sale on the street and was just having a look around the neighbourhood. Diane was so stressed that a vague similarity made her think she was the woman from the charity shop. A stupid coincidence, nothing more. Emma was singing the chorus of a nursery rhyme, she joined in and, a few minutes later, had cheered herself up a little.

Pulling into a space at the supermarket, she helped Emma climb down by herself, still enjoying this new game, but when Diane insisted on holding her hand as they walked through the car park, Emma's mood changed. *I don't need this*, she thought, rubbing a hand across her forehead where tension was starting to throb. Honestly, she was getting more stubborn every day. Just like her father.

Diane pointed toward the shopping trolleys. 'Do you want to sit in the seat?' She took a deep breath and, using the arm on her uninjured side, managed to get Emma into the seat without causing too much discomfort and her child's face was suddenly cheerful once more.

As she steered the trolley into the supermarket, she tried to busy herself with her list but couldn't help herself looking for that navy coat, that sleek bob. She knew she was being irrational, but she couldn't stop. Her hands were slick on the handle of the trolley, her stomach a tight knot. She looked down at the trusting face of her daughter and forced herself to smile. She was being ridiculous. Crazy. She needed to relax. Was this how it started the last time? With paranoia? Was she having another breakdown? If only she could remember.

Suddenly, she felt soft warm hands on hers and, looking down, saw Emma's two chubby hands, grounding her. *Emma*. Three weeks in that clinic, missing her every moment, and months before that where she couldn't remember being with her. She wasn't missing out on any more. Taking a deep breath, she smiled down at her. 'How about we get some ice cream to have later, would you like that?'

'Banana ice cream!' Emma squealed, her face lighting up with her smile.

Diane bent forward and planted a kiss on her soft curls, breathing in her smell, feeling a lump in her throat at her absolute unconditional love. 'Let's go then,' she said, pushing the trolley ahead, keeping her eyes on her daughter. Nothing else mattered.

The pleasure and excitement in Emma's wide eyes as she took the cold tub of ice cream was just the remedy Diane needed. She'd had a bad morning. There was nothing wrong with her that spending time with this gorgeous, enchanting little girl wouldn't heal.

Emma dropped the tub of ice cream into the trolley and rubbed her cold fingers, the look on her face making Diane laugh. She took her hands in her own and rubbed them. 'Better?'

Blonde curls bouncing, Emma nodded. 'It hurt,' she said, continuing to look at her fingers with a hint of suspicion.

'We'll get our revenge when we eat it later,' Diane said, ruffling her hair. Feeling so much better, putting the earlier silliness aside, she pushed the trolley forward. 'Let's go home.'

She headed towards the checkout and unloaded her purchases onto the conveyor belt. She'd forgotten to bring bags, of course, so had to buy two, packing them up as the assistant took her money and handed her the change.

'Thanks,' she said with a nod, and pushed the trolley away. 'We'll have a bowl each as soon as we get home,' she said, to Emma. 'Maybe, we'll even…'

The words died on her lips as she caught sight of a woman in a navy coat standing near the exit. Her heart in her mouth, for one terrifying moment she thought it was *her* but then the woman turned to wave at another, both women soon smiling and hugging.

She was just being silly. *Paranoid.* Maybe it *was* happening again.

CHAPTER 5

Outside, she looked around, feeling her heart thump. Taking a deep breath, she moved as fast as she could to push the trolley through the car park, the wheels rattling noisily, her badly packed bags tilting so that items started to fall out and slide about. She didn't care, she just wanted to get to her car. Luckily for her, rather than being frightened, Emma thought it was a game. 'Faster, faster!' she squealed, waving her hands and chuckling when Diane did just that.

Unlocking the car with a press of the fob as she approached, she opened the boot and threw the bags in, ignoring the pasta packet that had somehow split open. It would be all over the boot before she got home, but she didn't care. The other loose items she flung in on top and banged the door shut. Lifting Emma out of the trolley with a wince, she pushed the trolley away from the car with her foot and left it there.

'I want to do it,' Emma complained as she dropped her into the child seat and strapped her in with shaking hands. Finally, standing at the open driver's door, one foot inside as if prepared to jump in and drive away at speed, she braved a final look around. The car park was busy, there were people everywhere, but there was no sign of anyone bearing the remotest resemblance to the charity shop woman. She sat in her seat, took a deep breath and clasped her trembling hands.

'Mummy,' Emma said, 'can we go now?'

'Of course, darling,' she said, twisting her hands together. 'Just give me one minute.' *Deep, slow breaths in, slower breaths out.* She'd attended various classes at the clinic, and each session started and ended with this simple relaxation technique. She'd used it ever since. Sometimes, it worked.

'Mummyyyy!' This time the word stretched out in the start of a whine.

Diane started the engine, took another deep breath and let it out. 'Off we go,' she said, with forced jollity, turning up the music to drown out her anxiety. She kept her eyes firmly on the road in front of her as she drove, ignoring the few people she passed. At this stage, she just wanted to get home.

Once there, she left the groceries in the boot and, ignoring the pain, lifted Emma out and rushed towards the door, struggling with her keys, afraid to put her down, afraid to look behind her. Kicking the door closed, she took a shuddering breath before hugging Emma tightly for a moment and letting her go.

But then, of course, Emma wanted her ice cream.

Diane knew her fear was irrational, but it just wouldn't leave her. Leaving Emma in the living room, she stood in the hallway with her hand on the front doorknob and took a deep breath. Then, with a speed she hadn't realised she possessed, she opened the door, jumped down the two steps and rushed to her car. She stumbled in her haste and almost lost her footing, a hand on the bonnet of the car saving her from a fall. Wrenching open the boot, she grabbed the shopping bags in one hand, banged the boot shut and ran back into the house.

She dropped the bags on the counter and took a deep, shuddering breath. 'It's just coming, darling,' she said, the promise keeping Emma sitting on the sofa, allowing her time to recover. Moments later, she left Emma happily watching TV with a bowl of ice cream and headed back to the lounge.

The mess the spilt coffee had made on the floor brought a frown to her face. It needed to be cleaned up before Paul got home. She was a good housewife; the house was always sparkling, clothes always washed and neatly ironed. There was a certain pride in keeping everything looking so well. Paul had never commented, but she knew he liked the way she ran the house and, after all she'd put him through recently, she wasn't going to let him down now.

She'd no intention of telling him about the calamity in the shop, or the woman who had caused her such distress. If she told him, he would worry; he might insist she go back to the doctor. The doctor might suggest she go back to the clinic; he'd certainly insist she go back on those awful pills they'd prescribed, the small red pills that looked harmless, cheerful even, but which had left her feeling dazed and apathetic.

A couple of days after her return from the clinic, she'd stopped taking them, telling Paul a few days after that, afraid he would insist she take them or, worse, that he'd take her back to that therapist she really hadn't liked at all.

She'd persuaded Paul at the time that she was better off without the pills, and she was…she was…but now…if she told him what was happening, Paul would insist she go back to see the therapist, who would just give her something else to take, brushing aside her concerns, as if it were nothing to do with her.

Tomorrow, she'd be fine. Her imagination was working overtime because of what had happened that morning. That was all. And she was still adjusting to Emma being in nursery…wasn't there something called separation anxiety? Of course, no wonder she was feeling so unsettled. She *would* be fine tomorrow. There was no point in worrying Paul.

Picking up the hand towel she'd dropped on the puddle of coffee, she wrapped it in on itself to stop it dripping and took it through to the utility room to put into the washing machine. At the sink, she turned the tap on, letting the water flow until it was as hot as she could tolerate with her bare hands and filled a bowl with hot soapy water to take back to the lounge. Emma, she was relieved to see, was still engrossed in the programme she was watching and didn't even look up.

She knelt down and started scrubbing to clean away all the evidence of her stupidity. It took quite a while, requiring a few visits to the utility room to empty out the coffee-stained liquid and replace it with clean water. Finally, she sat back on her heels and surveyed the area. It would just about pass, she thought, standing up, feeling the pain in her side as she did; how was she going to explain *that*? She wouldn't, she decided; it was painful, but not excruciatingly so; she'd take a couple of painkillers before he came home, and he'd be none the wiser.

Returning the bowl to the utility room, she spotted the shopping bags where she'd dumped them on the kitchen counter. It was something Paul always complained about. 'You put them on the floor and then put them on the clean counter?' He'd said it so many times that eventually she'd stopped doing it. He *was* right, after all. But bending up and down to empty the bag from the floor was a chore she didn't feel like today, especially with the gnawing ache in her side.

Unpacking the bags, she put everything away and emptied the spilt pasta in the bottom of one of the bags into the rubbish bin, shaking it down to the bottom where it wouldn't be seen. With the bags folded and stacked neatly in their drawer, she reached for the disinfectant spray to spray the counter, wiping away her guilt at the same time.

A cup of tea would have been perfect but, checking the time, she decided there wasn't any to spare if she wanted to get the lasagne made and in the oven. Paul liked his evening meal on time; he'd watch the six o'clock headlines and expect his dinner on the table at six fifteen. Usually, everything went to plan. Lasagne was a dish she'd made many times and normally didn't require much concentration. But today, the ragù caught on the bottom of the pan and the béchamel sauce boiled over in the microwave. She managed to rescue both, and, still a little worried she might have added salt twice, she slid it into the oven quickly and shut the door.

Her bruised side ached. Paracetamol wasn't strong enough; she'd stronger painkillers in her bathroom cabinet, so she went up, took two and looked at herself in the mirror. She looked tired, she thought, resting both hands on the basin and leaning closer to look at the fine lines around her eyes, wondering when they'd appeared. Paul would worry if he saw her so pale, so washed-out. Applying tinted moisturiser, mascara and some pale-pink lipstick, she stood back to check she looked okay just as a car pulled up outside. Paul. He was like clockwork. With a quick flick of a brush through her hair, she took a final look and headed downstairs.

'Hi, darling,' she said, reaching the last step, stopping as she saw that Emma had beaten her to it. She watched as he bent to tickle her, making her gurgle with laughter. He adored her, and she him.

'You go back and play while Daddy gets out of his suit,' he said, turning the child toward the open door. 'Off you go,' he added, patting her bottom.

With Emma on her way, he looked at Diane. 'Hello,' he said. 'You look a bit tired,' he added, his eyes lingering on her face. 'How was your first day?'

'It was good, busy,' she said, stepping off the stairway so that she was closer to him, breathing deeply, catching the lingering hint of his aftershave. Resting her head on his shoulder, she waited for his arms to pull her closer and, for a moment, stayed there feeling safe. It would have been good to tell him everything; they could have laughed over the mix-up in the shop, at her silly overactive imagination.

'It isn't too much for you, is it? Maybe it was too soon to go back to work, even in a voluntary position.' he said, pulling back and looking her over once more, concern in his eyes. 'I want you to get better, Diane. If it's too difficult…'

She should have said it was, should have said she'd give it up but the words wouldn't come to admit to such a failure. 'No, it's fine,' she said, planting a kiss on his cheek and moving away. 'Go, get changed, dinner is nearly ready.'

'What are we having?' he asked. 'Work was mayhem and I didn't get a chance to have lunch.'

'Lasagne,' she said, watching his face to see if he approved.

'Okay, good, I like that,' he said, and headed upstairs.

Diane stared after him for a moment. There was a time when he'd kiss her passionately when he came home from work, sitting on the stairs, filling each other in on their day. Before Emma came along, sometimes passion would take over, and dinner would wait or burn. Her sigh was loud and long. Now, he just worried about her.

She set the table, switching off the TV as she passed Emma – she hadn't thought to turn it off earlier – and handed her a book instead. Paul had probably already heard it, but at least if it were off when he came down, he might not make a fuss. She hoped not, she really didn't need any more stress today. Emma took one look at the book and her face creased into a frown. For a moment, she looked so much like Paul that it took Diane's breath away. Sometimes, she wondered if hair colour was the only thing her daughter had inherited from her. 'It's one of your favourites,' she said, pleadingly. To her horror, Emma's face tensed and her mouth opened. Waiting for the inevitable wail, she frantically flicked the pages of the book, causing a draft that made Emma's curls lift and her eyelashes flutter. Her face changed in an instant.

'Again!' she chuckled.

Relieved that the impending disaster was averted, Diane happily spent a few minutes flicking the pages of the book.

'Okay, last time,' she said, 'now just sit and read it until Daddy comes down.'

'Thank God,' she muttered, making her way back to the kitchen. Taking the lasagne out, she placed it on the hob while she quickly made a green salad, placed the salad bowl on the table and checked that everything was as it should be, everything in its place.

'Smells good,' Paul said coming in, sniffing the air appreciatively. He looked more relaxed, Diane thought as he took a seat on the sofa beside Emma and switched on the TV to catch the news. He always did once he changed his tailored suits for casual clothes, the long-sleeved grey T-shirt and sweatpants he now wore suiting him far better.

She took the plates from the oven and dished up the lasagne, giving Paul an extra-large helping. 'It's ready,' she said, raising her voice to be heard over the sombre tone of the newsreader.

Paul switched off the TV, picked Emma up and carried her across to her booster seat, pushing it closer to the table. 'There you go,' he said, putting the spoon into her hand and moving her plate nearer. Taking his own seat, he picked up his cutlery and started to eat.

'It's good,' he managed to say between mouthfuls, hoovering up forkfuls hungrily for a few minutes before asking, 'So how did your first day go?'

'Fine,' Diane lied, 'the other volunteers are very nice.' Feeling she needed to elaborate, she told him the story of the bondage items that had been sent in to them. 'Anne and I howled with laughter,' she said, dropping her eyes to her food quickly so he wouldn't see the sudden sadness that crossed her face. It had been a fun moment, forgotten in the wake of a terrible day. She'd miss going back there but returning wasn't an option. She was embarrassed, humiliated and ashamed. How could she possibly explain? She looked up to find him staring at her.

'You look tired, you're certain it isn't too hard?' he asked, furrowing his brow.

She shook her head, probably more emphatically than she should because he continued to stare at her for a few seconds before shrugging and continuing with his meal.

There wasn't another anecdote she could tell him about the job. She didn't want to talk about Red, Beth or Anne who she'd really hoped…no, she had to stop thinking about them. 'Emma enjoyed nursery today,' she said brightly, hoping Paul wouldn't notice how forced it was. It wasn't a great conversation opener, but it was the best she could do. And it worked; Paul's attention switched immediately to his daughter. 'So, what did you get up to, princess?' he said, smiling across the table at her.

Emma revelled in his attention and happily told tales of her teacher, her classmates and the various things she'd done. Much of it was garbled and made little sense, but he listened to her intently. Diane sat back and tried to relax but she couldn't. Luckily, they didn't notice; all she needed to do was contribute a chuckle now and then when Emma, or Paul, said something witty and she was okay. She'd only given herself a small piece of lasagne, but even that defeated her. Afraid Paul would notice, she forced herself to eat a few mouthfuls before covering the remainder with a few salad leaves. 'Would you like some more?' she asked, standing with her plate in her hand and moving across to the kitchen as if she were intent on getting more for herself.

'No, thanks, it's very nice but I've enough here,' he said without looking at her, his attention focused on his daughter.

'Maybe I've had enough too,' she said, covering the dish with tinfoil and putting it into the fridge. She scraped what was on her plate into the bin, rinsed the plate and put it into the dishwasher.

Filling the kettle, she switched it on. Paul liked coffee after his dinner. A glass of wine would have been her choice, but they had a rule: no wine during the week. Opening the fridge, she saw the bottle of Chardonnay they'd opened at the weekend and not finished. With the open door of the American fridge blocking her from Paul's sight, and without thinking, she took the bottle from the shelf, removed the lid and held it to her mouth. She took two gulps, stopped for a breath and took two more before returning the bottle to the shelf and replacing the screw cap.

'You ready for your coffee,' she asked Paul, taking out the milk with an unsteady hand and closing the fridge door. She was shocked at what she'd just done, but there was a small part of her that relished the breaking of the rules, as if, by doing so, she was taking back a little control of something. And in the hellish day she'd had, that made her feel better.

He mumbled an affirmative as he scooped the last of his lasagne up, the fork scratching the plate.

'Are you sure you don't want more?' she asked, wishing, not for the first time, that he didn't scrape his plate as if it was the last meal he was going to have.

'No thanks, just coffee,' he said, putting his cutlery down with a clatter and pushing the plate away.

Mimicking his actions, Emma dropped her spoon on her plate and pushed it towards his, reaching out to be taken out of her chair. He stood, lifted her down and sat again. With the taste of alcohol in her mouth, Diane held her breath as she put coffee in front of him and quickly removed the two plates.

'Come on, Emma,' she said, reaching for her hand. 'Let's get you into your pyjamas and then you can sit and watch TV with Daddy until it's time to go to bed.'

Upstairs, she left her daughter in her bedroom choosing which pyjamas to wear while she hurried into her ensuite bathroom to brush her teeth. Rinsing her mouth, she looked up and saw her reflection in the mirror looking guilty. 'How silly,' she muttered, grabbing the hand towel and swiping it roughly across her mouth, dropping it back on the rail as Emma came in, her favourite animal motif pyjamas clutched in her little fists.

A wave of love washed over Diane and she bent to pick her up and carry her through to her bedroom, dancing as she walked, Emma laughing, the pyjamas trailing along the floor. The bedroom was decorated with cartoon animal wallpaper she and Paul had chosen when they'd discovered she was pregnant. The shop sold furniture inspired by the paper and they'd bought the lot. There was a hippo-shaped bed, a monkey bedside table and a couple of giraffe chairs. It was a delight.

Diane lowered her to her bed and helped her to undress, feeling her soft, still-baby skin with the same delight she'd felt when she'd first clasped her to her chest only three short years before.

Her fingers lingered, a frown creasing her brow as the image of her naked new-born daughter flashed before her eyes. It seemed only like yesterday…

'Mummy, you're hurting me!'

Diane looked down at her hands grasping the child's arms. Letting go, she was horrified to see fading pale finger marks on her skin. Had she blacked out? Only for a few seconds, but she'd definitely gone somewhere else. Emma rubbed her arm and looked at her accusingly.

'Mummy's sorry,' Diane said, brushing her hands over her arms. The marks were gone. She hadn't hurt her, probably just scared her a little. She plucked her up into her arms again and snuggled her face into her neck, blowing raspberries against her skin until she giggled. 'Come on, sweet pea,' she said, and carried her downstairs.

As they entered the family room, Emma squirmed to get down and sit beside her father. Paul, putting his coffee into his other hand, opened his arm out wide to allow her to snuggle to his side, wrapping his arm back around her.

For a moment, Diane felt a soft brush of envy. Then she remembered the marks, however temporary, she'd left on Emma's skin and she felt a tremor of anxiety.

Where had she gone for those few seconds?

CHAPTER 6

Diane took her time tidying up. She cleared the table and loaded the dishwasher. Then busied herself getting ready for the morning, emptying Emma's bag, rinsing her juice bottle, washing out the bag itself even though it didn't need it. She'd do anything rather than think.

She was still pottering about, wiping a cloth over the clean countertop, when she looked around to see Paul standing, a sleeping Emma in his arms.

'I'll go tuck her in,' he said with a trace of a smile. 'She's out for the count.'

Diane forced herself to echo his smile, 'She sleeps so soundly,' she said softly. She reached a hand out and very gently brushed a curl from her forehead. 'Before you go,' she said, raising her eyes to his, 'can I ask you something?'

'Sure,' he said, with an encouraging tilt of his head.

'The last time…before my breakdown…' she gulped, trying to find the words. 'How did you know it was happening? I mean, what were the signs?'

He shifted Emma in his arms and buried his face in her hair for a moment before looking back at her. 'You know what the doctors say, Diane,' he said gently, 'you're supposed to let the memories come back—'

'I know, I know,' she said, interrupting him in frustration, 'they're supposed to come back naturally.'

'Has something happened?'

She heard the worry in his voice, saw the sudden tension in his face. Hadn't she put him through enough already? She reached a hand up and laid it on his cheek. 'No,' she said firmly, 'it's just frustrating sometimes not knowing what happened, that's all.'

He put his free hand up to take hers and held it tightly for a moment. 'But you are feeling all right?'

'It's just been a long day,' she said, managing to smile, hoping she could keep it in place for long enough to reassure him.

She managed until he'd left the room. Throwing the cloth she'd been holding into the sink, she moved to the sofa and sat in the still-warm seats they'd vacated, letting her head flop back and eyes close. It would be several minutes before Paul came down. *If* he came down. He didn't always, sometimes he went to his office to check emails, got caught up in work and forgot she was downstairs waiting for him.

Tears were close. She felt the warmth at the corner of her closed eyes before one squeezed out and trickled slowly down her cheek. Pressing her thumb and first finger into the corner of her eyes, she took some deep breaths and got them under control. After a few minutes, she lifted her head and ran her hand through her hair. She needed to think.

Perhaps she should make an appointment to see that therapist again? The corners of her mouth drooped at the thought. She hadn't liked him; had found his manner condescending, his eyes cold. Maybe she should find someone else?

Much of the year before the breakdown was a mystery to her, huge gaps in time when she couldn't remember anything. The doctors had promised the memories would come back in time. *Don't force them,* she'd been told, *they will come back.*

And if she asked Paul, as she had today, he'd say the same thing, quoting the doctors or quoting research he'd read about *Spontaneous Recovery*. It all sounded very good except it wasn't happening. She could remember almost as little today as she did when she left the clinic a month ago and any memories that had returned were wrinkled scraps that made no sense. But despite the gaps, the frustration of not being able to remember things, and the sometimes-frightening sense of loss at these gaps in her life, she'd felt fine. Getting on with her life, keeping up with the housework, sticking to her routines. Until today.

The TV flickered through programme after programme that she didn't watch. She could have switched it off, but the sound of voices was comforting. The silence might not be. Paul didn't return; she heard his footsteps move about upstairs for a while and then nothing.

At ten, weary, she stood, switched everything off and headed up the stairs. She looked in on Emma who was curled up, fast asleep, and then knocked gently on the door of the room Paul used as an office. She opened it slowly and peered around the edge. 'I'm off to bed,' she said.

'Goodnight,' he said, looking up briefly from his laptop. 'Sleep well.'

Diane closed the door and headed to the room they hadn't shared since her return from the clinic. She needed space to recover, he'd said, moving his stuff into the spare room.

It had been difficult to see the logic behind his decision at the time; surely it would have been better to resume as normal a life as possible? But at that point she didn't really know what was good for her. Whatever had happened, she'd obviously shocked, maybe even frightened Paul, who'd suddenly started treating her like this fragile, breakable thing. Kisses she'd remembered as being passionate had become sexless. They barely touched her skin and never ventured towards her mouth – as if the temptation to go further would be too much.

She wanted to tell him she wasn't so delicate, that she was getting better every day, that sleeping wrapped in his arms would be the best medicine of all. She missed the closeness and, if she were being brutally honest, she missed the sex. But the pills had made her too tired to argue and she'd accepted this new way of living without question.

When she'd stopped taking them, a week after leaving the clinic, she'd felt better, more energetic and had put a hand around his neck to draw him close. 'I miss you,' she'd said. He'd kissed her gently on the cheek, pulled away and looked at her with concern. 'Don't rush. You need to get stronger, Diane. The doctor said you need plenty of rest.' How could she argue when she saw such concern on his face? 'Soon then,' she'd said. But that was three weeks ago, and he still treated her like an invalid and slept in the spare bedroom.

With a sigh for the way things used to be, she headed to her room. If there were a night she needed a sleeping tablet, this was it. She opened the ensuite bathroom cabinet, eyes scanning the rows of packets. Before the clinic, the only medication she'd ever taken was Paracetamol. Now sleeping tablets, antidepressants, and the stronger painkillers the doctors had prescribed for the pounding headaches she'd had in the clinic were all lined up in the cabinet.

She took out the packet of antidepressants. She'd spent the weeks since she'd stopped them proving that she was better off without, and now everything was falling apart. With a sigh, she put them back; she wasn't going back on them. Not yet, hopefully not ever. She was grateful, however, that the therapist had insisted on writing a prescription for sleeping tablets. Sometimes, just knowing they were there helped her to get to sleep and she'd only taken one or two since she came home. She took out the packet now, pulled out a card of tablets and pressed one from the foil, hesitating a moment before pressing a second.

Finally, she took out the packet of painkillers. The directions on the packet said to take one or two, she took two. Throwing all four tablets into her mouth, she scooped water from the tap with her hand and swallowed them down.

Brushing her teeth, cleaning her face and moisturising, she threw her clothes off and onto a chair in a careless heap and climbed, naked, between the sheets. With a weary sigh, she closed her eyes to wait for the tablets to kick in. She'd have a good night's sleep and tomorrow, everything would be normal.

CHAPTER 7

She felt groggy the next morning, her eyes heavy. Looking at her reflection in the bathroom mirror, she groaned before reaching for the concealer to hide the dark circles under her eyes. It was tempting to pull on the same clothes she'd worn yesterday, but they were creased. Her pallor and dark circles might escape Paul's notice, but wearing yesterday's crumpled clothes certainly wouldn't. As far as he knew, she was heading to the charity shop after dropping Emma off and she needed to keep up the pretence until she found a way to tell him.

Dressed in clean clothes, she went into Emma's room and ran a gentle hand over her curls. 'Time to get up,' she said softly. As usual, she woke almost immediately and stretched her arms over her head. She was an easy child in the morning, happy to wear whatever Diane chose, dressing without fuss in the pink corduroy trousers, long-sleeved T-shirt and raspberry-coloured jumper she took from the chest of drawers. No longer a baby, soon she wouldn't need her help at all. The thought sent a frisson of sadness through her.

Ten minutes later, they were downstairs, Emma rushing ahead, already babbling to her father about what she was going to do in nursery that day. If Paul noticed anything amiss with Diane, he said nothing, concentrating his attention on his daughter, listening to her every word. Relieved, Diane organised breakfast, setting a bowl of cereal and a glass of milk in front of Emma, noticing with surprise that Paul had almost finished his. She checked the clock, eight thirty. It was later than she'd expected. She felt her gut clench with anxiety. She would have sworn her clock said eight when she left her room. Had she lost time somewhere? Another blackout?

'I'm off,' Paul said, putting his bowl into the dishwasher. 'Have a good day, I'll see you tonight.'

She felt his kiss on her cheek, conjured up a smile and said goodbye, her eyes wandering to the clock again.

Leaving Emma to eat her cereal, she nipped back upstairs to make the beds. It didn't take long, a shake of a duvet and plumping of pillows on the single bed Paul now slept in, a quick tidy of Emma's. She'd already straightened her duvet so gave the room a cursory glance, startled when she saw the time. The alarm clock was an old battery-operated one that Paul was constantly saying should be thrown out, but it kept good time. It said eight o'clock. It took a few seconds before she let her breath out in a relieved laugh. She hadn't had a blackout. It had stopped, that was all. A simple problem that new batteries could fix.

Emma was just finishing her breakfast when Diane arrived back downstairs and she smiled at the white milk-moustache on her upper lip. 'Well done,' she said, taking the glass and bowl away. She dropped them into the sink and turned on the tap, leaving them to be dealt with on her return. After all, she had all day to fill. 'Right,' she said, wiping Emma's face with damp paper towel before helping her into her coat.

Diane lingered at the nursery after dropping her daughter off, spending a few minutes chatting to Miss Rogers. She was pleased to find that the teacher seemed fond of Emma and that she was settling in well. She then looked around, hoping to strike up conversation with some of the other parents, but most were rushing off to start a day's work. As she should be, Diane thought sadly before brushing away the feelings of self-pity. It was stupid, she had so much to be grateful for.

Back at home, she took out her mobile to ring the shop, hesitated, and put it down. She was too humiliated; they'd guess when she didn't turn up that she wasn't coming back. If they rang, she wouldn't answer. She didn't want to have to explain her decision; just the thought of speaking to them made her skin prickle with shame. Making a cup of coffee, she switched on the radio, listened to a chat show and tried to think of how she was going to fill her day. She'd look for something else soon, but not today.

Lost in her thoughts, the doorbell startled her. She put down the near-empty mug she'd been cradling for the previous half hour and stood still. She waited a minute, hoping whoever it was would just go away, but it rang again, for longer this time.

The door to the hallway was shut. In a moment of bravado, she opened it and stood in the doorway looking towards the front door. It was solid wood, no glass panels to help her out, no indication of what lay on the other side.

The fear that it was the woman from the previous day was irrational…crazy, even. But who else could it be? She wasn't expecting anyone. She'd no friends locally to drop by. Moving forward, one shaky step at a time, she reached a hand to the wall for support and then grabbed hold of the newel post. The front door was now within arm's reach; with a final, deep, steadying breath she gripped the doorknob and wrenched it open.

Whatever words were on the tip of her tongue died as she looked into the startled eyes of the woman who stood in front of her, her hand raised as if to ring the bell once more.

'Anne?' Diane started to laugh and stopped herself abruptly, holding a hand over her mouth. 'I'm sorry,' she said after a beat, standing back and waving her inside. 'This is a bit of a surprise,' she said.

Anne, as usual, was wearing black, her hair tied up on top of her head with a garish red and orange scarf, escaped curls dancing around her face. 'I was in work this morning,' she said, 'Red was so upset when you didn't turn up. She wanted to explain that everything was okay, that—'

Diane interrupted her. 'There wasn't money missing when she totted up yesterday, was there?'

Anne shook her head, sending tendrils of hair swinging. 'No, there wasn't.' She stretched out a hand towards Diane's defensively crossed arms. 'I didn't think you'd taken those books, but you rushed away so fast it made you look guilty, you know, and Red has been let down by people before.'

Diane looked down at the hand resting on her arm. 'Come on inside,' she said and led the way into the family room, waving Anne towards a seat at one end of the L-shaped sofa and taking the other end for herself. 'I rushed away because I was embarrassed,' she said quietly. 'It was obvious what you all thought.' She held a hand up when she saw Anne was going to interrupt. 'Obvious to me, anyway. It was too late then to explain what had happened, that a woman wanted to buy the books and changed her mind after I'd keyed in the price. I had no idea how to void a transaction and was going to wait until after Beth came back but then, stupidly,' she ran a hand over her hair, '*very* stupidly, I decided the easiest thing was to buy them myself. And that's what I did.'

It was mostly true. She'd left out the part about the strange look the woman had given her. And, of course, she'd no intention of mentioning the rest of yesterday's very bizarre events.

'How did you know where I lived?' she asked, when Anne said nothing.

'Red told me,' she said, tucking a rebellious curl into a fold of the scarf. 'She's really sorry about it and hopes you'll consider coming back.'

'She sent you around to plead with me, did she?' The words were tinged with bitterness, and edged with sadness.

'I wanted to call around,' Anne said. 'I told her that you and I got on so well it might be better coming from me.' She met

Diane's gaze squarely. 'I am right, aren't I? We got on really well. I thought we might become friends.'

Diane had thought the same. Standing, she moved over to the kitchen to switch the kettle on. 'Would you like a drink? I was just about to make one.'

Anne smiled before standing to unbutton her fitted black coat. She took it off, flung it over the back of the sofa and sat with a more relaxed expression on her face. 'I thought you were going to throw me out,' she said with a slight laugh.

Diane took down a couple of mugs and put them on the counter before looking across to meet Anne's eyes. She did her best to smile, feeling a lessening of the tension that had been twisting her gut tightly since the day before. 'I almost did. Tea or coffee?'

'Coffee, milk, one sugar.'

Diane took her time, the ritual of making the drinks giving her time to think. She added milk to both and sugar to Anne's, watching the woman from the corner of her eye. She brought the coffees over and put one in front of Anne, sitting herself down on the far end of the sofa with her own mug cupped in both hands.

'I *am* sorry,' Anne said softly, reaching for her coffee. 'Won't you reconsider and come back to the shop?'

'No, I wouldn't feel comfortable there now,' she said. And it was the truth. Apart from the wrongful accusation, she'd be constantly worrying about *that* woman coming into the shop. But Anne didn't need to know that. 'I'm going to look for a job.' She smiled briefly. 'One that pays.'

Anne picked up her coffee and sipped it before saying, 'Red said you'd worked in IT before you had your daughter?'

Diane's eyes narrowed. 'Wasn't my interview with Red confidential?' she said, more sharply than she had intended, regretting the words when she saw the embarrassed blush.

But the blush wasn't embarrassment, it was annoyance. Anne put her coffee down with as close to a bang as you could get with an almost full mug. 'We were talking about how best we could use our new volunteer, actually,' she said, her voice defensive. 'We were going to wait until you'd settled in and ask you to update our web page.'

It was Diane's turn to blush. She put her coffee down. 'I'm sorry,' she said, 'I've had a bad couple of days.' She watched Anne's face relax a little as she reached to pick up her coffee again. It looked as if she'd accepted her apology. Relieved, Diane sat back. For a moment, she was tempted to tell her about the strange woman; it would be good to share with someone. She had no friends in London and although she still occasionally met up with some of her Bristol friends, it was so infrequent that they never really made it past polite small talk. She picked up her coffee with a sigh. No, she couldn't tell her. She'd already made herself out to be paranoid, she didn't want Anne to think she was crazy. *Maybe she was.* She batted away the thought and pinned a smile in place as Anne put her mug down again, looked at her watch and jumped to her feet.

'Gosh, is that the time? I said I'd only be gone twenty minutes,' she said, with a smile. She grabbed her coat and put it on, fastening the overlarge buttons down the front.

Diane stood. 'Thank you for coming,' she said politely. 'I'm sorry how things worked out. Tell Red…tell her I was grateful for the opportunity.'

Anne finished fastening her coat and moved into the hallway where she turned to say goodbye. 'Maybe we could have coffee sometime?'

Surprised, Diane nodded quickly. 'I'd like that,' she said. Maybe, after all, they could be friends.

Reaching up to readjust her headscarf and then lifting both hands in acknowledgment of what a pointless exercise it was, since curls fell out faster than she could put them in, she said, 'How about Friday, then?'

Diane smiled, genuinely pleased. 'Okay,' she said, 'Friday it is.'

The Housewife

They arranged to meet at eleven in a coffee shop Diane had heard of but had never visited. 'The Birdcage, Friday at eleven,' she repeated as she opened the door. 'See you then.'

She shut the door with the smile still on her face. What an unexpected visit. There was a bounce in her step as she went back to clear away the mugs. Honestly, that something so simple could cheer her up so much. She needed to get out more, make new friends. Anne was a good start.

She wondered about her. Perhaps she was right to be wary, after all, she knew absolutely nothing about her. They hadn't had much time to chat in the shop during the one morning they had worked together. She tapped her fingernails on the countertop. Friday, she'd find out about her then.

It was soon time to leave and pick up Emma. Grabbing her keys, she closed the front door and headed off. Almost without realising it, her eyes flicked up and down the street. For the first time, she wished they didn't live in such a quiet area. She was barely on nodding terms with most of her neighbours, and only knew their names because of wrongly delivered post. The only one she saw regularly was the elderly Mrs Prescott who lived across the road and walked the twenty minutes to the nearest shop every day, always nodding with age-old graciousness when she saw Diane.

Today, there was no sign of anybody. She climbed into the car and drove to the nursery, pulling in and reversing into a parking space. Arriving too early, she sat in her car listening to the radio, humming along to a song she remembered from her youth, fingers tapping the steering wheel in time to the music.

When the song ended, she checked the time. Twelve forty-three. Any moment now, the nursery door would open. Other parents had arrived, the car park filling up around her. Looking out of the windscreen, a sudden lull in traffic allowed her to see across to the other side of the road.

The sharp intake of breath was loud and automatic. Her hand flew to cover her mouth, pressing hard against her lips to suppress a scream as she stared at the tall slim woman with the smooth bob.

How could it be?

And in the blink of an eye, as if to prove her right, there was suddenly nobody there.

CHAPTER 8

If she couldn't see her, she wasn't there. Diane knew she was falling back on a child's reasoning, but she didn't care. She wasn't there now, she'd never been there.

Moments later, with Emma strapped into her seat, she drove the short distance home with tunnel vision, barely reducing speed as she pulled into her driveway. Safely inside the house, she locked the front door, sliding the safety chain she rarely used into place, and stumbled into the family room, closing the door and leaning against it.

She glanced toward the telephone. Maybe she should ring the police? But Paul would find out. Then she'd have to tell him about the fiasco in the charity shop and he'd wonder why she hadn't told him already. She pasted a smile in place as Emma appeared from the downstairs cloakroom, her trousers around her knees and a grin on her face. Diane bent to help her with her clothes, the buttons on the trousers difficult for little three-year-old fingers. She kissed her on top of her head as she fastened them.

'Hungry, sweetheart?' she asked.

'Tommy says he gets cornflake sandwiches for his lunch,' Emma said, toddling over to her chair.

Diane helped her up, the twinge in her side telling her she needed to take more painkillers. Cornflake sandwiches? She was almost tempted. Instead, she took a carton of soup from the fridge, opened the top, put it into the microwave and switched it on.

Five minutes later, they were both sitting down to mushroom soup and cheese sandwiches. When they were finished, she gave Emma a glass of milk and switched the kettle on to make coffee.

The half-empty bottle of wine called to her as she put the milk away. She took it out and poured some into a clean mug, stopping when it was half full, only to swear under her breath and fill it to the brim. She threw the mug of coffee down the drain and sat opposite Emma, sipping the wine.

She was still drinking it twenty minutes later, listening to Emma's soft snuffle as she slept on the sofa. It was having its effect. Her ribs still ached, but she felt more relaxed. Debating the wisdom of taking painkillers on top of the wine, she decided against. Anyway, the pain focused her even as the wine relaxed her. She'd almost convinced herself that the woman she'd seen outside the house yesterday had just borne a similarity to the charity shop woman, but now she knew she was wrong. It had been her, and it was her outside the nursery today. Was she, for some reason, following her?

Finishing the mug of wine, she returned to the fridge and took out the bottle. There wasn't much left, maybe a quarter of a cup? Unscrewing the lid, she emptied it into her mug and stood leaning against the counter while she drank. She needed to know if the woman was outside now. Holding the mug in one hand, she ran a hand over her face and moved away from the counter. Alcohol-induced bravery; she'd better act while it was still working.

The blinds in the lounge were open, so she sidled into the room, edging around the wall to the window. Stepping to one side, she could see quite a way up the street. There was nobody to be seen. Reaching out, she grabbed the cord and shut the blind before walking across to the other side. Draining the mug, she waited a beat before carefully raising one slat to peer out. Nobody. There was nobody there.

She wasn't sure if she felt relieved that there was nobody there, or annoyed. Had the woman been standing there, while Emma was safely asleep, she might have gone out and faced her. *Might have found out if she were real.* She dropped the slat and headed back to the family room, leaving the blinds shut.

Emma woke just as she went through. She bent down to kiss her on the cheek, pulling back quickly when the child's nose crinkled up at the smell of alcohol on her breath. Reaching for the remote, she switched on the television. 'Watch TV for a while,' she said, brushing away the feeling of guilt. She wasn't giving her cornflake sandwiches, she was just letting her watch TV. She'd play with her later. When she didn't reek of alcohol.

She went to her room and brushed her teeth for several minutes, swirling the minty paste around her mouth before spitting it out. Then, because her side ached, she popped two painkillers. Looking in the cabinet mirror she saw her reflection; it looked as bad as she felt. She applied some make-up and brushed her hair. She didn't look a lot better but it was all she could do.

Back downstairs, parental guilt reared its head and she switched off the television and spent the next couple of hours playing with Emma. It was impossible to spend time in her company without feeling better. Buoyed by her infectious laughter, Diane lost herself in the world of dolls and purple stuffed toys, and closed out reality.

It was almost five before she stood up, suddenly aware she'd given absolutely no thought to dinner. A quick search of the freezer turned up a chicken crown she'd bought some time before. Hoping she could cook it from frozen, she turned it over to read the instructions, a sigh of relief escaping when she saw she could. She checked the clock. Just perfect. Deciding to do roast veg to go with the chicken, she peeled and chopped a selection, poured some olive oil into a metal dish and threw the lot in using her hands to coat them all in the oil. Checking the time again, she spread a tea cloth over the tray and put it to one side.

Next, she took the empty wine bottle and half filled it with water before screwing the cap back on and returning it to the fridge. Paul wouldn't want wine until Friday, so she'd have to replace it by then. Back in the lounge, she lifted one slat and peered up and down the street again. Still nothing. Relieved, she opened the blinds. And, finally, she took the safety chain from the front door and fetching her house keys she unlocked the main lock.

That was it, wasn't it? Everything was the way it should be. She held a hand to her head. It felt muggy; she wasn't used to drinking in the middle of the day. She leaned against the door for a moment with her eyes closed, feeling incredibly weary.

Her eyes snapped open to the sound of a baby's cry from the other room. Tutting, she pushed away from the door and headed towards the family room to switch off the TV. Emma, the little monkey, must have found the controls again; she'd have to be firmer about the rules.

But she was shocked to find the television blank and Emma sitting on the floor surrounded by her toys, happily playing. Diane rubbed her eyes. Seeing things and now hearing things? She gave a heavy sigh that drew Emma's attention. The little girl looked at her with a serious expression and said, 'Have you got a pain, Mummy?'

'No, darling,' she said, managing a reassuring smile. Dismissing her foolishness with a shake of her head, she went into the kitchen to finish preparing dinner.

With Emma playing quietly again, a check of the clock told Diane she'd half an hour before Paul was home. She made a mug of tea and with a last glance at Emma, headed into the lounge to relax. At the door, she stopped with her hand on the doorknob, suddenly strangely nervous about opening the door. With a grunt of annoyance at her hesitation, she flung the door open with unnecessary force. It banged against the wall making her swear softly and hope the handle hadn't caused damage to the wall.

She was being silly. With only a moment's hesitation, she went in to sit on the pale blue sofa that sat against the far wall, facing the window. It used to have two huge turquoise feather cushions, one propped on either end, now there was only one. She'd asked Paul if he knew what happened to the other, but he'd just looked at her blankly and shrugged.

'Did it get damaged or stained, maybe?' she'd persevered and then, with a frustrated shake of her head, she'd added, 'I don't remember.'

'It's just a cushion,' he'd said dismissively, turning away.

She'd searched the house for it before accepting it was gone. Somewhere in those missing hours, she guessed, it had been damaged beyond repair and thrown out. She never mentioned it again, propping the single cushion in the middle of the sofa. It looked odd but, so far, she hadn't the heart to care.

Maybe she'd buy two new ones, she thought as she moved closer to the sofa, her mug of tea cupped in her hands. Her initial nervousness hadn't ebbed and now a lick of fear joined it to send goosebumps over her skin. What felt like minutes passed before she was able to take a single shaky step backward. Then another and another until she was back out in the hall. Reaching out with one hand, she grabbed the door and pulled it shut.

Back in the kitchen, she threw the tea down the sink. Had there been any more wine in the fridge, she'd have downed the lot.

It was just stress, and her overactive imagination playing tricks on her. That was all. She frowned; everything was fine until she'd seen that damn woman. She needed to find out who she was.

Most importantly, for her sanity, she needed to prove she was real.

CHAPTER 9

The next day, when she drove to the nursery to collect Emma, she looked around for the woman as she indicated and pulled into the car park. There was no sign of her and Diane breathed a sigh of relief, closing her eyes for a brief moment, opening them with an indrawn breath when she saw her, exactly where she'd been the day before. Diane tried to keep her eye on her for as long as she could but the to and fro of cars and people blocked her view and, almost as soon as she had appeared, she had gone.

Waiting for the nursery to open, Diane considered her next step. This was the second day she'd appeared. Tomorrow, she needed to be free to approach her, find out who she was and why she appeared to be following her. The woman might be some kind of crank; she wasn't going to risk approaching her with Emma beside her.

But there was no point in putting it off. She needed to find someone to take care of Emma for a few hours. When she appeared, chatting to a boy her size and age, Diane guessed he was Tommy of cornflake sandwich fame.

The woman who came to pick him up looked frazzled and unkempt, her jumper creased, a stain on the leg of her jeans, but her face was pleasant; there was a smile on her lips and her eyes looked kind.

'You're Tommy's mum?' Diane asked as Emma came running towards her.

The woman looked up from greeting her son and weighed her up before answering. 'That's right,' she said, 'Rose Metcalf. You must be Emma's.'

Diane nodded. 'Diane Andrews,' she said. 'Emma is always talking about Tommy. I was wondering if he'd like to come back to ours for a couple of hours? You know, like a play date.'

Rose looked puzzled for a moment. 'Do you mean today?'

The idea had just come to Diane and she hadn't really worked it through. She needed someone to mind Emma while she followed the woman; if she had Tommy today, couldn't she ask Rose to take Emma tomorrow? Or the next day? She moved restlessly from one foot to the other.

Rose tilted her head to one side, considering the idea. 'As it happens,' she admitted, 'I've got a dreadful migraine. It was a struggle to get here and I wouldn't mind a couple of hours' peace and quiet to let the medication kick in.'

Diane grinned. Serendipity. 'Fantastic,' she said. Catching Emma by the hand, she moved out of the way as other parents led their offspring from the school. 'I'll come and take your car seat,' she said, 'and I'll drop it and him back around four thirty, if that's okay? I'm glad I can help. What's your address?'

Rose put her hand on her son's head. 'You hear that, Tommy? You're going to go with Emma and her mum for a couple of hours. Be good, won't you?'

Diane hoped this was going to work. She'd never had another child in the house before and it felt so wonderfully normal, but also a little daunting. It was also her first connection with one of the other mothers; if it went well, maybe they would become friends. But first, she needed to get her life sorted out.

Rose took a scrap of paper from her car and scribbled down her address. 'It's just around the corner from where Miss Rogers lives, actually,' she said, handing it over. 'She has that lovely house next to the ugliest church I've ever seen, you should drive down and see it.'

Diane nodded as she took the address from her and tucked it into her pocket. 'We'll see you later then. I hope you feel better.'

As it turned out, she needn't have worried. Tommy was a polite and easy child to entertain and, despite his predilection for cornflake sandwiches, he ate the soup and ham sandwich she put in front of him without a murmur.

It was probably cheating slightly but, for peace, she switched the TV on and parked both children in front of it after lunch. Emma, as she usually did, fell asleep almost immediately. Tommy was made of tougher stuff, but nodded off eventually.

When they woke an hour later, they played quietly until Diane told them it was time to go. Strapping both children into their seats, she put Rose's postcode into her satnav and followed the directions until she was pulling up outside her house. The Metcalf residence was a detached house on a very prestigious road, the house set well back behind stone walls with wrought-iron gates left open to allow entry. Indicating, she pulled in and drove up the curved drive, stopping in front of a truly beautiful house. Diane admired the square bay windows set either side of the ornate, panelled front door.

Getting out, she stood and admired the grounds and house for a few moments until the two children signalled, loudly, their desire to get out. Tommy, having opened his own straps, scampered out as soon as she opened the car door. Emma wasn't far behind.

The woman who answered the door looked like a different person to the one Diane had met earlier, her hair neatly brushed, subtle make-up enhancing very pale blue eyes, a crisp white shirt and well-fitting jeans replacing the scruffy pants and jumper she'd worn at the nursery. 'Are you feeling better?' Diane asked as both children ran inside.

'So much better. I can't thank you enough, you were a lifesaver.' Rose stood back and waved Diane in. 'Won't you come in for a cuppa?' she said.

It would have been wonderful to see inside the house, and to sit and chat, but Diane was suddenly embarrassed at the request she was about to make, feeling a little guilty that she had a motive behind helping this pleasant, friendly lady out. 'Perhaps another time?' she smiled. 'You have a beautiful home, I'd love to see the interior.' Nervously, she flicked her hair behind her ears. 'Actually, something has come up, and I was wondering if you could collect and take Emma for a few hours tomorrow? I know it's a massive favour.'

If Rose was taken aback at the quick request to return the favour, she was too polite to say so, but her voice was noticeably cooler when she replied. 'Oh! Well, yes, of course.'

'Great, thank you so much,' Diane said, feeling a slight blush rising in her cheeks. 'I'll just get Tommy's car seat and, in the morning, I'll give you Emma's.' She felt she should make some attempt to restore good feeling. 'When I pick her up tomorrow,' she said, 'perhaps we could have the cuppa then?'

Rose's eyebrows lifted. 'Unfortunately, that won't be possible,' she said. 'If you could make sure you're here by,' she looked at her watch pointedly, 'four thirty-five. I've got an appointment to go to with Tommy that we can't miss.'

Diane gave an embarrassed laugh. 'Yes, of course,' she said, and then added, 'It's something very important, I wouldn't have asked otherwise.'

Rose said nothing. Diane guessed she'd never get to see inside the house and Tommy wouldn't be coming for a second play date. Feeling a little dejected, she retrieved the car seat and handed it to her. 'Thanks,' she said, receiving just a slight nod in return.

Emma, unfortunately, had followed Tommy into the house and Rose had to go looking for her, leaving Diane waiting awkwardly on the doorstep. Moments later, she came back with both in tow, the two children still chatting happily to each other.

'They get on so well,' Diane said, a note of regret in her voice for the way things were turning out. If only she'd been honest with

Rose from the very beginning, they might have been friends. But from the look on her face, she knew she wouldn't get a second chance to make that good first impression. With a sigh, she took Emma's hand. 'I'll see you in the morning then,' she said, turning away and hurrying back to the car.

That evening, Emma told Paul about Tommy's visit. He smiled at her and raised an eyebrow at Diane. 'Oh, who's this lad then?'

'Just a boy in her class,' Diane said making light of it. 'His mother wasn't feeling well and asked if I could take him for a few hours.' Fudging the truth. 'He and Emma get along well, so I thought there was no harm. They live in a fabulous house, one of those along Kingston Hill,' she explained, 'the ones behind those high walls. Beautiful house, Edwardian.'

'Very nice,' he said, pursing his lips, obviously a little impressed that his daughter was already mixing in the right circles.

'Actually,' Diane continued, consciously trying to keep her voice calm, 'she insisted that she return the favour and Emma is going there for a couple of hours after nursery tomorrow.'

'So soon?' Paul asked, unconsciously echoing Rose Metcalf's unsaid words.

'I know,' Diane said, not meeting his eyes, 'but she insisted, and I didn't like to say no.'

'I suppose it won't do her any harm,' he said, finishing his meal and pushing his plate away. 'Kingston Hill is very nice.'

There was nothing more said about it. He took Emma up to bed after the news and, once again, didn't return. For once, Diane was relieved. She'd called into the supermarket on the way home and bought a bottle of white wine, swapping it for the water-filled one in the fridge. With Paul gone, she opened it, filled a glass almost to the top and sat into the sofa, balancing it carefully. Switching off the TV, she took a long drink and sat back. Tomorrow, she would follow the woman, find out who she was, and put an end to whatever was going on. Feeling positive, she finished the wine and let her head flop back on the sofa. Then she heard it.

A baby's cry.

She sat up. The room was in semi-darkness, just one lamp to toss shadows into the corners. It was so quiet. Had she imagined the sound again? Then it came once more, a piteous wail that sent shivers down her spine.

When it stopped, she stood and switched on the main lights and waited for it to come again.

After twenty minutes of standing absolutely still, the only thing she heard was the creak of floorboards as Paul moved about overhead. She switched off the lights and tilted her head to listen again, but now there was just the deep silence of night. Dragging herself up the stairs on leaden feet, she felt fear gnawing at her grasp on sanity.

CHAPTER 10

Once again, she took two sleeping tablets and, with her side still aching, two strong painkillers too but it still took a long time before she fell asleep as she lay rigid, listening out for another cry. She'd checked Emma several times, standing beside her bed, watching her closely to see if, in her sleep, she cried out for her. But she slept soundly.

It was after one before she took the pills, and nearly two before she fell asleep, so when the alarm sounded at eight, she woke from the deep, medicated sleep with a jolt. 'Oh God,' she groaned, lifting a hand to her head and holding it there as she swung her feet slowly to the floor. It felt like someone was trying to poke her eyes out from the inside.

A shower would wake her up, but she didn't think she could cope with the noise. She ran a cold flannel over her face instead. It didn't help. A look in the mirror told her that make-up wasn't going to save the day this time either. She'd have to plead insomnia and hope it would account for the grey tinge to her skin, the tiny pinpricks of blood in the whites of her eyes, and the dark circles underneath that no concealer could hope to hide.

Pulling on navy jeggings and a pale blue jumper, she slipped bare feet into a pair of old pumps and went to wake Emma.

'You're not looking too well,' Paul said by way of greeting when she walked into the kitchen.

'I didn't sleep well,' she said. It wasn't a complete lie. She settled Emma with her breakfast before making some extra-strong coffee. It might help, it certainly couldn't make her feel any worse.

'Would you like me to take Emma to nursery?' he asked, finishing his cereal and dropping the bowl into the sink.

'No, that's okay,' she said, with a grateful smile. 'I'll drop her off, then come back and go back to bed for a couple of hours.'

It was what she should do. She tried to conjure up some enthusiasm for the plan that had seemed such a good idea yesterday. Seriously, what on earth did she think she was going to achieve by following the woman? *To find out if she were real.* Wasn't that the reason?

When Paul left, she made more coffee and took two regular painkillers to combat the ache in her ribs but, more importantly, the thumping headache that was preventing her from making sense even to herself.

Whether it was the coffee or painkillers, or possibly a combination of both, fifteen minutes later she felt a little better and with it came a renewal of her determination. Of course, she'd go ahead with her plan. She wasn't hallucinating, there had to be a reason that this woman was following her and she intended to find out what it was.

'Come on, Emma,' she said, bundling the child into her coat, grabbing her bag and hustling her out the door. 'Don't forget you're going to go to Tommy's house to play today. His mother will pick you up after school, okay?'

Diane didn't listen to her reply because she'd just realised there was a flaw in her plan. There were strict rules about collecting the children. Only a nominated person could, and, in Emma's case, that meant her or Paul. She could add Rose Metcalf to the list, of course, but she had to do it in person and it also had to be in writing.

'Fiddlesticks,' she muttered, switching off the engine and jumping out of the car. 'Be back in one second,' she called to Emma as she dashed back into the house. She needed paper and a pen. In the hall table drawer there were plenty of pens but no paper. Pen in hand, she dashed upstairs. She'd take some paper from Paul's printer, she decided, reaching for the door handle. She twisted and pushed, coming up against the door with an audible *oomph*. Puzzled, she twisted the knob again. The door was locked.

Confused, she tried to remember if she'd tried the door recently but couldn't. He didn't like his stuff being disturbed so she didn't clean the room and had no reason to go inside unless he was there. But she was sure he never locked it before. But then again, her memory was not something she could rely on over the last year. Maybe he'd always locked it? He did bring work home, maybe it was for security. Brushing the thought aside, she hurried to Emma's room, found a pink notepad and tore a page from it. It would have to do.

Back in the car, she groaned when she saw the time. She was going to have to get a move on. Normally a slow, careful driver who always stayed within the speed limit, today she edged over it for the ten-minute drive. She felt more alive than she had in a while. Taking control had become more important in her increasingly shaky life.

Diane approached the entrance to the school. Despite her speed, she was still a couple of minutes late and she could see Rose Metcalf standing by her car.

She parked and rushed over, leaving Emma still strapped in her seat. 'I'm so sorry. I'll have the seat out in a jiffy,' she said and rushed back to her car, opening the seatbelt to let Emma slide out and then disconnecting the straps that held the seat in place and rushing back, holding the child by one hand and the light but awkwardly shaped seat in the other.

Rose watched as Diane fumbled to connect the straps to the back seat of her car.

'Okay,' Diane said, standing back at last.

Rose gave a thin smile and turned to get into the driver's seat. 'Four thirty-five, okay? Don't be late,' she said, shutting her door without waiting for an answer. Diane barely had time to step away before the car reversed past her.

She hadn't realised her grip on Emma's hand had tightened until the girl squealed. 'Mummy, you're hurting me!'

'Sorry, sorry,' she said, and squatted down to access the damage, planting a series of kisses on the chubby hand. 'Better?'

Emma nodded.

'We'd better hurry inside,' she said, checking her watch. 'I just need to get something from the car first.'

Grabbing the paper and pen, she shoved them into her pocket and rushed Emma into the nursery. The reception area was empty apart from a receptionist sitting behind a curved desk. She wore a forbidding look on her face that increased as Diane rushed forward. 'I'm so sorry, I got delayed. Diane Andrews,' she said, and then tugged Emma forward, 'Emma, my daughter.'

The receptionist, a large name badge on her right breast proclaiming her name to be Debbie, looked at the computer screen, clicked a few keys and then looked back up to Diane with a smile that completely transformed her face. 'Miss Rogers' class,' she said, 'they've only just gone through.' She stood and pointed down the corridor. 'If you go down to the third door on the right, that's her room.'

Diane smiled gratefully, feeling tears gather at the unexpected kindness in the woman's voice and, without a word, took Emma to her class. Miss Rogers was equally pleasant, brushing off her apologies with a smile, and reaching for the child's hand to draw her inside.

Back at the reception desk, she withdrew the now crumpled sheet of pink paper and laid it on the desk to write out the permission slip for Rose Metcalf to pick up Emma after school. 'It'll probably only be a one-off,' she said, smoothing the sheet out and quickly writing out the permission slip before handing it across the desk. 'Sorry about the paper,' she said, with a rueful smile.

Debbie took it and read it as if pink lined paper was perfectly normal and acceptable. 'That's fine,' she said, nodding. 'I'll scan it into your file. It is valid for today only,' she said, with a return to her more forbidding expression, 'if you need Emma to be picked up by Mrs Metcalf again, it will require another permission slip.'

Only when Diane nodded her understanding, did the receptionist's face resume its friendlier demeanour.

Outside the school, she looked around before leaving the school grounds. The woman had stood directly across the road, so she needed to find somewhere she could stand unobserved to watch her. The problem was, she had no idea which direction the woman came from or which way she went. She appeared and disappeared, as if by magic. Diane had seen magicians at work; it was the art of illusion, dependent on the gullibility of the customer and on the ability of the magician to distract them from what was really happening. She had been distracted by children, cars and anxiety. Today, she'd be ready.

There was a house to the right of the school with a large garden, surrounded by a high brick wall. Just past it lay a row of shops. Diane was in luck. Between the garden wall and the shops there was an alleyway that she guessed was used for deliveries to the various shops.

She ducked inside it and peered out. The view to the path opposite the school was clear. Double yellow lines between the shops and the school meant it would stay that way. It was the perfect spot. She took it as a good omen.

Wandering back to her car, she considered what might happen. She'd get in position by about twelve thirty, in case she came early. This was going to be her only opportunity. Sitting into the driver's seat, she rested her hands on the steering wheel and chewed her lower lip as she thought. The woman might walk to a car. In that case, she needed to have pen and paper in her pocket so she could write down the registration number. She might walk to public transport. That would be better, she could follow her. The third possibility was that the woman could walk home. This was the option Diane was hoping for.

She switched on the engine and made the journey home.

The coat she'd worn that morning was too thin for standing in damp, shaded places. She swopped it for a warmer jacket with a hood. Putting it on, she pulled the hood up and looked at her reflection in the hall mirror. She grinned as she pulled the hood down, the thought crossing her mind that she was enjoying herself. *Doing* something rather than sitting back and accepting the status quo. It felt good.

Before she took the jacket off, she got a pen, another page from the pad in Emma's room, checked her purse to make sure she'd money and stuffed everything into the jacket's zipped pocket, closing it with a pat of satisfaction. She was ready.

Leaving the jacket thrown over the newel post, she went into the kitchen, made some coffee and listened to the radio, one eye watching the minute hand of the clock. She'd have had more coffee but she was jittery enough as it was.

The plan was to park her car in a nearby supermarket car park, ten minutes' walk from the nursery. There was no sign to say parking was limited, so it was probably safe to leave it there for as long as it took. Anyway, she had to be back to collect Emma no later than four thirty-five.

Finally, it was time to go. She drove to the supermarket, parked and, ten minutes later, approached the row of shops, glancing into them as she passed. The first was a butcher's, and beside it a busy newsagent. There were only four parking spaces outside and as soon as a car pulled away, another took its place.

Diane checked her watch. Twelve twenty-nine. With a final glance towards the empty nursery car park, she stepped into the alleyway. Positioned as it was between the high garden wall and the side of the shop, it was cold and damp and she regretted immediately that she hadn't worn gloves. She pulled up her hood, shoved her hands into her pockets and concentrated on the spot across the road from the school where the woman had stood.

There was five more minutes of calm before cars started pulling into the car park and she moved closer to the edge of the wall, her eyes narrowing to focus on that spot only a few hundred feet away. Rose Metcalf's blue Focus pulled in at exactly twelve fifty-five.

From where she stood, Diane couldn't see the children coming out of the nursery. She hoped Emma would remember she wasn't going to be there, hoped too that she hadn't made a huge mistake leaving her with a stranger. She shook the idea away; Rose was a good mother, you only had to see Tommy to know that. She'd be good with Emma.

Stupidly, she'd been focused on the nursery and when she looked back across the street she gasped. The woman was there. Where had she come from? She'd only taken her eyes off the spot for a few seconds. Diane rested a hand on the cold, damp garden wall and kept her eyes fixed on the woman, barely blinking in case, in that nanosecond when her eyes were shut, she disappeared as quickly as she'd appeared.

She wasn't wearing her navy coat this time. Instead, she was wearing a pale green puffa jacket and dark trousers. It was the first time since the charity shop that she was able to observe her. Nice-looking, she decided, but nothing out of the ordinary. Her sleek bob was, in fact, her best feature.

As the crowds of parents and their cars dispersed, she saw her look at her watch and then up and down the road, but it wasn't until every car had gone that she turned on her heel and started to walk away. Diane waited a few beats and then stepped out of the alleyway and crossed the road to follow her, adjusting her pace to match hers, keeping her hood pulled up.

Apart from the nursery, the area wasn't one she knew. She followed as the woman walked steadily, crossing roads, turning corners, never looking back. Once, at a pedestrian crossing, Diane had to stop and wait and then dash forward to cross before the lights changed.

After thirty-five minutes, just when she thought she was going to walk forever, the woman stopped outside a house. She opened the gate and walked up a short drive to a front door. Diane hung back and watched as the woman vanished inside and then waited a few minutes before walking past, her eyes scanning the house to see if there was anything to see. A house, not a block of apartments. It was just what she'd hoped for, she couldn't believe her luck. She took note of the house number and then walked to the end of the street to read the street name. *Bridgemead Street*. Pulling the pen and notebook from her pocket, she scrawled it down and put it away.

She took another look at the house when she passed it again but there was nothing to see and no car parked in the driveway to the side. A handsome, late Victorian house. Expensive. She checked out the neighbours as she walked past. The cars in some of the driveways were newish BMWs, top-of-the-range Toyotas and Fords.

Pleased with how things had turned out, she walked briskly back to her car. It was two thirty. She had almost two hours free before she needed to pick up Emma. With the address burning a hole in her pocket, she headed for home.

Her laptop was usually under the sofa in the lounge, but she'd taken it upstairs when she'd checked out the nursery and left it under her bed. She took the stairs in twos and, flopping onto the bed, reached underneath to pull it out.

It took a while to power up. It was old; she'd suggested buying a new one but Paul had laughed, saying it was good enough for the internet shopping she used it for. It was also good enough, it turned out, for investigative work. Within five minutes, and the outlay of a few pounds to the Land Registry, she knew the woman's name.

Sophie Redmond.

CHAPTER 11

Sophie Redmond. It was such an ordinary name. Too ordinary, she realised, doing an internet search and finding hundreds. Taking the laptop downstairs, she made some coffee and sat scrolling through a few, but none of the ones she opened were likely candidates, and there were hundreds more to look through. Tapping her nails on the computer, wondering how she could narrow the search, the time caught her eye.

'Oh no!' she yelped, jumping up. It was four thirty. She'd fallen into the computer black hole that sucks time away. No matter how fast she drove, she'd never make it to the Metcalf house by four thirty-five. It would have been sensible if she'd taken Rose's phone number, she could have rung and explained she'd be a little late. But, stupidly, she hadn't thought of it.

Dashing out to the car, she started the engine and reversed out onto the road, a car blasting its horn as it swerved out of her way. She sped off up the road, groaning when she saw the flash of a speed camera. How was she going to explain that to Paul? But it didn't slow her down.

It was four fifty by the time she pulled into the Metcalf driveway and, as she pulled up outside, the front door opened to a frigid-faced Rose standing with the car seat in one hand, Emma's bag in the other.

Diane braced herself for harsh criticism, but Rose merely handed her the seat and bag without saying a word. Turning, she called into the house behind her, 'Emma, your mother is here, at last.'

The child skipped toward the doorway, her face a beaming smile.

Diane looked at the woman gratefully. 'Some day,' she said softly, 'I'll explain everything to you and I think you'll understand.'

Rose closed the door as soon as Emma had crossed the threshold.

Diane sighed. Maybe she wouldn't understand, maybe no one would. Taking Emma's hand, she took one lingering look at the door before turning, getting into the car and driving away.

At home, she opted to make a cottage pie and, working quickly, she had it in the oven just as she heard the front door open. It would take another ten minutes, at least, to brown.

Emma, of course, hopped up and ran to greet her father, giving her time to rush over and switch off the TV just as they came into the room, Paul swinging Emma by both arms. 'Hi,' she said brightly, plumping up the cushions on the sofa and straightening the throw that was draped over the back before turning to him. 'Did you have a good day?'

Paul leaned in to give Diane a kiss on her cheek. 'I did, but you look a bit frazzled,' he said, his eyes narrowing as they swept over her. 'Have you been overdoing it?'

She ran a hand over her hair and tucked loose strands behind her ears. Pulling the hood of her jacket up and down would have made it a tangled mess, she should have brushed it when she came home. 'Emma was having such a good time with Tommy that she wanted to stay longer,' she said, the lie coming easily. 'I didn't have the heart to drag her away, so I've been rushing. I'm still a bit behind. Dinner will be another fifteen minutes.'

'That's fine,' he said, with a shrug, 'I'll go and get changed. I've some work to do anyway. I'll come down in fifteen.'

Emma had run back to the sofa. With the television off, she picked up the doll that Diane had left beside her.

'It's good that she's mixing with other kids,' Paul said, looking at her. 'Maybe these play dates will become a regular occurrence.'

'Maybe,' she said with a forced smile, turning away before he saw the truth in her eyes. She opened the oven door and peered inside, using the oven mitts to turn the dish around. It wasn't necessary, but it kept her busy until she heard his footsteps recede. Throwing the mitts on the counter she leaned on it and took a deep breath. Tangled webs, she thought before pushing away and busying herself with setting the table for dinner.

It was almost twenty-five minutes before the potato was brown and crispy on top. Taking it out, she left it to cool slightly while she called Paul down and settled Emma into her chair.

Over dinner, Paul quizzed Emma about her afternoon in the Metcalf house but she was tired so, apart from saying that Tommy let her play with his toys, she'd little information to offer. Diane tensed, waiting for his interest to switch to her. How stupid to say she'd had to wait? She hadn't thought it through because, of course, she'd have had to wait inside.

'So, what's the house like?' he asked.

'It's okay,' she said slowly, gaining seconds to put together an acceptable description of a house whose interior she'd only glimpsed. But she knew what he wanted. To know it wasn't as nice as theirs. 'We sat in the kitchen. It has small windows and low ceilings so it's a bit dark and gloomy. It made me realise how lucky we are with this room and all the light we get.'

It was the perfect answer; she could see him visibly relax. 'They should do what I did here,' he said, waving towards the windows. Talking about the changes he'd made to the run-down house he'd bought was one of his favourite topics of conversation. It required little input from Diane apart from a look of rapt attention and the odd murmur of agreement. She had little appetite and left more than half the small amount she'd served up for herself. This time, unfortunately, Paul noticed.

'You're not eating properly,' he said, using his knife to indicate her unfinished dinner.

She laughed. 'Well, I was naughty this afternoon,' she said, wondering at how inventive she'd become. 'Rose had the most delicious lemon drizzle cake and I pigged out and had two slices.'

The frown that had appeared between Paul's eyes faded. 'Two slices, that *was* piggery.'

'Well, it is my favourite,' she said, taking her plate to the kitchen.

The usual routine followed and, finally, with a sigh she barely kept hidden, she watched as Paul picked Emma up and headed upstairs.

He wouldn't be back. Although she half waited, half expected him to, she couldn't remember the last time he'd spent the evening with her. Not since her return from the clinic, certainly. The first few nights, she'd been so tired she'd gone to bed at the same time as Emma and after that he'd excused himself, saying he had work to do. Now, he didn't even make an excuse. Was it the same before the clinic? She had no idea. Memories of them sitting together on the sofa, her curled up in his arms, were sepia-tinged in her mind.

Heaving a weary sigh, she wondered if she should suggest again that he move back into their bedroom. Suddenly, Paul's face appeared in her mind, a look of derision in his eyes, his mouth a thin line. She blinked, startled. *Was that a memory?* Her forehead creased as she tried to bring it into focus but, if it were a memory, it faded like warm breath on a cold day. Memory or not, it was enough to make her decide to leave things as they were for the moment.

His not returning had one major advantage. She could have a glass of wine without fear of censure. A large glass in hand, she curled up on the sofa to consider what she'd do about Sophie Redmond. With the limited information she had, she couldn't think of any way to narrow down an internet search. It left her with the only alternative; to knock on her door and demand an explanation. Sipping her wine, she nodded. It seemed the simplest thing to do. Monday, she'd do it on Monday.

Tomorrow she was meeting Anne. The thought brought a smile to her face. It would be nice just to sit and chat with another woman. There was something about Anne that reminded her of her mother. They'd been close, and when she'd died, suddenly, fifteen years ago, Diane had been bereft. An only child, she'd moved into Bristol and used money her mother had left her to study information technology which had always fascinated her. Maybe, it was time to get back to it and meet new people? She'd thought she'd make new friends when she came to London, but she hadn't. Then, when Emma came along, she thought she'd make friends with other parents. She gave a rueful chuckle. That wasn't exactly turning out so well. Perhaps if she'd been honest with Rose from the beginning? Hindsight, she thought draining her wine, was a wonderful curse.

She wouldn't discuss her past or her recent worries with Anne though; she'd learned a valuable lesson from what happened with Rose, new friendships were fragile. She didn't want to see Anne's smiling friendly face become worried and cautious. For the moment, she'd keep her problems to herself.

CHAPTER 12

Diane had passed The Birdcage Café a number of times but had never been inside. It was situated between a bookshop and a delicatessen, the frontage of all three decorated with the same sage green and cream trim.

Inside, the green and cream theme continued in tartan-covered sofas, soft green blinds on the windows and green floral seat pads on chairs. It was all very pleasing, and Diane felt cosy and relaxed as soon as she walked through the door.

There was a table free in the square bay window; she took off her coat, sat and perused the menu written on a board above the counter, her eyes boggling when she saw the prices. It had been a while, certainly, since she'd gone out for coffee, but it looked as if prices had doubled since then.

She checked her watch. Five past eleven. She straightened the sleeve of the burgundy-coloured silk shirt she wore. She wanted to make a good impression on this first social outing. Paul had raised an eyebrow when he saw her. 'Very nice,' he'd said simply, making her smile.

Her eyes flitted toward the door. Maybe Anne had forgotten? At ten past eleven, she began to worry. She *had* asked her to meet, hadn't she? She'd not imagined it? She pinched the top of her nose with her thumb and middle finger as tears prickled.

At eleven twenty, she was just about to leave when Anne appeared, an apologetic look on her face, her mass of hair tied up with a vibrant orange scarf. Tendrils fell down to curl around her face in a way that looked artful but Diane guessed was purely accidental.

'I am *so* sorry,' Anne said, pulling out the chair opposite and collapsing into it, dropping a well-worn leather bag on the floor beside her. 'It was one of those mornings where just everything took longer than I expected.'

Diane couldn't help but smile. Honestly, she was just relieved the woman had turned up, that she hadn't imagined they'd agreed to meet. 'Sit and relax,' she said. 'I'll go and order. What would you like?'

'Just a black coffee,' Anne said, taking off her jacket and looking at her gratefully.

There were a couple of people before her in the queue giving Diane time to wonder about Anne. She'd no idea what she did for a living, if she did anything at all. Perhaps today, over coffee, she could ask.

The queue was slow-moving, the people in front ordering multiple items that the young woman behind the counter collected one at a time from the room behind. Nobody seemed to be in a hurry, the atmosphere pleasant and relaxed. Eventually, it was her turn and she smiled at the cheerful assistant and said, 'A large black coffee and a large skinny cappuccino, please.'

A few minutes later, she returned to the table in the window. 'Sorry,' she said, 'service is a tad slow.'

Anne removed both coffees from the tray and reached behind her to put it on an empty table. Turning back, she grinned, added sugar to her coffee, picked it up and took a sip before sitting back with a sigh. 'Gosh, I needed that,' she said, looking across the table. 'You okay?'

Diane shrugged and picked up her own coffee. 'Yes, thank you,' she said, between sips, wishing it were true. 'I've applied for a few jobs.' It was a lie she couldn't resist; she wanted to sound strong and dynamic. But the lie wouldn't hold up to further questions so she turned the conversation around and asked, 'What do you do when you're not volunteering or meeting people like me for coffee?'

'I write crime novels,' Anne said. 'Pretty successfully, actually,' she added without embarrassment. She sipped her coffee again. 'That's why I volunteer. I need to get out of the house and mix with other people. It keeps my ideas fresh.'

'A writer,' Diane said, impressed but not surprised; she looked the part. 'Do you write under your own name?'

'Yes, Anne Manners. I've written eight novels. After self-publishing the first, I was lucky to get picked up by Red Ribbon Publishers and was able to give up teaching and write full time.'

'Must have been very exciting,' Diane said, with genuine enthusiasm. 'I'd love to have something that motivated me that way.'

Anne tilted her head to one side. 'You have a daughter, don't you?'

With a slight reddening of her cheeks, Diane nodded. 'She's wonderful, and watching her grow is the best thing ever.' She wanted to add that she missed working and mixing with other adults, being intellectually challenged by stimulating conversation, but she didn't want to sound self-obsessed so, instead, she asked, 'Do you have children?'

A toss of tendrils. 'No children, no husband. And, before you ask, no cats or dogs either.'

Diane gave a laugh. 'You never married?'

Anne shrugged. 'I've had lots of relationships, but nobody special enough to spend the rest of my life with. But,' she grinned, 'I haven't given up hope yet.' Her grin faded, her face turning serious. 'How long have you been married?'

'Four years.'

'Have you been together a long time?'

'Four years.' Diane smiled at the look of surprise on her face. 'Paul and I got married just two months after meeting. I moved from Bristol to be with him and then I got pregnant almost immediately.' She remembered feeling as if she were on a roller coaster. Had she fallen off; was that why she'd had her breakdown?

She could feel Anne's eyes on her and forced herself to smile.

'And are you okay?' Anne reached a hand across the table and laid it gently on her arm. 'Forgive me,' she said softly, 'it's just, sometimes, there is so much sadness in your eyes.'

Feeling the warmth of her hand through the silk of her blouse, Diane felt suddenly choked with emotion. 'I've had a tough year,' she said quietly. She hesitated and then added, 'I'm recovering from…from a sort of breakdown.'

The hand on her arm tightened. 'Oh, my dear, I'm so sorry.'

Struggling for composure, Diane nodded before saying quietly, 'I thought you might know, I told Red.'

'She wouldn't have shared something private like that.'

A baby started to wail, startling Diane who immediately looked around, afraid she was imagining it. She was relieved when she saw a young mother frantically jigging a newborn in an effort to calm him. She smiled in sympathy as the mother gave up and took her baby outside to walk up and down outside the shop while her friends continued with their chat. She turned her attention back to Anne. 'I was in a clinic for a few weeks, but I'm doing fine now.' Maybe if she told herself this often enough, she'd start to believe it.

'That makes me feel even worse about what happened in the shop.' Anne frowned, taking her hand away and sitting back. 'No wonder Red was so upset.'

No wonder *I* was so upset, Diane wanted to say, but didn't. 'Let's talk about something else,' she said.

'Of course,' Anne said quickly. And for the next hour, they chatted about living in London, their favourite restaurants, their favourite movies. *Friendship*. Diane felt a frisson of pleasure. She'd missed this.

'More coffee?'

Diane looked at her watch. 'Gosh, no,' she said, grabbing her bag and coat. 'It's time I was picking up Emma. I'll have to dash.'

Anne stood and gathered her belongings. 'We'll meet again?'

'Definitely,' she said with a smile. 'I've really enjoyed this.'

'How about same time next week?'

Diane's smile was wide, crinkling up around her eyes. 'It's a date.' She turned and left the café, her feet barely touching the ground as she hurried to her car.

She was later than usual, pulling into the car park with difficulty as cars were already exiting, holding up traffic on the road until a car flashed her to enter. She gave a wave of thanks and pulled into a parking space.

The hint of a smile on her lips faded as she got out of the car and looked across the road expecting to see the woman in her usual place. It even crossed her mind to accost her there and then, this Sophie Redmond, whoever she was, but there was no sign of her.

She turned to look up the road in the direction she'd followed the woman yesterday, expecting to see her walking away. But the path was empty as far as she could see. Unnerved, she looked the other way, still no sign of her. She could feel fear slither down her spine and tried to shake it away. The woman *did* exist. Her name was Sophie Redmond.

The shout of *Mummy* brought her attention back to the reception area and Emma's smiling face and she rushed over to greet her with a hug.

Monday. She'd have her answers then.

CHAPTER 13

Paul usually looked after Emma on Saturday mornings. He'd take her to breakfast and then to the park or to London zoo, where annual membership allowed them to visit as often as they wanted. He liked to feel they got value for their money, so they went at least twice a month.

Diane, who wasn't keen on the concept of keeping wild animals behind bars, was quite happy to be excluded and waved them off with a sigh of relief. She loved spending time with Emma, but it was so much easier to get housework and shopping done when she wasn't with her, especially times like this morning when she had to visit a number of different shops. She'd struggled to stay on top of things since the clinic; today she was determined to catch up.

The one job she wanted to get over with first, the one she'd been putting off, was a visit to the dry-cleaner. There was only one in the area and it was in the same shopping centre as the charity shop. In fact, it was in the same row of shops, separated from it by the local branch of a bank that was destined to be closed.

The dry-cleaner opened at nine thirty, at which time she hoped Red would be busy inside the charity shop which opened on the dot of nine. Diane parked her car and approached from the opposite direction, two of Paul's suits draped over her arm. She hadn't realised she was holding her breath until she got inside.

The man behind the counter unfolded the two suits and looked them over with a practised eye, searching for stains, damage or missing buttons. Satisfied, he picked them up and folded the jackets and trousers separately.

'Do you want to pay now or when you collect?' he asked, writing out a docket.

'On collection,' Diane said, wanting to get away as quickly as possible. She took the docket and turned to leave, checking it automatically as she moved, her hand reaching for the door handle to open it before realising it was already being opened by someone on the other side.

There was a moment when neither she nor the red-headed woman on the other side of the door moved, their hands both on the door handle, eyes locked on each other, neither blinking. Finally, Red removed her hand and stood back.

Diane didn't have any choice. Taking a deep breath, she pushed the door open and faced Red, who stood outside with several garments hanging awkwardly over one arm. 'Hi,' she said, hoping to brush by without another word.

'Please,' Red said, extending her free hand towards her, 'wait a minute till I get rid of these so we can talk.'

Diane met her eyes and nodded, watching through the window while she handed over the clothes to be cleaned and tucked the docket into the back pocket of her jeans. Her lips were moving; she wondered if she were rehearsing what to say.

As soon as she was through the door, Red blurted out, 'I am so sorry, Diane, for the way I treated you.'

She saw the genuine remorse on her face. 'Anne told me,' she said. 'Perhaps we should just forget about it.'

One side of Red's glossy red lips crooked in a smile. 'I don't suppose you'd consider coming back?'

Diane had been happy for the short time she'd been in the shop, but knew she couldn't go back. She shook her head. 'No,' she said. 'I don't think so.'

Red sighed, as if this was the answer she expected. 'I'm sorry I didn't call around and apologise in person,' she said, 'but when Anne said she knew where you lived and was going to call on you, I thought it was best to leave it to her.'

A group of teenagers drifted toward them. Self-absorbed and very vocal, they walked around and between the two women as if they didn't exist, drowning them, just for a moment, in their conversation.

Diane needed to get away, to think about what Red had just said. 'I have to go,' she said abruptly, turning and walking away, raising a hand in acknowledgement as she heard a *goodbye* drift over her shoulder. Something was very wrong; lies blinded her, words were smudging the truth, confusing her. She wasn't sure what was real any more, what and whom to believe.

She felt tears burn as she made her way across the car park to her car, opening the door and almost falling into the seat. Leaning her head on the steering wheel for a moment, she swallowed and took deep breaths, then sat back and rubbed the corners of her eyes, careful not to smudge the mascara she had applied just hours before. Trembling, she rested a hand on her forehead to think.

According to Red, Anne had known where she lived.

But Anne had said she'd got her address from Red.

One of them was lying.

Neither had a reason to. Did they? Frowning, she couldn't think of one. And, anyway, did it matter?

Yes, she decided, biting her lower lip. It did. People didn't lie for no reason.

Her meeting with Red had been purely accidental; she couldn't have known that Diane would choose that morning to visit the dry-cleaner. But Anne had called to her home, had met her for coffee. She groaned and shut her eyes. She'd been so pleased to have a female friend to meet up with, she'd been overly chatty, answering any question she'd been asked. Thinking back, she couldn't recollect all of them. What exactly had she given away? And what had she learned in exchange? That Anne lived alone and wrote novels. That was it.

She felt the first stirrings of anger, something uncoiling deep inside. It was time to put an end to this. Being stalked and lied to, she'd had just about enough.

CHAPTER 14

She stopped at the supermarket on her way home, relieved that Paul and Emma were still out when she returned. Unpacking the boot, she brought the bags inside and left them on the kitchen floor; she took out the frozen items, put them away and left the rest. She needed a cup of tea before she finished.

The kettle on, she sat to wait for it to boil, enjoying a rare moment of quiet in an empty house. Then she heard something, a cry so soft she almost missed it, lost as it was in the hiss and gurgle of the kettle. Getting up, she switched the power off, tilted her head and listened. There it was again; the unmistakable sound of a baby crying.

She moved into the hallway and waited for it to come again, hoping to pinpoint it to a place. Maybe it came from outside? A neighbour, or a mother passing with a loud, noisy baby? Opening the front door, she looked out. But the road was empty.

When the heartbreaking wail came again, she shut the door and leaned against it, clamping her hands tightly over her ears but unable to shut the gut-wrenching sound out. It seemed to weaken her to her core. Unable to move away, held frozen by the sound, she slid down the door to the floor, her eyes tightly shut. That's when she knew, without a doubt, something was happening to her. Something terrifying and completely out of her control. She must be going slowly, quietly mad.

She was still there over an hour later when she heard the sound of a car pulling up outside. Scrambling to her feet, she ran trembling hands over her face and shot into the family room to take a quick glance in the mirror that hung behind the sofa. 'Normal,' she whispered to herself; a word that had suddenly lost all meaning.

She headed into the kitchen when she heard the front door open and busied herself with unpacking the remaining groceries. Emma came flying in, her voice high-pitched with excitement, Paul following a few steps behind.

'Hi!' she called out, from behind the open door of a cupboard. 'Did you have a nice day?'

'Yes, we did,' Paul said, picking up the kettle and shaking it before switching it on. 'The zoo was packed though. You just in?'

She looked around the cupboard door at him. 'Yes,' she said, 'just in.' She bent to take a packet of cereal from the bag at her feet and buried herself back in the cupboard. By the time she'd finished, he'd made his coffee and taken it back to the sofa to work his way through the newspaper, one section at a time, never skipping a page or reading them out of order. When he finished, she knew, the newspaper would be as crisp and tidy as when he'd started.

In the short time before they married, they'd been amused by their differences, attracted to traits that were so alien, so opposite to their own. He'd laughed at the coffee stains she left on the newspapers and the clothes she'd left lying about, she'd mocked his ordered and tidy habits, his insistence on a place for everything and everything in its place. Now, she sighed, they were just differences they'd learned to deal with.

Through the floor-to-ceiling windows that overlooked the back garden, she could see that the breeze had picked up. Feeling guilty, she thought of the dirty laundry spilling out of the laundry baskets upstairs. She should have done a wash and hung it on the line before she went out. If she had, it would be almost dry by now.

Without a word to Paul, she left the room, closing the door softly after her. In the hallway, she hesitated at the staircase and moved back to the door of the lounge. Almost hesitantly, she laid one hand flat on it, the white painted surface cool under her hand, and there it was, the same flicker of fear. She backed away.

Her step was heavy as she headed upstairs. In the bathroom, she sat on the edge of the bath and swallowed the self-pity that was choking her. There were possibly tablets that would help without making her so withdrawn. It was worth asking. But not yet. Everything had started with Sophie Redmond; maybe meeting her would bring it to an end. She had to try before giving in.

She blinked. Why had she come upstairs? It took a few seconds to remember, and with a sigh she grabbed the heavy laundry bag and took it downstairs. Separating the laundry automatically into whites and coloured, she filled the machine, added powder and switched it on. She'd do the rest later, or tomorrow. Sometime.

A glance at the clock told her it was time to start dinner. Fish pie. She'd bought all the ingredients, hadn't she? She looked in the fridge and breathed a sigh of relief. Thirty minutes later, it was in the oven. 'It'll be ready in twenty minutes,' she said, laying the table. A baby's cry startled her. It was higher pitched and louder than before. 'Did you hear that?' she said, the words out before she could stop herself.

Paul looked up from the newspaper, irritated. 'What?'

Diane swung around. 'It sounded like a baby crying.'

'Cats,' Paul said dismissively, returning to the paper.

She blinked, feeling incredibly stupid. Of course. Cats, or kittens maybe, their mewling could sound just like a baby crying. It made sense; she'd chased stray cats from the garden several times over the years. Why hadn't she thought of it? Sometimes, the answers to problems were simple. She had to keep that in mind.

CHAPTER 15

On Monday she woke early after a restless night where her stalker materialised as a zombie, with body parts falling off as Diane chased her down the street. She was too anxious and too tense to see the funny side, her nerves jangling as she woke Emma, helped her wash and dress and sent her downstairs. Paul was already rattling around in the kitchen; if she didn't appear after a little while he'd begrudgingly give Emma her breakfast.

She applied make-up a little heavier than usual and left her hair loose, fluffing it around her face hoping to disguise a noticeable gauntness in her cheeks. Wanting to feel mature and professional, she took navy trousers and a pale blue shirt from her wardrobe.

Dressed, she looked at her reflection. Boring, she thought, fluffing her hair some more and thinking of Anne's bohemian style with a tinge of envy. It wasn't something she could carry off, she told herself as she finished buttoning her shirt, and besides, she might be conservative, but at least she was honest. Anne's lie still cut her deeply.

Emma had almost finished her cornflakes by the time she went downstairs.

Paul looked up in concern. 'Are you feeling all right? You're looking very pale.'

'I'm so sorry,' she said, keeping her voice low and soft. 'I woke with a splitting headache and getting Emma ready was as much as I could manage. I knew you wouldn't mind giving her breakfast.'

'Of course not,' he said immediately. 'Poor you. Would you like me to take Emma to nursery?'

It was the second time he'd offered recently. It was kind, but she worried that he thought she wasn't coping. 'No, but thanks,' she said, 'I've taken some pills, it's already easing. A cup of tea and I'll be fine.'

She felt a little guilty as he insisted she sit while he boiled the kettle and made her tea and toast, putting it in front of her with an assessing look. 'You do look pretty ghastly,' he said, 'are you sure you'll be okay? Why don't you ring the shop, say you're not feeling well?'

Lies and their ramifications, she thought, giving him a smile of reassurance. She never used to lie so much. 'I'll be fine,' she said, picking up a piece of toast and hoping that was the truth.

Moments later, he pressed his lips to her cheek, gave Emma a hug and left. Diane threw the barely nibbled toast onto the plate and pushed it away. She picked up her tea and sipped it, restlessly glancing at the clock. It was too soon to leave.

'Finish your milk, darling,' she told Emma, who was playing with her spoon, tapping it on the bottom of the empty bowl. 'Would you like some more cereal?'

Blond curls danced as Emma shook her head. Putting down the spoon, she picked up the glass of milk in both hands and drank deeply before placing it carefully on the counter. She grinned at Diane, a moustache of milk above her top lip.

Smiling back at her, Diane left her to finish it while she tidied up and organised everything for the day, putting a snack and a drink into her small bag, fetching their coats, grabbing her bag and keys.

Opening the front door, she automatically glanced up and down the road. It was, as usual, drearily quiet. Apart from Mrs Prescott, she couldn't remember when she'd last seen someone on the street. When she'd moved here, she'd hoped there'd be some community spirit, but the neighbours tended to keep to themselves and, as far as she knew, there were none with young children. When she mentioned it to Paul, he told her she'd get used to it, that she was in London now, not Bristol.

He was wrong, of course. Reading online London magazines, it didn't take her long to discover that there were many parts of the city with a strong community feeling. Just not here. She guessed it wouldn't have been high on Paul's list of priorities when he'd bought the house. A suggestion that they move to a more family friendly area after Emma was born was met with reluctance. He liked the area, and loved the house. 'We won't get anywhere better,' he'd said, 'you'll soon get used to it.'

She hadn't but she didn't mention moving again.

She pulled out of their drive into the line of traffic, Emma babbling away happily in the back. Outside the nursery, there was the usual chaos of cars pulling in and out. She waited and pulled in in turn, parking in the first space she spotted.

'Okay,' she said, undoing Emma's seatbelt. 'I'll see you later.' Bending, she hugged her daughter to her for a moment. 'Love you, my darling,' she said, pressing her lips to her head.

'Love you too, Mummy,' Emma beamed before scampering down from the seat.

Diane walked over with her and stayed waving as she and her classmates filed inside. From the corner of her eye, she could see Rose Metcalf looking over at her but when she turned, the woman quickly looked away.

With a shrug, she returned to her car and sat inside. It was just after nine fifteen. Would Sophie Redmond be at home? If she worked, she'd possibly have left by now, but Diane didn't think she did. What kind of job could she have that would enable her to pop up at all times of the day?

She'd be at home, Diane was sure of it. In an hour, she'd have this business sorted out, once and for all. Optimism. It was time she had some of that.

With traffic being heavy, it took her longer than she expected to drive to the house. She passed it by, darting a quick look to see if there was any sign of life. There was, of course, nothing to see. There was also, she realised to her annoyance, nowhere to park and she tutted with annoyance as she was forced to go further and further away, finally finding a space and pulling in.

It took ten minutes to walk back to the house. A long street of identical houses, Sophie Redmond's was almost the last before a T-junction. As she got nearer, Diane could feel her heart thumping. She wiped clammy hands on her trousers and swallowed, her mouth uncomfortably dry, her tongue feeling overlarge. She hadn't rehearsed what to say. There wasn't much *to* say until she got the answer to the question: *Why?*

Her pace slowed as she approached the house, hands now curling into fists so tight that her nails were close to piercing skin. She felt the pain, almost relishing it as proof that she wasn't dreaming all of this.

The houses were fronted by small gardens surrounded by iron railings. At one time, she guessed, they'd have had iron gates too, but many of these were now either missing or had been replaced. She couldn't stall any longer and, stopping outside Sophie Redmond's house, she unlatched the original iron gate and pushed it open. She left it open; she had absolutely no idea what the next few minutes were going to bring; a quick exit might very well be required.

The garden was a neat and tidy rectangle of grass. There were no flowers but no weeds either. The dark green front door was imposingly dressed with a brass letterbox dead centre and a brass doorbell set to one side. On one side of the doorstep, looking oddly lopsided, a terracotta pot held a sad-looking bay tree.

Diane lifted her hand to ring the bell. It was trembling, she noticed, as if it were someone else's hand. She dropped it, took a deep breath and raised it again, extending her index finger to press the bell before she had a chance to change her mind.

She heard its chime echoing inside and took a step backward, stumbling as she stepped off the doorstep onto the path behind. Several minutes passed. She was just about to give up and leave when she heard a noise from behind the door. The distinct sound of a safety chain being undone was followed by a rattle as the doorknob was turned and the door swung open.

Diane let out the breath she'd been holding.

CHAPTER 16

The frail, elderly lady's hesitant smile dimmed and her hand, joints swollen with arthritis, clutched the door frame tightly. 'Can I help you?' she asked, in an accent that spoke of private schools and old money.

With difficulty, Diane conjured up a smile and tried to marshal her thoughts. This twin-set and pearled woman, looking like she'd stepped straight from an Agatha Christie novel, was definitely not the woman she was looking for. The Land Registry gave the name of the owner of the house, but no details of who lived there. Maybe she had a daughter?

'I'm sorry,' she said, feeling for the right thing to say. 'You must be Sophie Redmond,' she said. When the woman inclined her head, she continued. 'I was looking for your…daughter.'

A slight frown appeared on the woman's face. 'Suky?'

Diane went with it. 'Yes, is she home? I wanted to have a word. It's important,' she added, seeing the woman's face harden. Had the circumstances been different she would have admired the way she lifted her chin and seemed to straighten her backbone. Women of her era, despite their gentle exterior, were tough as old boots. She kept her lips curved in a smile and waited for the answer.

The woman's free hand moved to her pearls, fingers moving over them as if for reassurance. Her lips moved silently before she dropped the beads and looked straight at Diane. 'Suky died in a car accident, eight years ago.'

Diane cringed under the weight of her look and the unfathomable pain in her eyes. 'I'm so sorry,' she said, reaching out to touch the hand that still clutched the door, an automatic gesture of sympathy she immediately regretted when Sophie Redmond pulled away. 'I assumed the woman was your daughter, my apologies. Perhaps she's just a friend?'

The older woman's eyes narrowed. 'What are you talking about?' she asked bluntly.

'I was following a woman. She came in here. I need to speak to her.'

'I'm afraid you're mistaken, I live alone.' As if she suddenly realised that this wasn't the sort of information you gave to a total stranger on your doorstep, a flash of fear crossed the woman's face. She started to close the door, sheltering behind its solidness. 'Please leave now,' she said, with a quaver in her voice.

It was all falling apart. 'She was here,' Diane said, putting a hand on the door, feeling the pressure as it was pushed closed. With a hint of desperation in her voice, she added, 'Please, I need to speak to her.' Before the door shut, she tried one last time. 'I'll come back later, maybe she'll be back then? I don't mean any harm, honestly. I just need to speak to her.'

The door shut with a loud click followed by the distinct sound of a key turning in the lock and the safety chain being attached. Pushing open the letterbox flap, she bent down, put her mouth close and said, 'I didn't mean to upset you. I just need to talk to the woman who visits you.'

Did she really expect an answer? She moved away from the door, over to the square bay window and peered in. All she could see was the back of closed shutters. She stepped back and looked up at the upstairs windows. If the woman was looking down on her, she couldn't see.

Finally, because she couldn't think of anything else to do, she crossed the small garden, and stepped out onto the footpath, closing the gate after her.

For several moments, she stood looking at the house. The charity shop woman had definitely gone inside, hadn't she? *Hadn't she?* Anxiety twisted her gut and a wave of nausea swept over her. She reached out to hold on to the railing, praying she wasn't going to faint. Slow, deep breaths in, slower out. She knew the mantra.

After a few minutes, she let go and straightened slowly, relieved when the nausea faded. She looked at the house again. Had she imagined it all? Seeing her, following her? She swallowed the lump in her throat and began the walk back to her car.

She was halfway along the road when a police car pulled up just ahead. She didn't pay it much attention, although they were now an increasing rarity on the streets. When two policemen got out and stood on the path looking down the street toward her, she still didn't give them much thought.

It was only when she was almost upon them and they made no attempt to move out of her way that the truth dawned. They were there for her. She almost laughed, would have done, perhaps, if either of the two men had shown the slightest trace of amusement. But their faces were set and grim.

Shoving her hands into the pockets of her navy jacket she tried for casual with a breezy 'Hi!'

Both officers stared at her, their sharp eyes taking in every detail. Obviously deciding she wasn't a dangerous villain, their stance relaxed a little. One took a small step towards her. 'We've had a complaint that you've been harassing a resident,' he said.

Harassing? 'I think there's been a bit of a misunderstanding,' she started, taking her hands from her pockets and holding them out palms up. 'I was looking for someone. A friend I'd lost contact with.' The lie came easily. 'I thought she lived there.'

The policeman weighed up what she'd said. She could almost see the cogs going around behind his steely grey eyes.

'Mrs Redmond said you asked to speak to her daughter, Suky, who's been dead for several years.'

Dammit! She tried an understanding smile. 'I think she got a bit mixed up,' she said, with what she hoped would be seen as an understanding shake of her head. 'It was she who mentioned her daughter's name.' Well, that much was true. 'My friend's name is Suri. I suppose they do sound alike.' She was babbling. Giving an indulgent laugh, she stopped.

'Can we have your name, please?' the officer said, taking out a notebook and pen.

Diane tried another laugh. 'Seriously?'

'We *have* had a complaint,' he said, nodding back to the house at the end of the street.

'Yes, of course,' she said, trying to show there was no hard feelings, that she was a law-abiding, upstanding citizen eager to assist the police in the performance of their duties. 'It's Julia,' she said, the lie out before she could wonder why she was lying, and then because she couldn't think of another surname that went with it, she added, 'Roberts.'

'Julia Roberts.' He wrote it down and then looked up at her. 'Seriously?' he said, echoing her. 'Can I see some ID, please?'

She clutched her handbag. 'Is this absolutely necessary?' she asked. 'I have explained the misunderstanding.'

The policeman's eyes narrowed. 'Is there a problem with providing some ID?' he asked.

There wouldn't have been, if she hadn't lied. And just why had she done that? With the eyes of the two men on her, she opened her bag and took out her purse. She pulled out her credit card and handed it to him.

He took it, gave it a quick glance and then flicked it with his thumbnail. 'So, either you're Diane Andrews and you lied to us about your name, or you're Julia Roberts and you've stolen this bag. Which is it?'

Feeling about five years old, Diane hung her head. 'I'm Diane Andrews,' she said. Remembering she had her driver's licence in her bag, she rummaged inside and found it. 'See,' she said, handing over the photographic evidence. 'Me.' She shrugged one shoulder. 'I really don't know why I lied, there was no reason.'

'It happens more often than you'd believe,' the officer said, jotting down the details and handing her back the licence and credit card. 'I don't know what your problem is,' he said, 'and to be honest, I don't really care. But Mrs Redmond is a vulnerable old lady. She's recently spent a long time in hospital and she doesn't need people causing her aggro, okay?'

She nodded. There didn't seem to be anything else to do.

'You can go,' he said, 'but don't let us see you around here again.'

They parted to let her pass, standing so intimidatingly close she could feel the warmth of their bodies and smell the mix of their cologne. She walked as quickly as she could, feeling their eyes on her with every step. Concentrating on putting one foot in front of the other, feeling awkward and stiff-legged, she reached the end of the street, resisting the temptation to run to get around the corner out of their line of vision.

She made it around, legs weak and trembling, and collapsed on the first wall she came to, dropping her head into cupped hands.

'Hello, are you okay?' The voice was concerned.

Diane lifted her head and looked at the young man who stood in front of her, his head tilted in concern. 'What…what time is it?' she asked quietly.

He checked the time on his mobile. 'Twelve thirty,' he said.

Twelve thirty! She must have been sitting there for at least an hour. She'd blacked out.

'You want me to call someone for you?' he said, waving the phone.

She shook her head and stood. 'Thank you, no, I'll be fine.'

With a shrug, he left, sauntering down the street with an easy self-confidence she envied. It was going to take her longer than thirty minutes to get to the nursery. She was going to be late. Picking up pace, she made it to the car. If she hurried, she thought, she'd only be a few minutes late. Indicating, she pulled into the heavy traffic.

Unfortunately, she didn't know the roads, took a wrong turn, and looked around realising she didn't know where she was. She pulled in to the side of the road. The satnav would get her to the school but, first, she'd ring the nursery and let them know. Picking up her bag, she searched for her phone, a sick feeling in her stomach when she realised she didn't have it.

There was nothing she could do except try and get there as quickly as possible. She switched on the satnav, her clumsy, damp fingers keying in the wrong postcode twice. Finally, she got it right and pressed GO before pulling out into traffic.

The arrival time in the corner of the small screen told her the bad news: twenty minutes late. She remembered reading that they were strict about late collection and groaned. Of course, the arrival time depended on traffic behaving and it didn't; coming to a halt when she was still ten minutes away. She watched the arrival time move from one twenty to one twenty-two, then one twenty-five. It was one thirty before the traffic cleared and she finally pulled into the deserted car park and switched off the engine. Staff, she knew, parked in a small area at the back of the building. The main door was shut tight. With an unsteady finger, she pressed the doorbell and waited, biting her lower lip, moving restlessly from foot to foot.

She heard movement on the other side of the door as it was unlocked slowly, as if the person on the other side was making a point. Diane hadn't met the manager, Susan Power, since the first morning. She remembered her as a pleasant, approachable woman with a genial manner. Something had changed, or she was very annoyed.

'It's twenty-five to two, Mrs Andrews,' she said without any preliminary greeting. 'We have, as you are aware, strict rules about being late.'

'I'm so sorry,' Diane said, ready to plead. She'd tried to think of an excuse that would be acceptable on the way and offered it now. 'I'm never late, honestly, but this morning it was one thing after another and then my car got blocked in by two other cars and I couldn't get out.' She reached a hand towards the manager. 'I forgot my phone, so I couldn't ring you to let you know. I really am so sorry. It won't happen again.'

The sound of a car pulling into the car park distracted both women. Diane saw a look of satisfaction on Susan's face. Turning, she saw why. The car that was parking beside hers was Paul's.

Her face fell and she scrambled for an excuse that *he* would swallow. She couldn't think of any and the truth was out of the question. He'd probably been worried sick too. After all, she was never late. But any concern for her was quickly replaced by annoyance when he saw she was all right. 'Mrs Power,' he said, ignoring her. 'I'm so very sorry we've caused this upset.' Without looking at her, he said, 'Go home, Diane. I'll bring Emma.'

Humiliated, unable to think of a word in her defence, she looked down. There was an uncomfortable moment of silence before she nodded and returned to her car. Starting the engine, she looked out the window. Whatever Paul was saying, Susan Power was nodding along, her face grim. As she continued to watch, she saw the manager's face turn to look at her, her expression unreadable.

She drove home and let herself in. Needing something to do, she put the kettle on. She'd make a pot of tea, it would be ready by the time Paul and Emma were home.

Less than five minutes later, the front door opened and she heard Emma's cheerful voice with relief. She brought the teapot, mugs and milk to the table and waited for them to come through. Emma, as usual, dashed through first. Diane looked at her face closely, looking for signs that her enforced detention had upset her. But all she saw was the child's usual sunny smile.

It showed how serious Paul was taking the situation that he immediately switched on the TV, flicking stations until he found something suitable. 'Sit and watch this,' he told Emma, giving her hair an affectionate tousle, 'I'll get you a glass of milk and something to eat.'

Ignoring Diane, he moved to the kitchen, poured a glass of milk, peeled and chopped an apple and put it into a bowl before bringing both over to her. 'There you go,' he said.

Diane poured tea into two mugs, added milk to both and pushed one across the table to Paul as he pulled out a chair and sat opposite her.

'What the hell is going on?' he said quietly, picking up the mug and cradling it between his hands. 'You're never late, Diane.'

She'd expected him to be angry, so was caught unprepared for the weariness in his voice. For the briefest of moments, she thought about telling him the truth, but it had gone past that stage. Anyway, she was no longer sure what the truth was.

'I'm sorry,' she said, putting her tea down and reaching a hand across to lay it gently on his arm. He didn't brush it away. Taking this as a good sign, she continued, 'I should have listened to you this morning and taken the day off. My headache never really went away completely so I came home early from the charity shop, took a couple of painkillers and lay down for a nap. I didn't expect to fall into a sound sleep and when I woke, I was horrified to see what time it was.'

So many lies, she was becoming quite adept.

Or maybe not.

Paul brushed her hand away. 'You told Mrs Power that your car was blocked in and it took ages before you could get it out. So, which is it?'

She tried a laugh, but even to her ears it sounded false. 'I didn't like to tell her I'd fallen asleep,' she said. 'I thought saying I was blocked in was better.'

'Couldn't you have come up with something better?' he said, with a heavy sigh. 'Who, for goodness sake, gets their car blocked in?'

'I'm sorry,' she said again.

He lifted a hand to stop her. 'It's not me you need to apologise to. Mrs Power was very annoyed. They are very strict about time-keeping, Diane.' Draining his tea, he put the mug down and stood. 'Right, I'd better get back to work. They weren't impressed that I had to leave so suddenly.'

Since he was virtually his own boss, this didn't ring true, but she wasn't really in a position to complain. 'I am so sorry,' she said again, wondering how often she'd have to say it before the stern look on his face faded. More than she had so far, she guessed.

Sighing, she watched him go before throwing the remainder of her tea down the sink and putting both mugs into the dishwasher. Emma was still glued to the television, so she sat down on the sofa beside her, pulled her into the crook of her arm and let her head flop back. She let her thoughts wander where they would. And that was all over the place. She tried to get them in order. Her stalker. Not Sophie Redmond, that was definite. But she had seen her go into that house. *Hadn't she?* She slapped the doubt away.

Everything was confusing and unsettling and her failure to achieve anything that day was a staggering blow to her hope to get at the truth. Colour flooded her cheeks when she relived the humiliating scene at the nursery. And then she remembered the look Susan Power had given her. Just what had Paul told her to make her look at her so strangely?

The cry made her eyes snap open. It was a piteous sound that made the hair on the back of her neck stand on end. *Damn it*, she thought, she really didn't need this now. Despite what Paul said, she knew no cat or kitten made that sound.

She went to the kitchen, took the bottle of wine out of the fridge, unscrewed the cap and held the bottle to her mouth, gulping mouthfuls clumsily, wine spilling from her mouth, down her chin and dripping onto her shirt. After a few mouthfuls, she stopped and put the bottle away.

She was seeing things, hearing things; fooling herself that they might be real. She'd tell Paul and go back to see that therapist. She'd even take the damn pills, if he insisted. It was time she faced the truth; she was having a relapse.

CHAPTER 17

The wine, drunk on an empty stomach, hit her quickly; it made her woozy, but also, eventually, calmer. She wouldn't tell Paul yet, after all, there were still things she needed to find out.

She needed to play normal for a while longer. The smell of spilt alcohol wafted from her shirt. With a glance to make sure Emma was settled, she headed upstairs, had a quick shower, brushed her teeth and changed her clothes.

Passing the lounge, she felt rising anger and, reaching out, she slammed her hand on the door. The noise was loud and brought Emma running from the sofa.

'What's wrong, Mummy?' she asked, her face serious.

Annoyed with herself, Diane rushed to gather her into her arms, hiding her face in her curls. 'Nothing, my little lamb,' she said, picking her up and cuddling her. 'I accidently banged into the door. Silly Mummy.'

She carried her back into the family room, put her down on the sofa and sat beside her. 'I'll read you a story, shall I?' she asked, reaching out for the remote and switching off the TV.

'Ooh yes, please,' Emma said, sliding from the sofa and toddling over to the bookshelf where she pulled out a book and brought it back. Diane grinned when she took it from her. A story of princesses and magical creatures, it was Emma's favourite and she invariably chose it. There was time and plenty to explore the wider literary world, she thought, as Emma snuggled beside her to hear it read for what must be the one hundredth time. She opened the book and read the first four magical words, *Once upon a time…*

She dreaded Paul's return, but when he did there was no mention of the early afternoon's drama. She was pleased, but not really surprised. Since her return from the clinic, she noticed he didn't challenge her about anything. Truth be told, they didn't talk much at all. Once more, she debated telling him everything, but she saw a weariness on his face that was new, her heart breaking as she realised she was the cause.

It made her all the more determined not to tell him her worries. She'd give herself this week to sort things out; it hadn't been a good start, but there were a few days left.

She waited until he'd gone upstairs with Emma almost asleep in his arms and stood listening in the hallway as he moved around. Then she heard the quiet click as the door to his office was opened and closed. With a sigh of relief, she opened the fridge, took the bottle of wine and brought it and a glass back to the sofa with her.

Switching off the TV, she poured the wine and sat back. *What a goddamn awful day*, she thought, taking a mouthful of wine.

The first glass was followed by a second.

The day had been an unmitigated disaster. She sipped her wine, trying to relax but there were too many thoughts chasing their tails in her head. One in particular, more terrifying than them all, was that this was all in her mind and she was heading for a breakdown. How long would she need to spend in the clinic this time? Weeks? Months?

Then she thought of Anne's lie. If she was imagining some things, she wasn't imagining that. Why had she lied? Perhaps she should concentrate on that, on the one thing she knew was real. Friday's arrangement seemed a long time away. She supposed she could ring and ask her to meet earlier. Considering the idea for a moment, she shook her head. What was that phrase they used in the military? Ah yes, she needed to regroup. She needed a period of calm where everything went as it should, the way it used to. Days where she could concentrate on being the perfect wife and mother, stock the cupboards, get the laundry finished, do some ironing. By Friday, if no other disasters occurred, if nothing else happened to unsettle her, she'd have regained some equilibrium.

Swirling the wine in her glass, she thought about the strange sensation in the lounge. If she were imagining the woman and the cry, was she also imagining that? Taking her glass with her, she opened the door into the hall, holding her breath as she took the few steps to the lounge. Her heart beat a loud tattoo as she laid a hand flat against the door and let her breath out slowly. With the fingers of her other hand almost crushingly tight on the stem of the wine glass, she lifted it to her mouth and took a sip.

There was nothing wrong here.

Sliding her hand across to the door knob, she gripped it tightly, turned it, and then, very slowly, eyes wide, heart still beating out its rhythmic drumbeat, she opened the door and stepped inside.

There was nothing here to frighten her, she thought, reaching for the light switch but, then it came, a feeling of intense fear that erupted from her core to send her staggering. The glass fell from her hand, shattering as it struck the doorknob on its way to the floor, sending glass and wine flying. She turned to hang onto the door frame, legs barely holding her up, and bit her lower lip to stop the sob escaping.

Oh God, please don't let Paul have heard.

She stood there without moving for several minutes, praying he wouldn't come down to investigate. When he didn't, when she knew it was safe, she pushed away from the door and made her way on unsteady feet back into the family room and shut the door.

In the kitchen, she took out another glass and brought it back to the sofa. Without sitting, she picked up the bottle, filled the glass and drained it in two long gulps before collapsing onto the sofa, the glass dropping from her hand to land with a soft clunk on the rug.

It was a long time before she moved and when she did it was to bury her face in her cupped hands. She tried to think but the wine had fuzzed her head. There was something at the edge of her mind…something. The more she clutched at it, the further away it bounced and even when she managed to catch it, it didn't really make sense. Everything began after she'd seen the woman in the charity shop. So, the woman, the cry, her fear of the lounge, were they linked in some strange way? Or was it the alcohol blurring her mind, making the impossible vaguely probable?

She thought of the days and weeks where there were huge gaps in her memory and squeezed her eyes shut tightly. Were they linked in some bizarre way to something that had happened during one of those gaps? If only she could remember, maybe everything would make sense. A shiver ran through her. Perhaps, whatever it was, it was so bad that her mind preferred to have a relapse rather than having to deal with it.

She picked the glass up from the floor, put it on the table and grabbed the bottle. It was empty. She consoled herself by thinking it hadn't been full to start with, she'd had a glass from it the night before. Carefully, she stood, took the glass to the kitchen, rinsed it, dried it and put it away. The bottle went into a cupboard with the rest of the empties gathered over months. She'd get rid of them tomorrow.

The smashed glass in the lounge could stay there until the next day but, even with her brain befuddled, she was concerned that the smell of spilt wine might drift into the hallway and draw Paul's attention in the morning. Reluctantly, with a roll of kitchen towel in her hand, she went back to mop it up. At the doorway, she took a deep breath and went in but, despite alcohol- induced courage, her eyes darted around anxiously and she chewed her lip. She focused on the spill, using reams of paper to wipe it up as quickly as she could. Finally, she sprayed some neutraliser spray into the room and closed the door. Switching off lights, she headed upstairs, holding on tightly to the banisters. Overcompensating for her unsteadiness, she placed each foot carefully, swaying dangerously when she was almost on the top step.

In her bedroom, she stripped, dropped the clothes where she stood, climbed into bed and pulled the duvet up, then pulled it higher as a flicker of fear uncurled. What if, this time, it was much worse? What if, this time, she never got out of the clinic? Pulling the duvet over her head, shutting the world out, she shivered.

CHAPTER 18

She felt wretched when she woke; head thumping, stomach nauseous. She swallowed two painkillers, gulped down some water and hoped they'd make a difference.

Downstairs, she fixed Emma's breakfast, putting a bowl of cornflakes and a glass of milk in front of her, forcing herself to sound bright and cheerful. She wasn't sure she was fooling Paul.

'What are you doing today?' he asked, slipping on the jacket he'd left on the back of the chair.

'Just the usual,' she said, 'the charity shop and picking up Emma. Nothing else planned.' She held a hand toward him, waiting until he caught it before continuing. 'Don't worry, I slept really well last night and won't be coming home for a rest. There'll be no problems. I promise.'

As he dropped her hand and turned to go, she added, 'I thought I'd take Susan Power some flowers as an apology, what do you think?'

'That would be nice,' he said, giving her a kiss on her cheek before picking Emma up and giving her one on the top of her head. 'Goodbye, princess,' he said, putting her back into her seat.

When he'd gone, Diane left Emma to finish her breakfast and went to sweep up the broken glass in the lounge.

With a dustpan and brush in her hand, she stood at the door without opening it for several minutes. It would be nice to get this done but she was conscious of the time constraints. It definitely wouldn't do to be late to nursery today.

Taking a steadying breath, she opened the door, looking around the room before stepping slowly over the threshold. Almost immediately, she felt her heart rate increase and beads of sweat forming on her forehead as her body was consumed by absolute and inexplicable dread.

She thought it would only take a few seconds but, looking around, she groaned. The glass had smashed into smithereens and there were pieces everywhere. Backing up, she shut the door. It was, definitely, a job for later.

There was no sign of the manager when she arrived at the nursery but that wasn't out of the ordinary. She greeted the teacher, kissed Emma goodbye and returned to her car, exhausted already by the effort of appearing normal. The thought worried her. Was that what she was doing? Trying to appear normal?

She dropped her head back against the headrest for a few seconds, conscious of the other parents mulling around the car park. She didn't need someone coming over to ask if she was all right. Didn't need to give them more ammunition than she'd already done.

Starting the engine, she left the car park and headed home.

There was no point in delaying the inevitable so, with reluctance, she picked up the dustpan and brush and headed back to deal with the glass. Apart from the glass, the room looked the same as it always had. It was her response to it that had changed, her heart already thumping, perspiration trickling down her back.

It took a few minutes to sweep up the glass. The feeling of terror had settled into an old friend by the time she'd finished. It didn't get worse, or go away, it was just there, a sinking sensation that made her feel nauseous. From being her sanctuary, a room where she could chill, it had become a place of conflict, and she'd no idea why.

With the glass swept up, she closed the door behind her, emptied it into the utility room bin and then sat, wearily. She'd had too much to drink the night before, but one thought stood out. She'd decided that everything that was happening was connected in some way. This morning, her head clearer, she wondered if she'd been right.

She still believed the woman was the key to it all. She just had to find her.

On Friday she'd sort out the lie Anne had told. At least, she hoped she could; that there was a simple explanation she could believe. If there were, if they continued their budding friendship, maybe she could enlist her help. Perhaps she'd even take Emma for a few hours so she could follow the woman again.

If she followed her to the same house, it would be proof that Sophie Redmond had lied. That she was in on it all.

As that thought crossed her mind, her eyes opened in disbelief. Did she really believe there was a big conspiracy against her? Why, for goodness sake?

But she gave it some thought. Because of something she had done during those days and hours she'd forgotten? She groaned. Perhaps she was drifting down the avenues of paranoia because, even to her, her reasoning sounded crazy. What could she possibly have done?

It made more sense if she could believe she'd made a mistake and had followed the wrong woman. Or that her stalker was visiting the older woman.

She frowned. Was that it?

What was it the policeman had said to her? That Mrs Redmond had recently spent a long time in hospital? Yes, that was it. So maybe, just maybe, she had someone going in to care for her; a district nurse or social worker. Any one of a number of people could be calling on a vulnerable older woman just out of hospital.

Diane's face brightened. It would also explain why the woman was able to appear at all times of the day. Because she was out and about, not chained to an office desk. It made sense. But it also made it very difficult to find out where she lived; she could be calling to several houses during the course of her working day. If she'd ever any hope of solving this mystery, she needed to be free to follow her, and that meant finding someone to take Emma for the afternoon.

Rose Metcalf? If she went around and explained that she was desperate? She pictured the woman's face, the derision. No, that wasn't an option. Anne? No, until she sorted out that lie, she couldn't trust her.

There was another possibility, of course. A babysitting service. She'd never used one, Paul didn't approve of leaving their child with strangers. Well, it was all right for him, she sniffed, he had her.

Returning to the family room, she pulled out her laptop and switched it on. There must be dozens of babysitting services in the area. After doing a search, she sat back. Not dozens, no, but there were three. She looked into each, finally deciding on one that looked to be the best, Unicorn Care Services. It was, of course, also the most expensive. She'd have to find a way of paying for it without Paul knowing.

Wanting to sort out the situation with Anne first, she decided to wait until the following week. She sent Unicorn Care Services an email telling them what she needed. Someone to pick up Emma from school on Monday, take her home and stay with her until she arrived back. Frowning, she realised it meant getting a spare front door key cut. She knew Paul had one, but she had no idea where he kept it and couldn't come up with a good enough reason for asking for it.

There was a shop that cut keys in the shopping centre near the charity shop. Reluctant as she was to go near it, she couldn't think of anywhere else. A quick online search showed the next was several miles away.

She had time to go and get that done now; it would be one thing sorted. There was a bottle bank in the car park too, so she could take the empties that were accumulating in the kitchen cupboard.

Fetching a strong canvas bag, she opened the cupboard and began to load the bag. Far more empty wine bottles than she'd anticipated, counting ten as she squeezed the last bottle in. A distant memory of her mother saying, *it's rude to count*, came to her down memory alley, making her smile. Her mother, dead now fifteen years, had lived by maxims like it. As she closed the cupboard and lifted the bag to take it to the car, she acknowledged that her mother hadn't been referring to empty wine bottles.

The bag was heavy, rattling as she walked to the car. She needed to put it down to open the boot, the bottles shifting and rattling as the bag sagged on the ground and then again when she picked them up and put them in the boot. It was as if they were warning her that she was drinking too much. She sighed and closed the door; they were right, she was.

At the shopping centre she kept her head down as she walked to the shop to get the key cut.

'It'll be ready in twenty minutes,' the man behind the desk said, taking it with a nod. He made out a numbered docket, attached half to the key and handed the other half to her.

Diane hadn't expected to have to wait that long. She checked her watch. There was plenty of time, but she didn't really want to hang around there. 'You couldn't do them straight away, could you?' she asked, thinking *nothing ventured, nothing gained*. It was an expression her mother used often. She wondered why she was coming into her head so much the last couple of days. She'd been the salt-of-the earth type, widowed when Diane was only five, bringing her only child up with lots of love and lashings of common sense. She could have done with her now, she thought with a pang.

'Afraid not,' the key cutter said, without any semblance of apology. 'It'll be twenty minutes, at the earliest.'

'Okay,' she said, with a quick smile. 'I'll be back then.'

Returning to her car, she lifted the bag from the boot and carried it to the bottle bank, separating the green, brown and white bottles and dropping them into their respective holes. She remembered Beth, in the charity shop, telling her that when the lorry came to pick them up, they were all emptied into the same place and smiled sadly. She'd enjoyed her stories.

Her eyes drifted across to the centre. You couldn't see the charity shop from where she stood but she imagined it; Beth chatting, Red sitting in her office, maybe Anne going through donations, laughing at something she'd found. Her lips curved into a smile as she thought of the box of bondage stuff before she shook her head and looked away.

She went back to her car, throwing the empty canvas bag into the footwell of the passenger seat. There was another twelve minutes to wait. She could go and have coffee but was afraid of meeting Red or any of the other volunteers. Perhaps she could get a takeaway coffee and a magazine to pass the time, but there was still a risk of bumping into one or other of them. Instead, she switched on the radio and resigned herself to waiting where she was.

With one minute to go, she climbed out and headed back to the shop, hoping they'd be ready.

She was in luck, the man looked up as the door opened and gave her a nod and a smile. 'Just done,' he said, polishing a key and putting it on the counter. 'There you go.' He placed the original key beside it. 'I'd advise you to try it when you get home,' he said. 'It should be okay but if it catches at all, just bring it back and I'll give it another rub.'

Diane picked the new key up and looked at it. It looked perfect. 'Thanks,' she said, handing over the money.

Putting the original key back on her key ring, she put the new one in her pocket and headed back to the car. It was time she headed for the nursery. She'd sat back into the car when she remembered she'd told Paul she'd bring flowers for Susan. Damn it, she could have got them while she was waiting. With only a few minutes to spare now, she considered forgetting about it. But she knew he would ask, and she'd told enough lies lately.

Dashing back to the supermarket, she picked up three bunches of flowers willy-nilly and took them to the self-scan checkout to pay.

'Would you like those gift-wrapped?' a hovering assistant asked with a smile.

Yes, if she'd come in ten minutes before instead of sitting in her car doing nothing, she thought, annoyed with herself. 'No thanks,' she said, taking her change from the slot and putting it in her purse. The three bunches dripped water as she rushed from the shop.

Back in the car, she shoved them into the canvas bag. When she mentioned flowers to Paul that morning, she'd planned to buy a proper bouquet of flowers, arrive early, find Mrs Power and present them to her with another apology. Now, however, she'd only minutes to spare before Emma would be out. She'd just hand the lot to the receptionist and ask her to hand them to the manager with her apologies.

Not nearly as good, but it would have to do.

She should have put a plastic bag around the bottom of the flowers, of course, because the canvas bag had simply soaked up the water. It wasn't precisely dripping, but the large dark circle proclaiming it was wet shrieked that she'd not really made much effort.

She looked at it in dismay and then took it and headed into the school just as the main doors opened. Waving to Emma's teacher, she pointed toward the reception desk, squeezing her way past and stopping in front of the desk, the disreputable bag in one hand.

Debbie looked up, her default forbidding expression softening when she saw Diane. 'Good morning, Mrs Andrews,' she said, an unusually sympathetic look in her eyes.

Wondering how much she knew about what had happened the previous day, Diane pasted on a smile. 'Could you give these to Mrs Power for me, please,' she said, handing the bag over the desk. Unfortunately, the canvas bag chose that moment to reach its maximum soakage and a large drop fell from it onto the pile of papers on the desk.

Diane watched in horror as another gathered. She moved the bag away but wasn't quick enough and the drop fell onto the computer keyboard.

There was a moment's melee with both reaching to brush off the drop, hands clashing, sounds of dismay from Diane, of annoyed disbelief from the receptionist who dabbed at it with a wad of tissues she pulled from a box. 'For goodness sake,' she muttered, turning her attention to the paperwork where the drop had formed a wet patch out of all proportion to its size.

'I'm so sorry,' Diane said, her face a picture of consternation.

The wet canvas bag still hung from one hand. She hovered for a moment, but at a sharp glance from the receptionist who was peeling the wet pages apart, she shrugged and backed away a step. She turned to see where Emma was, her vision blurring as tears gathered.

Unfortunately, it was Rose Metcalf who first caught her eye, a look of disapproval on her face. She'd obviously seen the whole ridiculous episode. Gripping the bag tighter, Diane moved to where Emma was chatting to children whose names she didn't know, just grateful that Rose's Tommy wasn't one of them.

'Hi, sweetie,' she said, taking her hand. Looking neither right nor left, she left the area, Emma's hand in one of hers, the other still clutching the dripping canvas bag.

Once Emma was strapped into her seat, she threw the bag into the boot. She'd throw the lot into a rubbish bin somewhere. At least, she thought, when Paul asks, she could say, hand on heart, that she did buy the woman some blasted flowers.

Starting the engine, she fastened her seatbelt, and only then did she look across the road. *She* was there, standing across the street, staring.

It was hard to make out her expression, and it was probably Diane's imagination, but she was sure she was laughing.

CHAPTER 19

Determined to be ready for Monday, on Thursday she wrote out a notification for the nursery and delivered it in person to the receptionist when she went to pick up Emma. 'I'm sorry about the mess I made, Debbie,' she said first with an apologetic smile.

'It was just one of those things,' the receptionist said. 'I'm sorry too that I was so uptight about it. I'd had a tough day and it was the proverbial straw.' She never mentioned the flowers, neither did Diane. Paul had asked, of course, and she had told him she'd bought her three bunches and delivered them with profuse apologies.

It wasn't a complete lie. She was getting good at fudging the truth.

'On Monday Emma will be picked up by a lady called Milly Anderson,' Diane said, handing over the slip. 'Just on Monday, the other days it will be me as usual.'

The sheet of paper was taken and checked before she received a smile of acknowledgment. 'That's fine,' Debbie said. 'I'll let Miss Rogers know.'

'Thank you,' she said and then went to collect Emma, holding her hand tightly as they headed across the car park.

She ran a weary hand over her face and sat in the driver's seat. She looked across the street expecting to see *her* standing there but, this time, the road was empty.

'There's a funny smell,' Emma said, crinkling up her nose

Diane started the engine. There *was* a funny smell, and she knew what it was. She'd left the flowers in the boot and the weather had been warm for the last couple of days.

Back at home, she settled Emma with a glass of milk and a sandwich and went back to the car with a black rubbish bag in her hand. Opening the boot, she reached in and took out the canvas bag. The flowers had wilted, their stems enclosed in plastic and, still damp, had turned into a gloopy mess. She bundled it all into the black bag, tied the top tightly and dropped it into the rubbish bin, pushing it down as far as she could.

The erratic nature of the woman's appearances and the sound of the cry were beginning to take its toll. She was restless the rest of the afternoon, almost expecting something to happen. Hugging Emma, she derived pleasure and comfort from her warmth. With her curled up in the crook of her arm, she read book after book and when Emma became bored with being read to, she switched on the TV, happy to watch children's programmes with her…anything as long as she didn't move away. Finally, though, it was Diane who had to move to make dinner. She didn't have the heart to turn the TV off and Emma was still glued to it when Paul came home.

'I thought we'd agreed not to allow her to watch television during the afternoon,' he said, picking up the remote and switching it off.

Normally, she'd have made up some explanation. Today, she ignored him and concentrated on stirring the casserole she'd just taken from the oven, the steam rising from it to dampen her face.

Surprised not to get an answer, he stepped into the kitchen and stood looking at her. 'Everything okay?' he asked.

'Fine,' she said, making it clear that everything most certainly wasn't.

'The TV?' he said, ignoring the warning signs.

She put the lid back on the casserole with a loud bang and returned it to the oven before turning to him abruptly. 'Give it a rest, will you? It won't do her any harm, now and then.' Seeing that he was going to argue the point, she held a hand out, 'Please, Paul, just leave it.'

'Are you feeling okay?' he asked again, a frown between his eyes.

'Just tired,' she said with an attempt at a smile.

'Maybe you're doing too much,' he said quietly. 'You've not been yourself since you started that job. Perhaps it was too soon, after all.'

It was a perfect opportunity. She could agree, say it was too soon, talk about leaving. Admit to being a failure, admit she wasn't coping; that, in fact, she didn't know what the hell she was doing any more.

'I didn't work today, Paul, I'm just tired,' she said, her voice thick, 'dinner will be ready in five minutes.'

He took the hint and left to change. Over dinner, he asked pointed questions about what she did in the charity shop on the days she did work, forcing Diane to become more inventive.

'Over the weekend a lot of stuff had been donated so I spend most of my mornings going through it. Some of it was just rubbish but there was some good stuff that will sell,' she said, her eyes on her dinner.

'Such as?'

Such as, such as? For a few seconds she couldn't think of a single thing. 'Handbags,' she said eventually, making a big deal of chewing and swallowing to explain her hesitation. 'Some very nice, designer handbags.'

'Really? So, what will they bring in?'

Diane had no idea if they'd ever received designer handbags and what they'd sell for if they did. But she guessed he didn't either. 'Forty pounds each, easily.'

It looked as if he were going to ask more awkward questions, but just then Emma dropped her spoon and started to cry. The rest of the meal was spent chatting with her.

Unusually, after dinner, Paul said he had an important phone call to make. 'I'll be tied up for a couple of hours,' he said. 'I'll leave you to put Emma to bed, if that's okay?'

Without waiting for an answer, he kissed the top of Emma's head and left the room. She watched him go with a slight frown between her eyes. He often worked in the evenings, and at the weekends if he was particularly busy. But he'd never missed the opportunity of putting Emma to bed for the sake of a phone call. Whoever he was ringing must be very important.

She reached to take Emma from her chair, a slight twinge in her side reminding her to be careful. Cuddling her, she sat on the sofa, keeping her on her lap, and pressed the remote to switch the TV back on. She flicked channels until she found a documentary about animals and they watched it snuggled together, Emma's eyes round with delight, laughter pealing as monkeys cavorted across the screen.

They didn't move until it was over, about fifteen minutes past Emma's usual bedtime. Switching off the TV, Diane stood with her in her arms, her daughter's chubby hands wrapped around her neck. Upstairs, she watched as she brushed her teeth and washed her hands, her little face so serious and intent. It was a nightly ritual she loved but she hadn't actually put her to bed in a long time, that pleasure having fallen to Paul. Cosy in pink pyjamas, Emma climbed under the duvet and reached her hands up. Diane bent and allowed the little fingers to clasp her face. 'Love you, Mummy,' Emma said, her long eyelashes fluttering and drooping closed as she bent to place a gentle kiss on her cheek.

'Love you too, my little angel,' she whispered, staying on her knees beside the bed to watch innocence sleep.

Emma's eyes fluttered open. 'I'm not an angel, angels are in Heaven, like Jane,' she mumbled before her breathing became heavy.

What? Diane blinked. *Angels are in Heaven, like Jane.* She wanted to wake Emma, ask her what she meant, but then shook her head. It was probably something Miss Rogers had told her. Maybe some children's story she'd never heard before. Putting it out of her head, she took a final look at her sleeping daughter, stood and left the room. Switching off the bedroom light, she left the door ajar and turned on the light in the hallway.

The door to Paul's office was shut. She wondered about the important phone call and stepped closer to the door, resting her ear against it before she realised what she was doing. She couldn't hear his words clearly, but she could make out the tone of his conversation and the timbre of his voice. It sent her spinning back to when she still lived in Bristol; the hours they had spent on the phone in the evenings desperately missing each other, the longing in their voices, the words of love they'd used.

She pressed her ear to the door, harder, but it was an old, solid door and she couldn't make out any words. But the timbre of his voice, she remembered that. Shaking the quiet voice of suspicion from her mind, she headed back downstairs, thought about having a glass of wine, and then switched on the kettle instead. She needed a clear head in the morning. Anyway, those rattling bottles had told her she was drinking far too much.

With a mug of tea in her hand, she switched off the lights and sat on the sofa, putting her feet up on the coffee table. She sipped the hot tea and slipped down in the seat until her head was resting on the back of it and closed her eyes. Immediately, she heard the distinct sound of a child's cry.

Instead of jumping up, as she usually did, she sat and listened, her eyes now squeezed shut as if she were afraid to open them. It was unmistakeably a child's cry. There was a plaintive note to it, the slight hiccup of an infant who has cried for too long, or in vain. It was a sound that made her heart ache, the soft hiccup of a child crying out for succour. Any mother would run to pick her up and offer comfort, ease the child's pain and distress, feed her, keep her warm. Any mother. But Diane didn't stand. She knew there was no point; if she did, the sound would stop. And wanting it to stop, contrarily, she found she wanted it to continue and became lost in this loop.

So, she stayed in her seat and listened as it came again and again until, she realised, she was crying too, silent tears that ran down her cheeks, dripped off her chin and fell into the now-cold tea she still clasped in her hands.

Eventually, it stopped. But the ensuing silence gave her no comfort. Instead she was filled with an overpowering feeling of intense sadness and bottomless regret that she couldn't begin to explain. She put the mug down, swung her feet to the floor and went to the fridge, sitting moments later, a large glass of wine in her hand.

CHAPTER 20

It was bright, so it must be morning. She was in her bed but, the problem was, she'd no recollection of getting there. Closing her eyes, she dragged her mind back to the night before. The baby's cry. The sadness. And hadn't she gone to get a glass of wine? Had she drunk more? Had she drunk the whole bottle? Was that why she couldn't remember coming to bed? She sat up in alarm.

The clock told her she had time to spare, and when she listened, she could hear the hum of the power shower in the main bathroom. Throwing back the duvet, she swung her legs to the floor and stood, grabbing the robe from the back of the door and pulling it on as she crept downstairs.

She opened the door to the kitchen quietly, shutting it behind her with an agonisingly loud click. Her wine glass was on the coffee table, half full. Picking it up, she took it to the kitchen, threw the contents down the sink, washed the glass, dried it and put it away. Then she ran the tap for a few minutes to get rid of the smell of alcohol.

Opening the fridge, she took out the bottle. It was three-quarters full. Frowning, she held it up to the light to check. It looked as if she'd only poured the one glass and of that she'd only had half. Could she have blacked out again? She put the bottle back in the fridge and went back to her room. Leaving her robe on, she crawled under the duvet, shut her eyes and tried to remember – but there was nothing.

She rolled over in despair; the more she pulled at the strings of the tangle her life had become, the tighter it seemed to get. She needed something to hold onto or she was in danger of losing her grip completely.

Focusing on one thing, she thought about her meeting with Anne later that morning. She would take control of one tiny part of her life and find out why she'd lied.

She was late arriving at the café, and heard her name called as she pushed the door open.

'Diane!'

She spotted Anne waving from a table at the back. Lifting a hand in acknowledgement, she negotiated her way past an array of pushchairs and, reaching the table, was pulled into a hug she wasn't expecting. There was comfort in it, but she pulled away. 'My turn to apologise for being late,' she said, 'I had a rough morning.'

'It's no matter,' Anne said, releasing her and sitting back into her seat. 'I thought maybe you weren't coming.' Her smile was genuine, spreading to her eyes, making them twinkle.

'No, I've been looking forward to it,' Diane said truthfully because despite the lie she'd caught Anne out in, she *had* been looking forward to seeing her. She looked at her with admiration. In the black harem pants, fitted military-style jacket and glaring neon-orange scarf wrapped turban-like around her head, she should have looked ridiculous, but she looked amazing.

Taking in her empty, foam-stained coffee cup, Diane asked, 'Another? My treat to make up for being so late.'

'Great,' Anne said with a smile and indicated her cup. 'I'm on cappuccino this morning.'

The queue to be served was short but it was still several minutes before Diane returned to the table, a large cup and saucer in each hand. 'Here you go,' she said, putting one carefully down in front of Anne before pulling out the seat opposite.

There was a moment's silence as they each lifted their coffee and sipped. Anne put hers down first, rested entwined fingers on the table in front of her, and said, 'So, how are you doing?'

Diane held her cup a moment longer. Wouldn't it be wonderful to tell her everything, to offload the whole sorry tale? Maybe, it would help? But maybe Anne would join the obvious dots and think her crazy. Taking another sip, she put the coffee down. 'Great,' she replied, injecting more energy into the one word than was necessary and then, 'I've been so busy recently.'

'Life's like that sometimes, isn't it? Periods of mania interspersed with periods of calm. Of course,' Anne added with a faint smile, 'writing is always like that. I'm desperately trying to get a book finished and then it's done and there's this lull before the editor sends it back to me and then mayhem while I do the edits.'

'But you love it,' Diane said, seeing the passion in her face.

Anne grinned. 'Wouldn't do anything else. I was born to be a writer.'

They chatted about books and movies for a while. They had similar taste in books but when Anne said she preferred foreign films, Diane shook her head. 'I just want to relax,' she said, 'not to have to read everything.'

'You don't even realise you're reading after a while. Seriously,' she argued, 'come with me sometime, I bet you'll be hooked. There's more subtlety in their work than you find in US or UK-based movies.'

'That would be lovely,' Diane said, checking her watch. 'Listen, I have to leave soon to pick up Emma, but there's something I need to ask you.'

Anne looked surprised at the sudden seriousness of her voice. 'Sounds ominous,' she said, with a slight tilt of her head.

Diane pushed her cup out of the way and leaned forward onto her crossed arms. 'You told me that Red had given you my address,' she said, keeping her voice low. 'But I was at the dry cleaner last week. The one near the charity shop is the only one in the area so I had to go there, and I bumped into her.' She dropped her eyes for a moment and then looked back at Anne, holding her gaze. 'She didn't give you my address, did she? You already knew it.'

Anne looked taken aback, and suddenly much older. She pulled back from Diane's stare and folded her arms across her chest, hugging herself. When she didn't say anything for a few minutes, Diane knew she'd have to push more. She wasn't leaving until she knew the truth. 'How did you know?'

A pause, and then a sigh. 'I'm sorry. I've always been intensely curious about people,' Anne said. 'I suppose it's part of being a writer.' Uncrossing her arms, she rested both on the table, mirroring the way Diane had sat moments before. 'I like to know the nitty-gritty; the stuff people don't tell you about themselves when you first meet. To put it in more unflattering terms, you'd describe me as a nosy parker.'

'A nosy parker?' Diane repeated. It wasn't what she had expected to hear. It sounded so mundane.

'To get right to the point, I was curious about you and read your personnel file.'

Not so mundane. Diane looked at her in disbelief. 'You read my personnel file? How?'

Anne shrugged. 'Red often leaves the shop and never locks the office; we all have to have access to it in case someone comes to pick up all the black bags of stuff that are stored there. She keeps her files in the locked drawer of her desk but the keys hang on a hook in the footwell. I think probably everyone knows they're there.'

'But not everyone would take advantage of that fact and read confidential documents.'

Anne didn't look embarrassed. 'No,' she said, 'probably not.'

'So that's how you knew my address?' It wasn't a big conspiracy, just a little, sordid nosiness.

'I felt so sorry for you that day,' Anne said, shuffling in her chair. 'I'd intended to call around anyway, but when Red discovered the cash was correct, she wanted to apologise. But then something came up and she didn't have time. When she heard I was going to visit you, she asked me to tell you she was sorry. She probably assumed you'd given me your address. When you asked, it seemed simpler to say she'd given it to me. I didn't think it mattered all that much.'

It was more likely that she didn't think she'd be found out. 'I see,' Diane said. There wasn't much else to say. 'Well, I'd better be going.' She didn't add it had been good to meet her, didn't suggest they meet again; was unsure if she wanted to. Suddenly, Anne's outfit, which had looked so bohemian and exotic when she'd arrived, just looked ridiculous.

'There's something else. Please wait, just a moment,' Anne pleaded.

'Just a moment then,' Diane agreed, 'I can't be late collecting Emma.'

'You told me you'd applied to three places and took the charity shop because it was the only one who replied, didn't you?'

'Yes, that's right, so?'

'And not because your husband and Red are friends?'

Diane frowned, and clenched her bag tightly. 'What are you talking about?'

'It says in your personnel file that Red employed you on the personal recommendation of Paul Andrews.'

'That's impossible,' Diane said, standing. 'You're nosy, *and* a liar. Goodbye, Anne.'

Anne reached out and gripped Diane's arm. 'You may not think much of me right now. And yes, I'm a terrible busybody, or whatever you want to call me, but the one thing I'm not, Diane, is a liar. I don't know what's going on, but what I've told you is the truth. Red knows your husband.'

Diane held her hand up and backed away, turning and pushing through the crowded café. *Red knew Paul.* There was no reason for Anne to have lied this time, after all. And if she knew him, there was no way she wouldn't have told him about what happened, and about her quitting the job. But he couldn't say anything, could he? Couldn't admit that he knew, because then he'd have to admit to knowing Red.

Her head spinning, she sat into the car. Hadn't Paul been more interested in her work recently, asking probing questions about what she did, how many customers they had? Questions she thought were trying to show interest. Now, she wondered exactly what he was trying to do; to catch her out in a lie or to try to force her to admit the truth; that she didn't work there anymore.

In frustration, she banged her hands on the steering wheel. What the hell was going on? How was she supposed to clear up her mess of a life when, every time she tried, it just got worse? She'd pulled Anne up on her lie, only to discover a bigger lie underneath.

CHAPTER 21

She picked Emma up without a word to anyone, taking the child's hand, returning to the car, strapping her in, all the time thinking of Paul and Red. She remembered the laidback interview, her lack of surprise when she'd admitted she'd had a breakdown. Was it because she'd already known everything about her? Red, with her glossy red lipstick, sloe-eyes and vibrant red hair, so very glamorous, so very attractive.

It suddenly felt as if the ground had opened up beneath her feet, the bustle of the nursery silenced around her as she finally saw with blinding clarity what she'd been missing all along. She'd thought all this time that things were different with Paul because she was still recovering, that when she was better they would return to how they used to be – passionate, spontaneous, independent, carefree – but the awful truth now staring her in the face was that things were different because they had changed.

There was no reason for Paul and Red to keep their relationship a secret unless they were having an affair. Her eyes narrowed. Or was there? It was curious that of the three emails she'd sent, Red was the only one to reply. She'd given the links to all three positions to Paul and he'd seemed happy that she was looking for something to do – but maybe he wanted to keep an eye on her and had made sure the others hadn't replied? He kept insisting she was doing fine. Perhaps she wasn't doing well at all. Hallucinations, blackouts, paranoia. And now this.

The car behind blasted its horn and she looked up startled. She pressed the accelerator too fast so that the car jumped forward and then stalled. The car behind leaned on the horn for longer, startling Emma and making her cry. With pandemonium erupting all around her, all Diane could do was stare at the steering wheel in front of her, her mind a blank, unable to remember how to start the car and, for several seconds, she had absolutely no idea what to do.

It would be easier to shut them all out; Emma, the car behind, Paul and Red, the charity shop, the whole damn all-too-confusing world. Emma's cry hit a new pitch and shocked her back into the present. A quick glance in her rear-view mirror told her the traffic was building up behind her. Turning the key, the engine started immediately and she moved on, indicated and pulled into a parking space. Undoing her seatbelt, she climbed over into the back seat, pulled Emma to her and soothed her as best she could. It took a while, but the tears calmed and the promise of ice cream eventually brought a smile back to her sweet face. Diane took in her daughter's perfect mouth, her button nose and big brown eyes. No, she decided, smoothing Emma's curls back and dropping a kiss on them. This time, she wasn't going to shut everything out, this time she was going to pull herself together and fight for what was most precious in her life: her daughter.

Back at the house, with Emma asleep on the sofa, she sat at the table and tried to put her thoughts in order. Was she getting near to the truth? Either Paul had arranged for Red to keep an eye on her and their relationship was all above board, or they were having an affair. In either case, he would know that she didn't work there any more. The thought that he knew and was amused at her lies made her stomach heave.

She suddenly felt weary beyond words. Too weary to face a truth that should have been obvious. She remembered the phone call. Had that been her? Hadn't she known, deep down, that things just weren't right?

But with everything that was going on, she wanted proof, she *needed* something solid to confirm her suspicions and make them real. Then she remembered the locked office door and her eyes narrowed; she'd have to get inside.

A quick glance towards Emma to see she was still asleep, she moved quickly, unlocking the back door and crossing the garden to a shed they rarely used. Most of the stuff stored inside predated her occupancy of the house. In fact, she guessed, some of the stuff predated Paul's purchase several years before. But she remembered seeing a rusty old biscuit tin full of keys. Nobody had been inside since and it was just where she'd seen it.

Brushing off the cobwebs, she grabbed it and headed back to the house. The utility room had a counter stretching along one wall. A handy place for folding and organising laundry. Today, it was empty. She put the tin down and looked inside.

There were at least fifty keys of various sizes and shapes. Taking a dirty towel from the washing machine, she laid it along the countertop and emptied them out. Working methodically, she'd soon discounted and removed keys that couldn't possibly work.

It left her with twenty, or so.

Surely one of them would fit. She threw them into a bowl and took them with her.

Checking on Emma, who was still fast asleep, she went up to the office and tried the door. It was definitely locked. Examining the lock, she tried to identify the most likely key from the selection she had. Trying one, then another, then another. The fourth key turned with a loud click. Holding her breath, she turned the knob and pushed the door open.

She wasn't sure what she'd expected to find. It wasn't even that long since she'd been inside, a week or so ago, saying goodnight to Paul. She remembered he'd barely looked up from his computer.

The blinds on the room's one window were closed, so she felt for the light switch, turned it on and squinted in the dazzling light as she waited for her eyes to adjust.

Moving around the desk, she switched the old desktop computer on and waited for it to power up. While she waited, she searched the desk drawers. The top drawer held the usual paraphernalia; paper clips, staples, elastic bands, all in their individual containers. To the front, neatly stacked, their passports. They'd taken out one for Emma the year before with some idea of going to France on a holiday. For some reason that she couldn't remember, they'd never gone. In the second drawer, there was a thick sheaf of papers. She flicked through them, her eyes widening as she took one sheet out and read it intently.

'Very interesting,' she murmured and returned them carefully to the drawer, checking that they looked exactly the same. The lowest drawer held a box file, inside there were more papers, but from a quick glance at the dates they were a little older.

She was just about to shut the drawer when the corner of a blue logo underneath the file caught her eye. Lifting the file slightly, she was able to pull out the two pages. It was an information leaflet entitled, *Being Sectioned (in England and Wales)*. Her eyes flicked over it and then, feeling sick, she put it back carefully and shut the drawer.

She turned her attention to the computer which had booted up and was requesting a password she didn't have. She tried Emma's date of birth, then her own, the date they married, the name of the street. No luck.

Giving up on the computer and switching it off, her eyes scanned the bookcase in the corner. There were accountancy, auditing and finance-related books that she guessed were relics of his college days. She'd bet he hadn't touched them in years. There were also a few folders. She took the first out and opened it on the desk. It was full of household bills. Council tax, electricity, gas, everything. Working as quickly as she could, she opened, flicked through and closed every folder until, at last, she opened the one she'd been looking for. Personal expenses. Every penny he gave her for household expenses was listed. Extra money he'd given her for Christmas gifts and birthday gifts, all with receipts stapled alongside.

Even gifts he'd bought her over the years, itemised and accounted for. The flowers, the diamond and ruby bracelet for their first wedding anniversary that she rarely wore, the simple silver bangle she'd chosen herself for their second. Every item listed, accompanied by every receipt. Wasn't it just a little bizarre? It showed a side of Paul that she never knew about, a side she certainly didn't care for. She turned the pages, fascinated. All the itemised expenditure for Emma's birth, more than three years ago, the furniture, the clothes, everything.

She noticed there'd been fewer and fewer personal expenditures on gifts for her in the last couple of years, with an understandable increased spend on Emma. She hadn't realised the educational toys he insisted on buying for her were quite so expensive.

Her eyes continued down the page, and then she saw what she'd been looking for. For several minutes, she simply stared at the few simple words that told her their marriage was over. There was a moment of intense pain as her world tipped and spun until somewhere deep inside, unacknowledged and ignored, she realised she'd already known. But still her eyes brimmed with tears as she read the receipt for the very expensive diamond and emerald earrings, purchased two months ago. She would imagine emeralds looked good on Red, and at that price they'd better. Closing the folder, she put it back exactly where she had found it, her mouth a thin line, eyes bleak.

Checking the room to make sure she hadn't left any evidence of her intrusion, she switched off the light, shut and locked the door. Picking up the bowl of keys, she was about to drop the key back with the rest when she changed her mind. She might need it again. Instead, she went to her room and put it into a drawer, pushing it to the back out of the way. She glanced over the clothes she'd left dumped on the bed early that morning, remembering her worry about looking good for her meeting with Anne. She didn't know what she'd been worrying about.

Emma was still asleep when she went downstairs. She really should wake her, but she needed a moment to absorb what she'd just learned, and time to put a brave face on it all.

She emptied the keys back into the old biscuit tin and returned it to the shed. Order restored in the utility room, she returned to the kitchen to switch on the kettle. Then, as images of emeralds and diamonds flicked across her mind, she swore softly and reached into the fridge for the open bottle of wine.

Grabbing a glass, she half-filled it and took a mouthful. By the time she'd finished it, a few minutes later, she felt a little calmer. Calm, but angry and unbelievably confused. Why would Paul arrange for her to work with his lover? Why would he take that risk?

Putting the wine bottle into the fridge, she took her glass to the window and looked out over the garden. It was a miserable day, dull and chilly. Perfect weather for finding out your husband was cheating on you and your marriage was over. Leaning forward, she rested her forehead on the window and shut her eyes, feeling the hot burn of tears run down her cheeks.

In the last month, with so much uncertainty in her life, Paul was the one constant, the one dependable. Now it seemed even that wasn't true. Maybe it never was. She sipped her wine. Was this why she'd had a breakdown? Had she found out or, worse, had he told her he was leaving her and she'd fallen apart? It was a horrible thought to think she'd been that weak, that dependent. Suddenly she remembered…something. Shutting her eyes tightly, she strained to grab the memory. The phone had rung, she was feeding Emma and wanted to ignore it but it might have been Paul, so she struggled to answer it, but it wasn't him it was a woman…she was annoyed that she couldn't remember any more. Was it a memory of something that had happened during those missing months? Or was it just something her mind was making up; after all, she'd not bottle-fed Emma for years.

Frustrated by the half-memory she turned, wiped her eyes with the sleeve of her jumper and looked at her sleeping daughter. She was the only good thing left in her life, the best thing to come from a marriage made in haste. It was the only thing left between her and Paul, they both adored her. She frowned. Now, more than ever, she needed a friend. Having just spent the last hour snooping on her husband, perhaps she shouldn't have been so critical of Anne's curiosity about her life; maybe they had something in common after all. Putting down her glass, she went up to her bedroom, retrieved her mobile phone and, taking a deep breath, dialled Anne's number.

'Hello?'

'Hi, Anne,' she said, relaxing. 'It's Diane. Listen, I wanted to apologise.' She waited a beat. 'Because you're right.' Another pause, while she gathered the strength to say it aloud, aware that once the words were said, they couldn't be unsaid. 'In fact, I think they might be having an affair.'

'Ah.' It was all Anne said. Nothing more; no shock, no sympathy, no lying reassurances that they'd be okay, that it was probably just a fling. Had she done so, Diane would have enlightened her. For Paul to spend three thousand pounds on diamond and emerald earrings, it had to be more than just a fling.

'To be honest,' Diane said as she finally admitted it to herself, 'I think I've been fooling myself for quite a while.'

Anne found her words, asking Diane the same question that burned through her. 'But why on earth would he want you working with her?'

She didn't know the full story and it was impossible to explain over the phone. 'Listen,' Diane replied, 'there are things you don't know, but I haven't time to tell you now. Can we meet again? Maybe tomorrow?'

There was a pause, before Anne answered. 'I'm really sorry, I can't. I have meetings booked with my editor that I can't change as it involves others too. In fact, the soonest I could meet is Tuesday.'

It was further away than Diane liked but she didn't have any choice but to agree. At least it gave her time to think things through. 'Okay, Tuesday, and I'll tell you everything then.'

She couldn't have said anything more appealing to the inveterate nosy-parker. 'In the same place?'

'Yes, but earlier, if you can. It's going to take time to explain.'

Agreeing on nine forty-five, Diane hung up.

Back downstairs, she finished the wine she'd poured. She was going to tell Anne everything. Funnily enough, knowing she wasn't all that perfect herself made it easier.

She washed the wine glass and put it away. Leaving Emma asleep, she got on with preparing dinner. Another casserole, easy food. Chop everything, dump it in a dish, empty a jar of sauce on top and bung it into the oven. It was done in ten minutes.

Before waking Emma, she ran upstairs and brushed her teeth, swirling the toothpaste around a few times. Looking at her reflection in the mirror, she sighed. The stress was getting to her. She looked tired, her hair needed washing; it was greasy, lifeless. Fishing a hair tie out of her drawer, she tied it back.

Rubbing Emma's back gently to wake her, she sat beside her and switched on the TV. 'Let's watch *Pet Zoo*,' she said, switching channels. Letting the sound drift into the background, her brain struggled to understand what was going on but, no matter how she looked at it, it didn't make any sense. It kept coming around to the same fact: Paul had encouraged Red to give her a job.

A shriek of laughter interrupted her thoughts, and she looked down at Emma who pointed at the screen, her eyes wide in wonder as a trio of young monkeys cavorted in a children's play area. She brushed one golden curl from the child's forehead and leaned down to kiss it in place. And then it hit her. They both adored Emma, was that the key? Feeling the soft, warm weight of the child in the crook of her arm, she looked down at her. She'd do anything for her. So would Paul.

Was that it?

That information leaflet with its official blue logo and crest, detailing everything he needed to know to have her committed. Hidden away until he needed it.

She shook her head slowly as a series of horrendous thoughts bombarded her. She'd dismissed the idea that it was a conspiracy against her, laughing at her own paranoia. But what if she'd been right? What if it was all a devious plot? And Paul getting Red to give her the job in the charity shop was just the first step. It set the scene. It was there she'd had her first meltdown after that strange woman had appeared. Red and Paul. Working together and conspiring against her.

If she was right, they were to blame for everything that was happening to her.

CHAPTER 22

She thought through this new and horrifying idea. If she was right, Paul was being very, very clever. He adored Emma. If he planned to divorce Diane, he'd want custody of her.

What better way to obtain full custody than to prove she wasn't a competent mother? She'd had a breakdown and there were huge portions of the last year that she couldn't remember. Hadn't she felt, over the last couple of weeks, that she was heading for another breakdown; feeling that edge to fall over was close and getting closer.

What if everything that had happened was designed to drive her straight back to that clinic?

Her eyes filled with tears as she considered all the things that had happened. That woman…not a stalker…someone planted by Paul to unsettle her. And how well it had worked. And that child's cry? A cat. He probably heard it just as clearly as she did.

She bit her lip and swallowed a sob. This was her husband, the man she loved. Love wasn't something that could be switched off at will. How could he do this to her, how could he be so cruel?

Easing Emma from her arms, she left her watching TV and went upstairs. She would not cry in front of her. Sitting on her bed, feeling hopeless and lost, she let the tears flow. The pain of his infidelity made her double over, his intention to destroy her made her moan with despair. She curled up on the bed, wrapped her arms around her knees, and sobbed.

It was several minutes before she regained control, but when she did, when she straightened, wiping her face with her hands, her eyes were hard. Knowledge was power; now that she knew what he was up to, she'd start to fight back. She'd put the pain of his infidelity, of his utter and absolute betrayal, to the back of her mind to be dealt with sometime in the future. She'd lost him; she wasn't going to lose Emma.

There was no point in challenging him. He'd just laugh and deny everything. Or tell her she was being paranoid. Keeping quiet and playing the game was the best way of ensuring he didn't win, and certainly the best way to make sure she did.

What could she possibly have done to warrant such treatment, such cruelty? How could their love have turned so toxic?

He thought she'd crumble, didn't he? It was time she showed him she had inner strength; she just needed to find it. An idea came to her that brought a slight smile to her lips. It was time to turn the tables, even just a little. Checking on Emma once again, she dashed back upstairs, had a quick shower and washed her hair. She chose her clothes carefully, blow-dried her hair and left it loose. Carefully applied make-up and she was ready.

The animal programme had just ended when she went back down. Switching the TV off, she settled Emma with some toys; the educational ones Paul had bought her. Once she began playing, she took a few photographs with her phone. She'd build up a collection of photos showing what a wonderful, caring mother she was and what a happy, contented daughter she had.

Emma was still playing happily when Paul came through the door. He looked down at her approvingly before turning to Diane, an eyebrow rising when he heard jazz music playing in the background. 'Nice,' he said with a smile. 'We haven't listened to that in a while.'

'I was in the mood,' she said, tossing her hair back and looking at him through her eyelashes, a flirtatious glance that had him blink and turn away, but not before she'd seen the puzzled look on his face.

Smiling, she took the casserole out of the oven, putting plates inside to warm while she finished setting the table.

'Finish up playing, Emma,' she said, putting knives and forks in place as Emma abandoned her game and headed over, climbing up into her chair without assistance. Soon they wouldn't need the booster seat at all; she was growing up so fast.

Switching the oven off, she stood for a moment, took a deep breath and then took wine glasses from the cupboard and put them on the table. She poured wine into both and put the bottle away. She certainly didn't want him calculating how much she'd already drunk.

'I fancied a glass of wine,' she said, pre-empting his objection to this unusual mid-week drink. 'I've poured you one too, but you don't have to drink it if you don't want.'

He had only glanced at her earlier but now his eyes lingered on the tightly fitting T-shirt she'd changed into, the low-cut neckline that exposed the curve of her breasts. She bent down to take the plates from the oven, keeping her arms close to her chest to increase her cleavage.

Straightening, she caught his stare. 'Breast of chicken casserole,' she said, resisting the temptation to wink, suddenly feeling as if she might be overdoing it. There was no point in going overboard. For the moment, she had him just where she wanted him. Confused.

She maintained a steady stream of innocuous chat over dinner; she told him about meeting Anne that morning and made up anecdotes about people who visited the charity shop earlier in the week without a hint of embarrassment at her lies.

'So, you still like it there?' he asked, picking up the wine she'd poured for him and taking a sip.

She sat back, hooking one elbow over the back of the chair. She could feel the fabric of her T-shirt stretch, saw his eyes flick down and away.

You bastard, she thought, forcing her lips to smile as she considered his question. 'Yes, it's perfect for me right now. I think when Emma goes to primary school, I'll probably look for something more challenging, or, what was it you called it?' she asked, faking a puzzled look. 'Oh yes, a proper job.' She gave him a bright, full-on smile.

After dinner, Paul went to watch the news. Diane made him some coffee and took Emma upstairs to get ready for bed. When she was ready, dressed in pale-yellow pyjamas with white ducks encircling arms and legs, she looked so adorable she picked her up and squeezed her.

'Mummy!' the child squealed, wriggling from her arms and toddling away to run downstairs and climb onto the sofa. She was cuddled up to her father by the time Diane came down.

She took her time tidying the kitchen and loading the dishwasher, but he was still sitting there when she'd finished, Emma curled up beside him, fast asleep. Tired and weary, the chill of his betrayal like a weight in her chest, she'd no energy left for pretence and games. Now, she just wanted him to go so she could have another glass of wine. She was aware she was drinking too much but it was a crutch she needed at the moment. When this whole horrible mess was cleared up, she'd give it up. Or, she tempered, she'd cut it down anyway.

She watched him stand and stretch and felt tension ease.

'Okay,' he said, bending to pick up the sleeping child. 'I'll take her up to bed.'

There was a strange look on his face that Diane didn't like. Maybe, she thought with a flash of horror, she'd come on too strong. She was damned if she was going to sit wondering and waiting. 'Will you be coming back down?' There was no invitation in the question, no hint of flirtatiousness this time in her voice.

He looked perplexed. 'You're in a strange mood today,' he said. 'Is everything okay?'

'Everything is hunky-dory,' she said, pasting a smile in place. 'Why wouldn't it be?'

'That's okay then,' he said, with a shrug. 'No, I won't be down, I have a lot of work to do.'

She waited until she heard his office door close before pouring herself that much-needed extra glass of wine and collapsing into the sofa.

Another mouthful of wine and she put the glass down. She sat for a long time without moving, trying not to think, trying to give her poor, abused brain a rest. She still loved him – love wasn't something you could switch off that easily – but now that the initial shock had eased, it wasn't as painful as she would have thought. She frowned, wondering if perhaps, somewhere in those forgotten months, she'd been aware of what was going on. With a sigh, she shook her head. She loved him and would have remained faithful to him. Betrayal wasn't in her nature. She'd thought it wasn't in his. Perhaps, she'd never really known him at all.

Suddenly weary, she finished the wine and rinsed and put away the glass before switching off the lights. She stood in the darkness for a few seconds before turning to leave the room, pulling the door shut behind her. Upstairs, there was no light from under the office door or Paul's bedroom door. She'd no idea of the time, but it must be later than she'd thought.

Slipping quietly into Emma's room, her breath caught when she saw how the light from the hallway made her curls shine, turning them into a halo around her face. Her angelic daughter, there was nothing she wouldn't do for her. Unfortunately, she knew that Paul felt the same.

With a heavy heart, she went to bed and tossed and turned until morning. Bleary-eyed, she finally gave up at six, threw on a robe and padded barefoot down the stairs. She made a pot of coffee, set a tray with a china mug and a jug of hot milk and took it to the small table near the window. Pulling back the curtains, she sat into the comfortable bucket chair to drink it, forgot about the weekend that loomed ahead and watched the day dawn. It would be hours before Paul was awake, at least two before Emma was. Just for a few hours, she would pretend that all was right with her world.

CHAPTER 23

Nothing untoward happened over the weekend; there was no sign of her stalker, no further sound of a baby's cry. Diane no longer went into the lounge so she had no idea if that feeling of terror still persisted.

She took several photos of Emma: having her lunch, playing with those ridiculously expensive toys, turning the pages of her favourite book. 'One more,' she said, as the child's eyes began to droop. Finally, she took one of her curled up on the sofa, asleep.

Ammunition. She needed to gather as much as she could.

She didn't continue her game with Paul. The more she thought about it, the more devastating his betrayal and his willingness to destroy her to get what he wanted. She didn't know who the man she'd married was, and found it hard to bring herself to look at him.

He commented a number of times on how quiet she was. 'Are you sure you're feeling all right?' he asked for the second time on Sunday evening. 'You sure you're not overdoing it in that shop?'

She looked at him and saw the look of concern on his face. If she hadn't seen the information sheets on how to have her sectioned, if she hadn't seen the receipt for those expensive earrings, she might have been taken in. Her mouth twisting in disgust, she quickly turned away. 'I'm fine,' she replied.

She was tempted to pour wine at dinner again that night, but dismissed the thought. After all, she didn't know what kind of ammunition Paul was trying to collect; she didn't want any talk of alcohol abuse. She'd wait until after he'd gone to his office.

Did he spend hours on the phone to her when he was up there? She'd heard the one call, guessing now that he'd been speaking to Red; he probably did every night. Maybe that was a special one, a birthday…an anniversary. Bitterness coursing through her with biting sharpness, she wondered when he saw her. He hadn't spent a night away from home since her return from the clinic. Had he done so before? She couldn't remember.

She didn't have any wine that night. Tomorrow was going to be a busy day; she needed a clear, rested head for all the private eye stuff she'd planned. It was the worst thing to think, of course. Immediately, she started to worry about not sleeping. How could she follow the woman for miles if she was as weary as she'd been the last few days?

She didn't want to take sleeping tablets as they left her groggy the next day, but she did have some painkillers that made her sleepy. She rummaged in her bathroom cabinet, found a packet and quickly took two.

Then she lay on her bed and tried to sleep.

She tried the mindfulness technique she'd been taught, but her mind refused to stay focused on the moment, drifting along all the different tangles of her life, attempting, almost pathetically, to unravel them.

If she could just unravel one part, she hoped the rest would come undone and maybe the gaps in her life for the last year would close over.

She'd really like that.

And on that thought, she fell asleep.

CHAPTER 24

She dressed with care the next morning. It was a grey, miserable day, the road and pathways puddled from overnight rain. In black jeans and a long-sleeved black T-shirt, she looked at herself in the mirror. Dressed for action. A pair of comfortable walking shoes and she was set.

Paul's eyebrows rose. 'You going to a funeral?'

'Anne always wears black,' she said, 'and she always looks so sophisticated. I thought I'd give it a go.' She was getting so good at blending lies and truth it worried her. Maybe they were very alike, after all.

'Anne?' he queried, picking up the kettle to pour boiling water into a mug.

She moved around him to take a mug from the cupboard, spooned instant coffee into it and held it out to him, waiting until he'd filled it before answering. 'The woman from the charity shop I met for coffee on Friday. I told you about her.'

He shrugged. 'It's hard to keep up with you.'

Biting her lip, she stirred her coffee and added milk. His comment had been carefully neutral, too carefully. He didn't believe her. She could see the sneering disbelief in his eyes and turned away before he could read the hurt in hers.

He gave Emma her usual cuddle before leaving. 'Be good, princess,' he said, ruffling her curls. Diane received her usual dry kiss on the cheek. She wondered why he bothered going through the motions.

Once he was gone, she concentrated on getting ready for the day. 'Okay, Emma,' she said, crouching beside her. 'When you come out of school today, Mummy won't be there to meet you. A very nice lady called Milly will bring you home instead and stay with you until I come back, okay?'

Emma's little face took on a serious expression as she digested this unusual change to her routine. 'Will she give me my lunch?'

Diane hugged her. 'Yes, of course she will.'

Dropping her off at the nursery, she mentioned to Miss Rogers that she'd arranged for someone else to collect her daughter and headed to the offices of the babysitting service, where she handed over the key to the receptionist and asked her to confirm that everything was arranged for that afternoon.

Back at home she waited restlessly until it was time to leave. She'd decided to walk this time, had calculated the timing perfectly and stepped into the same alleyway at twelve thirty. It was damper and colder than she'd remembered. Shuffling from foot to foot and rubbing her gloved hands in an attempt to keep warm, the time passed slowly. The traffic on the road was fairly constant, but when she saw it build up, she knew it was almost time, the cold and damp forgotten as she concentrated her attention on the path across the road from the nursery.

She breathed a sigh of relief when she saw the woman approach at five minutes to one. The same sleek bob, this time wearing a short, boxy jacket over dark trousers. Her unremarkable face was exactly as she remembered. As before, she was coming from the opposite direction, walking without haste. Diane felt anger bubble, her hands clenching. How dare she be so casual about what she was doing? Maybe, she should just forget about this stalker angle and go and face her now.

Face her, and tell her she knew what she was up to. The idea lingered for a moment. But then she shook her head. If she confronted her, Paul would know the game was up. But he might come up with something else. No, she needed proof, something she could take to a solicitor, something that would give her some clout when they went to court to fight for custody of Emma. No, she'd stick to her plan. Find out who she was, and go from there.

It wasn't until all the cars had left that she saw her turn and walk back the way she'd come. Relieved to be on the move, her hands, despite the gloves, numb from the cold, Diane followed her. She didn't pay much attention to where she was going, concentrating on maintaining an appropriate distance without losing her. She closed the distance at junctions and increased it when she spotted pedestrian crossings.

She was getting good at it. She was still congratulating herself on doing such a good job when she saw the woman cross the road and head down a quiet residential road. A road she recognised. The road where Sophie Redmond lived. Shaking her head in disbelief, she crossed the road to follow. She should have considered this, of course, and slowing her pace more, she watched the woman open the garden gate and vanish into the house.

Diane wasn't supposed to be on that street but, realistically, what were the chances of that police car just happening to pass by? Slim, given it was a relatively safe, affluent neighbourhood, but it still wasn't the best place for her to hang around after the warning she had already received. She bit her lip and kept walking. This had to work. There was only so much more she could take.

At the end of the street, she looked back down the length of it. She could wait here; if the woman left and came this way, she could just duck around the corner. If she went the other way, she could run to catch up.

After another ten minutes, she decided to walk the length of the road again, just to keep warm. She pushed away from the thigh-high wall she'd been leaning on, her gaze drifting over the garden behind it to the house. A net curtain at the window twitched and Diane raised a hand in friendly greeting, and quickly moved on.

And then she saw it. A police car at the junction, indicating to turn. The same police officers? She'd no idea but, in a few seconds, they'd be on the road and see her. That net curtain twitcher must have rung them. If it were the same officers, there was no way she could explain why she was back on the street that made any sense. And there was no time to get away. In desperation, she swung her legs over the wall beside her, dropped down and lay flat on the grass on the other side.

She waited a moment, ears pricked, and heard the sound of the car travelling slowly down the road, past her and stopping at the end. Then she heard the unmistakeable sound of two car doors bang. Her cheeks reddened at the thought of them wandering along the street and seeing her lying there in a stranger's garden. But there was no sound of footsteps, and, after a few minutes, she relaxed. They must have gone inside the house where she saw the curtain twitch.

Damp was seeping through her clothes and woodlice ran across her fingers and hands, but she didn't dare move until movement in the window of the house behind caught her attention. Looking up, she jolted as she saw a pair of startled eyes looking back. When the face vanished, she knew she had a choice, stay here and be caught, or run like hell.

Jumping up, she swung her legs back over the wall and started to run up the road as fast as she could, throwing a glance at Sophie Redmond's house as she passed and cursing her luck. When she got to the junction, she stopped for a breath. She looked back down the road just at the same moment that the two police officers had come out of the house and were staring up. She watched them rush to get into their car and didn't wait to see more.

Panic-stricken, she ran across the road, causing cars to brake suddenly and horns to blare. It was a main road, and there was nowhere to hide as far as she could see. She was running as fast as she could, but she wasn't a fool, they'd be behind her in seconds.

She looked from side to side as she ran, looking for a laneway, anything that would take her off this road. From behind, she heard a siren, they'd reached the junction. She only had seconds.

Then she saw it. On the other side of the road, a narrow walkway between houses. She dashed across, waving a hand at an approaching car that braked with a squeal of tyres, seeing the police car approaching from the other direction, close enough so that she could see they weren't the two police officers who'd stopped her before. It wasn't much of a consolation. Then she was in the walkway and running as fast as her legs would take her, surprised at how fast she could go when under pressure.

But they'd be after her, and she guessed they could run faster.

A minute later, just when she was thinking she'd have to give up, and hearing heavy, fast footfall closing in behind her, the walkway opened onto a path in a large, modern housing estate with no front gardens, and multiple ways through. Chest heaving, she ran like hell down the first road she came to, then took the next and every one after, hoping she wouldn't end up back where she started, or that they wouldn't choose a road that would make their paths cross.

Exhausted, she stopped for a moment, and listened. She couldn't hear anything, but she doubted they'd given up. She needed to get out of sight.

At the bottom of the road she was on, an end of terrace house looked uncared for, weeds high in the pots that stood on either side of the front door. It didn't look the kind of house where people were interested in what went on. And it had a side gate that was hanging askew.

With a quick look around to make sure nobody was watching, she slipped through and gently pushed the gate shut. Legs wobbling, she slid to the ground and leaned back against it trying to catch her breath, her face wet, nose running. With a dirty hand, she wiped both and rubbed her hand on her even dirtier jeans.

She looked down at herself, she was filthy. And it had all been for nothing. Hot tears of self-pity rolled down her cheeks.

She had no idea how long the police would search for her. Probably not for long, but she wasn't risking moving for at least an hour. What a catastrophe. She gave a laugh, and then a slightly louder one, then harder and harder until she was laughing hysterically, gasping for breath and leaning against the fence for support. She was losing her grip; that edge was getting so close.

With a gulp, she stopped abruptly and wiped a hand over her face. She was cold, filthy and hungry having stupidly skipped breakfast and lunch. Stupid. She let her head rest back against the rotting wood of the door and closed her eyes.

Now would be a good time for a blackout, but instead, when she was fairly sure they'd given up the chase, she pulled out her phone and called for a taxi. Twenty minutes, they said. She kept an eye on the time, and when fifteen minutes had passed, she moved out front, her eyes scanning anxiously, ducking back behind the gate when a car passed. The next car that turned down the road was the taxi. She had removed her filthy jacket in case the driver asked questions, climbed into the back with a quivering sigh and gave the driver her address. She was asleep before the taxi had turned onto the main road.

'We're here.'

Woken suddenly, Diane blinked groggily, confused by the battered car parked behind hers on their driveway until she realised it must be the sitter's.

'Keep the change,' she said, handing over the money and climbing out of the taxi.

Relieved to hear the sound of laughter as she gently opened the front door, Diane shut it quietly and tiptoed up the stairs. She didn't want either Emma or the sitter to see her in the state she was in. Stripping her clothes off, she washed her face and hands, eyeing the shower with longing. With a sigh, she pulled clean clothes on, brushed her hair, put her purse and mobile into a handbag and headed back downstairs where she opened the front door quietly and closed it with a slam.

'I'm home,' she called, heading to the family room and opening the door with a smile pinned in place.

'Mummy!' Emma yelled in delight. 'We're doing painting.'

Milly Anderson stood, an embarrassed blush on her face.

Not surprising, Diane thought, taking the mess in with a look of surprise. There seemed to be paint everywhere.

'It's not as bad as it looks, honest,' Milly said, holding up two paint-splattered hands. 'When we're done, I just roll everything up and take it away, see,' she pointed to the large sheet that seemed to cover half the floor, 'everything is contained. And it all washes off. I'd planned to give Emma a bath when we were done, put her in pyjamas and wash her clothes out.'

'See, Mummy,' Emma held up her painting.

Diane bent down to look. 'That's amazing,' she said. 'It looks like she's having fun,' she said to Milly with a smile. 'I'm going to leave you to it. I've had a shattering day and I'm going to head up and take a bath. Can you stay until five thirty?'

Milly nodded. 'That's the time I was expecting to leave, Mrs Andrews.'

She left them and headed back upstairs. She turned the hot tap on full and stripped while she waited for the bath to fill, adding scented bath foam to the running water. When it was ready, she dipped a hand in, added cold water and then stepped in with a groan of pleasure.

She stayed in until the water turned cold and then climbed out. It would have been nice to pull on a pair of pyjamas and a robe, to slouch for the evening and have dinner on a tray in front of the television. She grinned when she imagined Paul's horrified face if she even suggested such a thing.

Searching her wardrobe, she pulled out a pair of jersey pants that were the nearest to pyjama bottoms she had, and a jumper that had gone soft and baggy with age. They'd do just fine. Comfortable, she headed downstairs.

Milly had worked a miracle while she'd been upstairs; the family room was back to normal. No sign of paint on any surface. Emma, who'd been showered, glowed in pink bunny-rabbit pyjamas.

'I have no idea how you managed to tidy all that up so well,' she said to Milly, who was standing in the kitchen with a mug in her hand.

The sitter grinned. 'Years of practice,' she admitted.

Diane gave a faint smile and checked the time. 'Well, thank you so much. I'm sorry it's a bit later than I promised.'

'Not a problem,' Milly said, emptying the dregs from her mug into the sink and dropping it into the dishwasher.

Diane watched as she enveloped Emma in a hug, speaking to the child with what sounded like genuine affection before waving to them both as she left.

Leaving Emma to play with her toys, she headed into the kitchen. Dinner, as she'd planned, was simple, and minutes later pasta was simmering, the cooked chicken chopped up and ready to be added with the sauce. With nothing more to do for the moment, she sat at the table and went over the day's events, her head in her hands. So, after that disaster, what now? It was a question she couldn't answer.

There was no way she could have hidden Milly's presence in the house. When Paul came home, Emma was full of chat about her paintings and insisted he admire them before he went to change.

'I'll explain when you come down,' Diane said. 'She had such a good time. I think she shows such flair for a three year old.' She watched as he picked up each of the paintings she had done, one by one, asking Emma what she had painted. Diane, leaning over to hear the explanation, was amused when she told them that the painting she'd been shown earlier was of her teacher, Miss Rogers, and her classmates.

For one brief moment, they were a happy family. But it didn't last; she looked at his smiling face from the corner of her eyes and she wanted to scream her pain and frustration. Instead, she bit her lip as he enthused over the paintings.

Over dinner, she unpacked her lie to cover Milly's presence. 'Miss Rogers asked if I was interested in having one of their trainee nursery teachers for a few hours. They were keen that they have more interactive one-to-one time with children.' She liked that line, thought it was just the kind of thing Susan Power might say. 'Of course, I jumped at the opportunity to have her, and Emma just loved it.

'Once I saw how good she was, I went and had the longest bath I've had in ages.' Keep lies simple and blend in as much truth as possible, that was the secret. She watched his face, there wasn't the slightest hint that he didn't believe her.

'You had fun,' he said to Emma, who was picking pasta up with her fingers and nibbling it with great concentration.

'Mmhh,' she said, and then elaborated, 'it was the best.'

Paul who didn't approve of her eating with her fingers, reached over, took the pasta from her fingers and put the spoon back in her hand. 'Maybe you should emphasise how beneficial it was to Miss Rogers when you drop her off tomorrow,' he said, looking at Diane, 'maybe she'd be kind enough to think of Emma again.'

'I'm sure they try to give everyone the opportunity,' she said, calmly. 'And I'm not sure how long they have trainees for. But,' she added, seeing that he was going to insist, 'I'll make sure that I tell her what a great opportunity it was, and how much Emma enjoyed it.'

He seemed to be content with this and concentrated on his dinner. Diane relaxed, relieved at how easily deceit came these days. She was glad that Emma had genuinely enjoyed Milly's care.

At least something good had come of it. It was, after all, the only success of the day.

Once Paul had taken Emma up to bed, she tidied up quickly and poured a glass of wine. She didn't even consider he might come down again. That ship, she guessed, had definitely sailed. Glass in hand, she switched off the TV and the overhead light and curled up on the sofa in the soft light of the table lamp.

It had been a hell of a day, she thought, shaking her head. She was no further forward in trying to find out how everything was tied together – or even if they were. Swilling the wine around in the glass, she weighed up her options. So far, following the woman had only ended up in disaster.

Maybe, she needed to cut to the chase and talk to Paul's lover, Red. She had *so* many questions for her.

Sipping her wine, a wave of sadness washed over her. She loved Paul; she wondered when he'd stopped loving her. His betrayal hurt, but what stunned and frightened her was his deviousness.

Just to get what he wanted.

She wouldn't have thought him capable, but then maybe everyone was. She thought of all the lies she'd told in the last few weeks. How far was she willing to go to keep Emma?

She wasn't sure, but she hoped she'd stop before trying to destroy someone. If she could prove that was what he was trying to do, she could stop him. But she needed proof.

So far, she'd not had much luck, but she had to believe her luck would change.

CHAPTER 25

When she woke the next morning, after yet another restless night, she remembered she was meeting Anne. Of course, she'd hoped to have some clarity after yesterday's attempt to follow the woman, had hoped to lay the whole sorry tale out for her. But she had nothing.

She should cancel, go directly to Red and get some answers. She couldn't go in the afternoon, not with Emma to look after. Lying in her bed staring at the ceiling, it suddenly dawned on her that she *could* do both. Perhaps, after all, Paul wasn't the only one who could be manipulative.

After she dropped Emma off, she drove to the café arriving just after nine forty and managing to get parking directly outside. Her good luck continued; she was the first customer and had her choice of tables. She'd have liked the one in the window but, for privacy, chose one in a corner alcove, dropping her jacket on the back of a chair and returning to the counter to order.

When Anne pushed through the door, their eyes met and Diane pointed toward the table she'd laid claim to and turned her attention to the server. 'An Americano and a low-fat latte, please.'

'Regular or large?'

Diane looked across the room to where Anne was making herself comfortable. 'Both large,' she said.

'I'll bring them over.'

Diane waved her thanks and crossed the café. Pulling out her chair, she sat and dropped her bag on the floor. 'Well, here we are again,' she said.

As an ice-breaker, it wasn't great, but Anne grinned. 'I was so pleased when you rang. I wasn't sure you'd want to see me again.'

'Because you poked around and read confidential papers?' Diane said with a shake of her head. 'Nosiness isn't one of my flaws but lying is a different matter. Recently, I've discovered I have quite a flair for it.'

Anne looked more than surprised. With her mouth slightly open, and eyes round, she looked stunned. 'Ok,' she said, with an embarrassed laugh, 'I wasn't expecting that.'

Diane laughed with genuine amusement. 'Wait until I tell you the rest.'

Their coffees arrived at that moment, oversized cups on small saucers, a plastic wrapped biscotti struggling to balance on the edge of each.

Diane unwrapped her biscuit, took it out and dunked it in her coffee before demolishing it in two bites. She brushed her fingers on the leg of her jeans before picking up her coffee. 'Well,' she said with a slight smile. 'Let me tell you my story.'

Anne was one of those unusual people who could listen without comment and, more importantly, without interrupting. She simply sipped her coffee and listened. When the cups were empty, she held up a hand, stood and went to order more.

Diane gathered her thoughts and waited for the coffee to arrive before continuing. An hour later, she took a deep breath and sat back. 'And that's it, so far.'

The café had filled as she told her story and they were surrounded by a cacophony of voices and sounds, but between them there was a silence that lasted for several minutes.

Anne ran a hand over her face. 'Let me see if I've got this straight,' she said, and then stopped again.

Diane held her breath. If she didn't believe her, she wasn't sure she could cope.

Anne leaned forward, fingers interlinked, thumbs tapping. 'Okay. So, you had a bit of a bad time over the last year, gaps in your memory, a spell in what very much sounds like a psychiatric institute of sorts. Then you decided to go back to work and took a volunteer role in the charity shop where you met Red. You'd never met her before, right?'

Diane nodded.

'Okay. And then this woman, that you'd never seen before, turns up, looks oddly at you and leaves you with those books. You never go back to the shop, but then you see the same woman in a number of places and she appears across the road from your daughter's school several times. First question. Why didn't you go to the police?'

It was a valid question. She tried to keep her voice calm as she explained. 'Paul would find out and worry, even more than he does already. Also, I know I had a breakdown last year, but I've no idea what led up to it. So, at first, to be honest, I thought I was imagining her.' Her voice dropped, the next words coming out hesitantly. 'It's hard to trust yourself when you know you've lost your way before.'

Anne looked at her thoughtfully for a moment before nodding slowly. 'Yes, I can see how that would be. But now,' she said, leaning forward, 'if you think Paul might be responsible for all these strange goings-on, why not go to the police now?'

Diane shook her head. She hadn't told Anne the humiliating and embarrassing story about her run-ins with the police, she didn't need to know every detail. 'I need more proof,' she said now.

'And you think he's doing all of this, all these dreadful things, to get custody of Emma?'

'In a nutshell,' Diane said, knowing how crazy she must sound.

Anne watched her for a moment. 'Are you still seeing someone from the clinic?'

Diane winced. 'A psychiatrist, do you mean? You think I'm paranoid?'

'No, no I don't. The bit about your irrational fear of the room in your house sounds like you're imagining stuff, but then we have to remember you have big gaps in your memory. Maybe something happened in there, and, somewhere deep in your mind, you're beginning to remember and it's scaring you.'

Diane nodded slowly. 'It was something that had crossed my mind, to be honest, but I don't know, Anne, everything seems to be connected. All I know for sure is, it started with that woman and it ends with Paul. And if I don't find some proof, something solid to make sense of it all, I'm afraid I'm going to fall apart and end up back in that clinic.'

Anne reached a hand across and rested it on her arm. 'I'm no expert, but considering all you've been through, you seem pretty together and strong to me,' she said with a quick smile. 'You don't strike me, at all, as someone who is falling apart at the seams.' She thought for a moment, then tapped the table with a fingernail as a thought came to her. 'Tell me again why they haven't filled in the blanks for you and told you what happened before your breakdown?'

Diane shook her head. 'They want the memories to come back naturally. It's called Spontaneous Recovery,' she explained, 'and is supposed to be better for me. They explained it as being a bit like why you are advised not to wake up a sleepwalker.'

'Right, and your doctor said that.'

'Yes,' she said, and then thought a moment. 'I think so. To be honest, the medication I was on at the time made me a bit groggy but Paul was with me at the final consultation before I was discharged. Any time I've asked since, he's reminded me of what they said; that I've to let the memories come back naturally.'

'It's convenient for him, isn't it? It keeps you unsettled by not knowing what happened.'

Diane's eyes widened. 'You think it's a *lie*? That he's deliberately hindering my recovery?'

Anne's hand tightened on her arm. 'Not a lie, no, I've heard about Spontaneous Recovery before, but it's very convenient for him and maybe he's playing on it.'

'He certainly uses it,' Diane said, remembering Paul's insistence that they had discussed sending Emma to nursery. She felt the warmth of Anne's hand. It felt reassuring. 'I would never have thought he could be so cruel, I wonder if I ever really knew him.'

'You were married very quickly…was it his idea?'

Diane hesitated, her mind slipping back to a different time. 'He said it made sense not to wait and I agreed.' But she'd been swept along by his love and enthusiasm. She remembered feeling overwhelmed by it all.

'He likes to get what he wants, doesn't he?' Anne said. 'And usually gets it. If he is really responsible for everything that is going on, it shows a very single-minded determination, a level of cruelty that is unforgiveable.' Her grip on Diane's arm tightened. 'You haven't thought this all the way through, have you?'

Confusion flickered across Diane's face. 'I'm not sure what you mean?' She looked at the hand on her arm then back to the other woman's face. She wasn't sure she wanted to know what she meant.

'Well, if it's really custody of Emma he's after, and if he's determined to get it, then there's only one way to make absolutely sure…'

Diane gasped. No, she hadn't thought it all the way through. Despite everything, it had never crossed her mind but now, of course, the blinding clarity of it seared her.

'If I'm dead,' she whispered.

CHAPTER 26

It made such perfect sense she couldn't believe she hadn't seen it for herself. But, of course, that was what he'd wanted, wasn't it? To keep her troubled and confused so she couldn't see what was going on. With her out of the way, Paul would have Emma and the house, no maintenance to pay to her, no worries she'd recover and fight for shared custody.

Paul, the man she loved. She shook her head, desperate not to believe he was capable of such a thing. 'I can't see it, Anne, he's not a violent man.'

Anne shrugged. 'If what you've told me is true, he doesn't need to be. He's using psychological warfare; he's hoping you'll do the job for him. If he succeeds completely, he has won; but if he succeeds even a little, he's still won. He'll have you sectioned, and then declared incompetent to have custody.'

Diane sat back in her chair, lifting her chin and straightening her spine. 'If he thought I'd take my own life, he doesn't know me at all; even at my lowest, the thought never crossed my mind. And if he's trying to push me over the edge, he won't succeed. I saw it recently, Anne, I looked over, but I didn't fall. If I didn't then, when everything was spinning around me, I am certain I won't now that I know what he is up to.'

'What are you going to do?'

'I've made a start,' she said, her voice grim, 'I've told you. If anything happens to me now, someone knows what's going on.' She rubbed her face with both hands and then dropped them onto the table. 'I want to go and see Red. The sooner I get all the facts, the safer I will be. I can't believe she knows what he's up to. Or am I being totally gullible?'

Anne shook her head. 'I've known Red for almost five years. I would have sworn she was completely honest and straight up. Mind you,' she shrugged, 'I'd never have believed she would go into a relationship with a married man. I always thought she was a bit,' she hesitated, seeking for the right word and then shrugged, 'uptight, for want of a better word.'

'There's only one way to find out,' Diane said. 'I need to speak to her.' She pressed her lips together. 'Finding out exactly what is going on has taken on a whole new urgency, Anne. I can't afford to wait. For me, and for Emma.' Lowering her eyes, she looked at the woman opposite through her lashes. 'I have a problem, though. I can't take Emma with me, and there's no-one to look after her. I was wondering – hoping, even – that you'd be able to take her for a few hours?'

For a moment, Anne looked a little taken aback, and then, slowly, she nodded. 'I don't have any experience with kids, but I suppose I could manage a few hours. And I agree, the sooner you get some proof of what he's up to, the better. For your own piece of mind, at the very least.'

Relief washed over her; she felt a little lighter now that she'd shared her turmoil with someone. It all seemed so simple having spoken to Anne. She played with her rings, twisting them around her fingers, the diamonds sparkling. She remembered Paul going down on one knee, the ring in his hand. A million years ago.

'You'll get through this,' Anne said softly. 'And I'll be here for you. Okay?'

For a moment, Diane felt anchored for the first time in weeks. 'Thank you,' she said, gratefully. 'That means so much. I've felt so alone in all this.'

'Well, you're not alone any more,' Anne said, emphasising every word. 'Together, we'll make sure this goes no further.'

Together; it was a comforting word. 'I'd better go,' Diane said, 'being late to collect Emma is definitely not an option.' Taking her jacket from the back of the chair, she slipped it on. 'So, it's okay if I bring her to you straight after nursery. I'll stop and pick up a sandwich or something for her lunch—'

'No,' Anne interrupted, 'I think I'll manage a sandwich for her. We can have a tea-party.'

Diane smiled. 'She'd like that and afterwards she'll just want to curl up and sleep for an hour or so. And when she wakes, she'll happily watch TV.'

She waited while Anne put on various layers of clothing, wrapping and draping cardigans and scarves and, finally, adding a hat that sat crookedly on top of her mop of hair, they walked out together. Reaching into her bag, she took out pen and paper. 'Okay, what's your address?'

'Turret House, Parkside Gardens,' Anne said, and then added the postcode.

Diane wrote it down, double-checking the postcode. 'I should be with you by one thirty at the latest.' Arrangements set, she reached for the handle of the car door. 'Okay, see you later. Thanks again.'

Suddenly, Anne threw her arms around her and pulled her into an unexpected hug. Diane tensed at first; it had been so long since she'd felt the full force of female friendship, but then she relaxed into it, taking comfort from it.

With a final wave goodbye, she headed off to the nursery, pulling into the car park with ten minutes to spare, long enough for Anne's words to finally sink in. Did she really think Paul would go that far? She sighed heavily. Unbelievable as it was, it did make a warped kind of sense.

The nursery doors opened at five to one, signalling to her and the other early birds to get out and migrate in that direction. She'd got into the habit of keeping her eyes focused on the door, ignoring the other parents. Rose Metcalf was friendly with many of the others; Diane guessed her own reputation was pretty muddy.

Back in the car, she checked across the road for the woman. She wasn't there but, rather than relief, her absence put Diane more on edge. Fastening Emma's straps, she said, 'I'm taking you to stay with a nice lady for a few hours while I go to a meeting.'

'Milly?' Emma's eyes brightened.

Diane smiled at her. 'I'm afraid not, but a lady just as nice.'

'Are we going to do painting?' she asked hopefully. 'I like painting.'

It was unlikely. 'No, I don't think so. But she'll let you watch TV, is that okay?'

Emma shrugged her little shoulders. 'Okay, Mummy.'

Diane put Anne's postcode into her satnav and, twenty minutes later, pulled up outside a large house on a pretty leafy street, her eyes widening in admiration. Nice area, nice house. She guessed Anne hadn't lied when she said she was a successful writer. Wide gates stood open, she pulled in and turned off the engine.

Close up, the house was enormous, a turret to one side giving the house its name. It was quirky, just like its owner.

Opening the car door, she undid Emma's straps. 'I'll be back in a couple of hours,' she said to the little girl who jumped down and, immediately grabbed her hand, a look of uncertainty on her face as she looked up at the house. Diane bit her lip. It had been easier leaving her with a stranger in her own home. This was different. She was being unfair to her, taking her to a strange place to stay with someone she didn't know, but this was something she had to do.

She'd make it up to her, maybe organise a painting afternoon the way Milly had done it. There was sure to be a worn sheet in the airing cupboard that she could sacrifice for a good cause. With that in mind, she squeezed Emma's hand and pressed the doorbell.

It was another minute before she saw a shadow appear behind the glass of the door and then came the distinct sound of keys rattling in the lock and the door was pulled open.

'So sorry,' Anne said, standing back and waving them in. 'I was getting an idea down, if I'd left it, it would have floated away, and I'd have spent the rest of the day fruitlessly trying to remember it.' She waited until they were inside a large hallway and closed the door. 'Come on in,' she said, leading the way past a dramatic curving stairway.

Diane looked around in pleasure when Anne brought them into a large bright room where the emphasis seemed to be on comfort. Skylights and floor-to-ceiling glass across the back made it, even on a grey day, full of light.

'This is lovely,' she said. 'What a great place to work,' she added, seeing, the large desk at the far wall, a comfortable swivel chair behind it angled to face the small but lush garden.

Anne smiled, pleased with her reaction. 'I had the garden designed last year. He managed to pack in an amazing array of plants and, when the sun shines, I can almost imagine I'm in the tropics.' Her eyes dropped to the child who stood slightly behind Diane. 'And you must be Emma,' she said. 'I bet you're tired after school.'

Diane almost grinned at the note of hope in Anne's voice. She supposed it was daunting looking after such a young child if you weren't used to it. 'Emma likes her nap. She usually just curls up on the sofa and I throw a rug over her.' Her hand rested gently on her head as she spoke.

'Well, I think I have just the spot,' Anne said, crossing the room to an old, worn sofa. 'This is where I take a nap when I'm exhausted,' she said. She picked up a blanket that was thrown over the arm of the sofa. 'And this is my cuddly blanket. You can borrow it if you like? But first we're going to have a tea party.' She waved towards the table where she had an array of food laid out.

Seeing the neatly cut triangular sandwiches, the little cakes, Diane was taken aback at her kindness. Emma looked up at Diane uncertainly before taking a step forward and taking Anne's extended hand.

'You can have your nap, afterwards,' Diane said, 'and when you wake up, Anne will let you watch TV, okay. And then I'll be back to pick you up a little while later.'

'Okay, Mummy,' she said, dropping Anne's hand and reaching up to grasp Diane around the neck in a hug.

She kissed her cheek and then the top of her head, and watched while Anne helped her into a chair and put a sandwich on a plate in front of her. 'Back in a second, sweetheart,' she said and followed Diane from the room.

'What you told me this morning has been going around and around my head,' Anne said, her voice sombre. 'Are you sure you shouldn't be going to the police?'

'And tell them what?'

'Just what you told me.'

Diane held her hands up. 'When I have proof of some sort, maybe, but right now, they'd think I was crazy.'

'You'll get your proof today,' Anne said firmly, 'I just know you will.'

Her sympathy and understanding were almost too much for Diane, who felt the prickle of tears. She swallowed. 'Thank you so much,' she managed, her voice choking, 'I don't know what I'd do without you.' Jumping into the car, she started the engine and gave Anne a wave before pulling out onto the road.

She hadn't given much consideration to what she was going to say to Red when she saw her. Maybe she should just ask her straight out and take her by surprise? It was melodramatic, but she needed answers fast. When she arrived, she parked, switched off the engine and sat for a minute taking deep, calming breaths before opening the car door and stepping out.

The charity shop had two customers, both browsing the book shelves. Beth, behind the counter, looked up as the door opened, a flash of recognition crossing her plump face. Diane gave a quick wave and then pointing to the back office, mouthed *Red*. Beth nodded and waved her on before turning her attention to one of the customers, who had approached the desk with a large pile of books that she dumped unceremoniously on the counter.

With a smile, Diane headed to the back of the shop. They were obviously behind with getting through the donated items; she could see several bags and boxes piled up through the partially open door. The other door, also partially open, was Red's office. Deciding against knocking, she pushed the door open only to find Red had her back to the door, a phone pressed to her ear. She didn't hear her enter and Diane, frustratingly, had no option but to wait until she'd finished her call and turned around to hang up the phone.

When she did, it was with a look of pleasant surprise rather than the shock she'd half expected. 'Diane,' she said, standing and coming around the desk with outstretched hands. 'How good to see you!' She grabbed her hand and shook it before indicating a chair. 'Sit. I'm so glad you called.' Returning to her chair, she gave Diane a warm, friendly smile and jerked her thumb toward a kettle that sat on a windowsill. 'Can I get you some coffee or tea?'

She shook her head. This wasn't going at all how she'd expected.

'I felt so badly about what happened,' Red said, slowly, her eyes fixed on Diane's. 'It was unforgiveable of me to jump to conclusions without giving you the chance to explain. You must have thought I was awful.' She shook her head slowly. 'I think I was just worried because I hadn't got around to checking your references.'

Now was her chance. 'Was that because you had a personal recommendation from my husband?' Red was still leaning forward, her face so close that Diane imagined she could feel the warmth of her breath. She waited for her face to change, to see a shiftiness in her eyes, a narrowing of her painted lips, maybe even a quickening of her breath. But there was nothing except a slight furrowing of her brow.

'I don't understand what you mean.'

Diane let out the breath she had been holding. 'My husband, Paul, didn't he ask you to give me a job?'

Red sat back. 'Is that what he told you?'

'No.' There was an uncomfortable silence. 'Tell me what your relationship is with my husband.'

'Relationship?' Red's voice rose an octave. 'I don't have any relationship with your husband. I've never even met the man.'

Diane sniffed. 'And I suppose he didn't buy you a pair of outrageously expensive earrings either.' She was disappointed to see that Red wasn't wearing them, in fact, she wasn't wearing any. Her eyes widened slightly when she realised her ears weren't even pierced. Perhaps they were clip-on. It didn't matter, she watched a quiver of dismay crossing Red's face. She'd hit home, she thought with satisfaction, and waited for the confession she was sure would follow.

'I am so sorry,' the voice was soft, gentle.

'Sorry?' Diane's eyebrows were almost in her hairline. 'You're having an affair with my husband and you think saying *sorry* makes it all right?'

Red shook her head. 'No,' she said, 'that isn't what I meant. I'm sorry your husband is having an affair. But it certainly isn't with me.'

CHAPTER 27

'I don't believe you,' Diane said, lifting her chin and trying to look braver than she felt.

Red sighed. 'If we were having an affair, he'd know better than to buy me earrings. I don't wear jewellery, of *any* kind, not since I had an unfortunate, and very painful, reaction to a bracelet my mother bought me many years ago.'

Diane sneered. 'Maybe there wasn't much time for talking in your relationship?'

Red lost a little of her calm. 'Listen, you're obviously upset, and I do feel sorry for you, but I really don't have to take these nasty accusations. I told you, I have never met your husband.'

'Then explain why it says on my application form that he recommended me for the job here.'

Red looked puzzled for a moment. Reaching into the footwell of the desk, she brought out a set of keys and inserted one into the top drawer. She pulled it open, rifled through files, pulled one out and slapped it loudly onto the desk.

With a quick look at Diane, she opened it, flicked through a couple of pages and then extracted two sheets stapled together at the corner. Her eyes flicked over the first page and then the second before she handed it over. 'Have a look,' she said. When Diane took it, she added, 'Read the instructions at the very bottom.'

She did as she was told. In small print at the bottom of the second page was written: *Each box must be completed. If there is no information, please add a comment. Do not leave a box empty.*

'Some head office genius came up with that. It's supposed to prevent us adding information after we've taken someone on. There are different forms for that, you see.' She shrugged. 'I do what I'm told, I fill every box. If you look on the second page you will see where it asks if there has been any personal recommendation. We get a lot of them, from local churches, women's groups, et cetera. Head office likes to hear that we play an active part in the community.' She waited a beat. 'When you sent an enquiry, I read it and forgot about it until the next day when I got an email from a Paul Andrews asking if we would consider his wife for the volunteer role. He mentioned you'd had a tough time but were getting yourself together and also mentioned you had worked in IT.

'I looked at your enquiry again and replied to you asking you to come for an interview. And that,' she said with firm emphasis, 'is the only contact I've ever had with your husband.'

Diane felt a wave of weakness rush over her and darkness creep around the corners of her vision. Her chest tightened and the room spun around her. Then, nothing. When she opened her eyes, she was on the floor on her side, something cold on her forehead, water from it trickling down her neck. Red, her face creased with concern, was kneeling beside her. 'You fainted,' she said.

Reaching up, Diane removed the wet cloth and sat up. 'I'm sorry,' she said, her voice trembling. 'Sorry for everything.'

Red put a hand under her arm and helped her to her feet and back into the chair she'd so dramatically exited, minutes before. Without asking, she switched on the kettle and spooned coffee into two mugs. When it was made, she added milk and sugar to both and handed one to Diane. Back in her chair, her coffee held between two hands, she looked across the desk at her and said quietly. 'It looks as though I'll have to put my keys in a more secure place from now on,' she said without rancour. 'I assume it was Anne?'

There was no reason to lie. 'Yes,' she said. 'She thought she was doing the right thing.'

'By reading my confidential papers or by sharing the content with you?' Her voice was heavily sarcastic. She obviously didn't expect an answer as she continued, her brow furrowed. 'Wasn't it a bit of a leap of the imagination, though? I wrote on your form that your husband had recommended you, so of course we must have been having an affair?'

'There is more to it than that, but I really can't go into it,' Diane said with a weary smile, her head pounding.

Red shrugged. 'Fair enough, as long as you're quite clear that I have never met your husband.'

'Yes, that's clear now. And again, I'm sorry.'

There was silence for a moment and then Red put her mug down with a firmness that indicated she'd made a decision. 'I've known Anne for a number of years,' she said, 'she's a lovely woman but she does tend to be overly dramatic at times. I think it's those fantasy novels she writes, I sometimes think she forgets what's real and what isn't.'

It was Diane's turn to look puzzled. 'I thought she wrote crime novels.' She was sure that was what Anne had told her when she'd asked.

'Crime with a strong fantasy element,' Red explained. 'I've read them, they're really good but I've noticed in the last three that the fantasy element is becoming stronger.' She hesitated. 'You've obviously become friends and I don't want to put you off her, but you strike me as being a little vulnerable so it's best to know these things.'

'Thank you,' Diane said, putting her mug down on the desk. 'I'd better get going.'

'Are you sure you're okay to drive? You look terribly pale.'

Diane forced a smile and stood. 'I'm fine, honestly. And again, I'm sorry.' She turned and left the office, closing the door behind her. Of course, she'd lied, she didn't feel fine at all. Swaying slightly, she took a step away, and then back into the room next door, leaning against the door frame, dropping her chin onto her chest.

Seconds later, she lifted her head, turning to listen as she heard Red's voice clearly through the thin partition wall. Only *her* voice. On the phone to someone. It was a short conversation. 'We need to talk,' she heard Red say bluntly and then, moments later, the single word *yes*.

There was nothing more. It was tempting to barge into her office and demand to know who she was talking to but, instead, Diane pushed away from the door and made her way from the shop.

CHAPTER 28

Diane sat in her car for a long time, trembling, and close to tears. Every time she thought she was getting to grips with some part of what was happening, it was all turned on its head. She was going around in circles, her world spinning out of control.

She started the engine, pulled out of the car park and was half way home before she realised she was on the wrong road. Swearing loudly, she looked for a place to turn. Seeing nowhere, she swore again and took advantage of a lull in the traffic coming toward her to indicate and throw the car into an illegal U-turn. The car behind, forced to slow down, blasted its horn. She gave an apologetic wave, got a rude gesture in return, and headed back in the right direction. Ten minutes later, she pulled into Anne's driveway.

This time, the doorbell was answered almost before she'd removed her finger, taking her by surprise. 'Gosh, Emma isn't giving you a hard time, is she?' she asked with an attempt at a laugh that failed dismally.

'Of course not,' Anne said quickly, 'she's a little angel. I was worried about you, that's all. You were longer than I expected.'

'Was I?' Diane said dismissively, pushing past her without looking and heading to the room at the end of the hallway where, inside, Emma was sitting cross-legged on the sofa watching TV. Stooping to give her a kiss, she looked across the room at Anne, who looked a little pale. 'I'm sorry I was so late,' she said, picking up the blanket that had fallen to the floor and twisting it in her hands as she spoke. 'It wasn't easy.'

'She admitted it?'

Conscious of Emma sitting nearby, Diane fought to stay calm, swallowing the *no* she wanted to shout out. 'It appears I was barking up the wrong tree,' she said.

Anne looked puzzled for a moment, as if she didn't understand the phrase. 'Barking up the wrong tree?' She thought for a moment. 'Are you saying she isn't having an affair with your husband?'

'That's exactly what I'm saying,' Diane said, letting the anger she'd felt since she realised Red was completely blameless colour her words. 'She's never even met him.'

'But the application form—'

She held a hand up stopping her. 'It meant nothing. She had to fill in something and Paul did email her to ask her to consider me for the job so…'

Anne paced the room and then stopped and turned. 'So, they were in contact?'

She threw up her hands. 'Yes, but it meant nothing. And, to add to the proof, she doesn't wear jewellery, ever. Why would he buy her expensive earrings?'

'Maybe he didn't know?'

All the anger left Diane in a whoosh and once again she felt drained and weak. Stretching out a hand, she grasped the back of a chair and, swinging the seat around, sat heavily. She could feel Anne's eyes on her, waiting. 'Red says you write fantasies,' she said, unable to keep the hint of accusation from her words.

Annoyance crossed Anne's face. 'Oh, I see. I write fantasies, so perhaps my idea that your husband is trying to push you over the edge is just that?' She paced the floor, pulling tendrils of hair from the bun she'd tied loosely earlier in the day. It made her look quite wild and, for a moment, Diane was nervous of her.

But then Anne turned, her eyes filled with tears. 'I'm not a liar, or a fantasist.' Her face hardened. 'Is that what she told you?'

'She said you sometimes confused what was real and what wasn't.'

Anne's eyes narrowed. 'She did, did she? You didn't really want to believe they were having an affair anyway, and now she's given you a reason not to. I wonder why she did that?'

'Oh, for goodness sake,' Diane shouted, startling Emma who immediately started to cry. Scooping her up, she lowered her voice as she stroked her little girl's head. 'Listen,' she said, 'I can't think any more today. My head is reeling. Meet me tomorrow morning, same time, in the usual place?'

She'd no idea why she wanted to meet her again; listening to her hadn't brought any clarity. But she needed to talk it out and at least she'd listen – she was kind. There was no time now, if she left immediately, she'd just be in the door before Paul and wouldn't have to explain where she'd been.

Saying a hurried *thank you so much*, she gathered Emma's belongings, rushed out the door and into the car as fast as she could, only to hit traffic the moment she got to the main road. It was five fifteen; she was running out of time. When the traffic ground to a halt completely, she gave a quick look around before pulling out her phone and hitting one of two speed dials she had set up on her phone, one to him, the other to emergency services.

'Paul,' she said, when it was answered. 'It's me,' she said unnecessarily, 'listen, I've been out in Anne's house and got delayed. You might be home before me, so I just wanted to warn you so you wouldn't be worrying. I'll get us a takeaway on the way home.'

Relieved that he asked no questions, she hung up and concentrated on the road. Thirty minutes later, takeaway bags hanging from her free hand bouncing against her thigh, she pushed open the front door. 'We're home,' she called. 'Go and find Daddy,' she said to Emma, who immediately rushed ahead.

Taking the bags into the kitchen, she put them on the counter, leaving them there while she took off her coat, dropping it and her handbag onto a chair. She could hear Emma's voice coming from upstairs, and the low rumble of Paul's voice as he replied.

She remembered she hadn't locked the car. Grabbing her keys, she pulled open the front door, held her key fob out and pressed, waiting to see the flashing light before dropping her hand.

And then she saw *her*. The light was fading, her features in soft focus, but there was no doubt. Diane stood and stared, refusing, this time to back away. Pulling back her shoulders, she refused to look intimidated outside her own home. She thought the woman would disappear as she always had before, walk away and not look back but, to Diane's horror, she lifted her hand and waved. Even in the dimming light, she could see the curve of her mouth. She was smiling.

CHAPTER 29

She was still smiling as Diane took slow steps towards her, stopping when she reached the gate and staring across the street. If she'd had to describe it, if someone asked her exactly what kind of smile it was, she would have had no difficulty in doing so. Because even in the failing light, she could tell it was cold and calculating. Despite a desire to rush back into the house and shut the door, she maintained her gaze, refusing to back down.

'I know about you,' she shouted, her words vanishing into the sound of the traffic that drove past. 'I know all about you.' Louder, the words fired across in fury.

Unfortunately, Paul chose that precise moment to come down the stairs, saw the open door and came to investigate. Emma was held comfortably in his arms, her plump hands around his neck. 'What on earth are you doing out there,' he said. 'Was that you I heard shouting?'

She turned to him. The shout that was on her lips died when she saw Emma. It would frighten her. Instead she quickly ran back to his side. 'Look,' she said, grabbing his arm and pointing across the road.

He looked over her head. 'At what?'

Diane spun around, dismayed. She was gone.

'What on earth is going on?' he said, stepping backward and putting Emma down. 'Go in and play until dinner is ready,' he told her, watching her scamper off with fond eyes before turning back to Diane.

'What's wrong, Diane? Was there somebody out here worrying you?'

She looked across the street again at the empty path and slowly shook her head. 'I thought—'

'You're overtired,' he said, interrupting her, taking her by the arm to lead her inside. 'You've been overdoing it.' It was a statement, not a question.

In the hallway, with the front door shut, she managed to paste a fair resemblance of a smile on her face. 'It has just been a long day,' she said. 'The shop was busier than usual this morning, so I was already tired, but I'd promised to call around to Anne's and the afternoon was gone before I realised it. Then, of course,' she brushed a hand over her hair and flicked it back behind her ears, 'I had to rush.'

She watched his face. He seemed to accept the explanation without question. 'It was a good idea to get a takeaway,' he said. 'We should do it more often.' Without another word, he headed into the family room and, seconds later, she heard him chatting to Emma.

She wanted to turn, open the door and see if the woman had come back, but she was afraid to. Afraid because, if she were, she'd not be able to stop herself, she'd cross the road and wipe that damn smile from her face. She could feel a scream building, deep inside, if she opened the door again, it would start, and she wasn't sure she'd be able to stop. And it would be all over then, wouldn't it? He'd have no difficulty in getting custody.

Moving away from the door, she passed the door to the lounge, eyes studiously averted. In the kitchen, she switched off the cooker, removed the warmed plates and spooned rice and the chicken jalfrezi onto a plate for Paul and the korma onto another for herself.

'It's ready,' she called, bringing the plates to the table.

As Paul tucked into his, she cut some of her chicken for Emma, giving her far more than she could eat, concealing that she'd kept little for herself. She tried a mouthful, chewing for a long time. It was probably lovely, if Paul's rapidly emptying plate was any indication, but her appetite had deserted her in the face of that smile. She struggled with another mouthful of chicken before giving up and pushing the plate away.

If Paul noticed she was unusually quiet, or that she ate little, he didn't say. Instead, he concentrated on his dinner and listened to Emma babble, answering her *why* questions with infinite patience.

After dinner, he had his coffee in front of the TV while she took Emma upstairs. What mundane lives they led, she thought, even as she enjoyed the child's squeals as she tickled her. Was it any wonder that Paul has started looking for his excitement elsewhere? She felt suddenly exhausted, keeping up this act of normality with him was shattering. She wasn't sure how much longer she could spend in the same house with him.

With her daughter's warm, small hand in hers she headed back downstairs where Emma instantly curled up beside her father and she got on with the even more mundane task of tidying up.

She was grateful when Paul stood and lifted the sleeping child into his arms. 'Goodnight,' he said, waiting until she had looked up before continuing, 'I hope you sleep well.'

'Thanks,' she said, surprised. It almost sounded as if he meant it and was the nicest thing he'd said to her in a while. 'And doesn't that say it all,' she muttered, opening the fridge and taking out a bottle of wine. She poured a glass and took it to the sofa. He'd left the TV switched on. Channel hopping, she found a house renovation programme and curled up to unpick her nightmare of a day under the guise of watching it.

But dry rot, crumbling plaster and rising damp only succeeded in reminding her of the mess she was in and she switched it off. Sipping her wine thoughtfully, she found it empty and reached for the bottle, wondering if she could really rule Red out. She had serious questions about her ability to judge, about her grasp of what was true and was a lie. Perhaps, it was someone at work, someone she'd never met at all. She splashed wine into her glass, spilling a little on the sofa and not really caring.

She trawled her mind for other women Paul had mentioned or encountered in the last few months and she couldn't tell if the list was pleasingly, or suspiciously short. He'd certainly had an effect on Susan Power, the nursery manager. The thought lingered before she pushed herself off the topic. She couldn't go around accusing every woman she'd met of sleeping with her husband, she'd look insane, and wasn't that exactly what Paul wanted?

Susan Power. What had Paul said to her that day when she'd been so late? Was it worth finding out? When she dropped Emma off in the morning, she'd go and ask her.

Topping her glass up again, she thought about Paul. A theory, that's all she had really. There was no proof he was having an affair. All she had was that pair of earrings and an overheard phone call. For all she knew, the earrings were for his secretary, a married woman with three kids and a husband she adored. Diane had met her once at an office party, had been secretly relieved when the stylish, and very attractive, woman had been so vocal about her family. Had it all been an act? That was three years ago, just before Emma was born. A time when she had felt unattractive, weary and obviously insecure. She hadn't been to another office party, unwilling in the first year to leave their precious baby with a sitter while she was so young. And since? She shook her head; she couldn't remember.

For all she knew, he could have a different secretary by now. It would make sense. Because, if it wasn't someone he worked with, when would he see her? Since her clinic stay, he'd been home every night.

And before that? Her brow furrowed. She'd tried to remember before, with little success. But now…hadn't there been a conference? She squeezed her eyes tightly, trying to drag the memory back and then groaned. It just wouldn't come.

She was frustrated and infuriated that, until now, she'd never had the strength or the resolve to insist that Paul fill in those missing weeks, those blank months in her mind. Now it was too late, he was using it for his own ends. 'Spontaneous recovery, my ass,' she muttered.

Reaching for the bottle again, she was horrified to find it empty. She got to her feet, swaying, and cursing herself for eating so little, she headed for the cupboard where she kept the empties. She opened it and bent to put the bottle inside and then straightened, brow creased. The cupboard was full. Hadn't she emptied it just a few days before? Yet, now, she had to push bottles back to make space for the one she'd just finished.

Closing the cupboard, she leaned on the counter and tried to clear her head as the wine sped through her bloodstream. Try though she might, she could not remember what day she'd brought the bottles to the bottle bank. A week ago, maybe. But now the cupboard was full. She was drinking more than she used to, but there was no way she was drinking that much.

The only logical conclusion was that someone, and of course she meant Paul, was putting bottles into the cupboard to mess with her head. The thought sobered her up almost instantly. Switching off the lights, she headed to bed.

Waking with a start, she looked at her bedside clock to see that it was just past 3 a.m. Listening for a moment, she waited, her eyes flickering shut only to fly open when it came again, the plaintive cry that had woken her. It couldn't be real; was it a dream, or a trick? Her eyes widened as an idea struck. Throwing back the duvet, she stood and, without bothering to throw on a robe, padded naked down the stairs.

Opening the door into the family room, she switched on the light. Where had she put her laptop? Then she shut her eyes. It would be where it was always kept for safety, under the sofa in the lounge. She hadn't put it there, but she knew Paul, ever security conscious, would have done so.

For a moment, she stood outside the lounge door. She'd not been inside in days. Maybe what Anne had said made sense and something unpleasant had happened here during one of her blackouts. Something so terrible, her mind still couldn't cope with it. She laid her hands flat on the door, fingers splaying, and closed her eyes. If she hoped that enlightenment would come by osmosis, she was disappointed. All she felt was the same quiver of fear.

She moved closer and pressed the length of her naked body against the door. Was she just going crazy? A smile wavered on her lips. If Paul happened to come down the stairs and saw her pressed naked against the door he would certainly think so.

She was about to pull away, when a memory flashed before her eyes. A happy memory, full of noise, light and excited voices. They were in the lounge; she was smiling at something Paul had said and Emma was dancing around, begging to see whatever it was Diane held in her hands…something just at the corner of her mind, desperate to find a way out…but it faded as quickly as it had come and, as it faded, a wave of intense, devastating sadness swept over her, such sadness she thought she would die from the hole it seemed to leave in its wake. She tried to pull herself from the door but found herself unable to move, as if glued to that faint trace of memory. When another crashing wave of sorrow hit her, she gave in to it and slipped slowly to the floor.

When she opened her eyes again, soft light poured through the fanlight above the door. Freezing cold, she felt physically sick. She tried to stand, but her feet were numb; trembling, she crawled on her hands and knees to the stairway and reached for the banisters to pull herself up, but she was unable to grip with her icy cold hands. With no other option, she crawled up the stairs, one step at a time, until she reached the landing.

She'd have liked to have called for help. For Paul to come and pick her up, bring her to bed and comfort her with the warmth of his body. For a moment, she rested on all fours, her forehead against the carpet. A howl built inside, it had an edge of madness that terrified her, she could feel it grabbing hold, trying to force its way out and she bit down on her lip, holding it in. Using the pain to focus, slowly, she inched herself towards her bedroom.

It was a struggle to clamber into bed, but she managed and pulled the duvet around her, over her head, around her feet. Her teeth chattered, her hands were so cold they hurt, and she couldn't feel her feet. How stupid she was to have gone near the lounge. She didn't want to think about what could have happened there. What awful thing could cause such sorrow?

Her teeth chattering, she lay awake until morning, too afraid to sleep, too terrified to think about what memories lay behind that door. She waited until her alarm went off before she rolled out of bed for a long, hot shower.

She dressed in warm layers: a silk vest, a brushed-cotton, long-sleeved T-shirt and a fine-knit jumper. Navy trousers and thick socks sealed in the warmth that was finally returning to her legs. Her reflection in the mirror almost sent her running. If Paul thought she'd looked shattered yesterday, what was he going to say today? There was nothing she could do about her red-rimmed eyes, but she made an attempt at concealing the dark half-circle under each.

Downstairs, once Emma was sitting with her cereal, she filled the kettle and popped a slice of bread in the toaster. Today, she needed caffeine, food and comfort, in any order they came. The toast came first since she'd forgotten to press the switch down on the kettle. Pressing it harder than it needed, she closed her eyes in frustration. She was so tired she couldn't think straight.

As soon as Paul left for work, she took out her mobile and rang Anne. 'Hi Anne,' she said. 'Something's come up, would it be okay if I called to yours to use your computer rather than going to the café.'

'Yes, of course,' Anne said. 'I'll see you when you get here. I'll be writing, so if I don't answer straight away, you'll know why.'

Hanging up, Diane drained her coffee and made another. She'd have to mainline it to keep awake for the drive to Emma's nursery, and she wanted to be alert enough to try and get a meeting with Susan Power.

With Emma dropped off with a smiling Miss Rogers, she headed for the receptionist's desk. 'Hi, Debbie,' she said. 'I wanted to have a word with Ms Power, would it be possible to see her today?'

Debbie looked up over the rim of her glasses and said, 'I'm sorry, she's not available. Is it something someone else can help with?'

'No, I'm afraid not,' she said. 'It's personal, and really important that I see her today, couldn't she could spare a few minutes?'

The receptionist's eyebrows rose. 'It's impossible—'

'Just a few minutes, please,' Diane interrupted, her voice cracking a little. 'It's important.'

'I can see that,' Debbie said quietly, 'but, unfortunately, Ms Powers is away at a conference in Leeds. She's not back until next week.' She looked down at her computer screen and tapped a key. 'I can put you down for a meeting on Tuesday, if that's any good?'

She rolled her hands into fists, feeling her nails make half-moon indents into the soft skin of her palm. 'Thank you,' she said, her voice tight with frustration.

Debbie's eyebrows rose at the tone, but she said nothing and looked down at the keyboard. After a moment, she looked up again. 'Ten thirty on Tuesday. I've put you down for a thirty-minute slot, unless you think you'd need longer.' Her voice was cool.

'Thirty minutes is fine. I'm sorry, I didn't sleep last night.'

The receptionist's face relaxed a little and then her sharp eyes took in the pallor that lay behind the poorly applied make-up. 'Are you sure you're okay,' she asked gently.

'Just tired,' Diane said, with a shaky smile.' Ten thirty on Tuesday. Thank you.'

She walked through the door to the car park feeling Debbie's eyes on her, praying that she would get to her car without collapsing.

When Anne opened her front door, she took one look at her, led her inside the house and over to the sofa. 'You look like you haven't slept a wink,' she said, fluffing the cushions behind Diane's head before pulling off her shoes. She took the blanket from the back of the sofa and draped it over her. 'Have a rest. I'll be over at my desk writing. When you wake, we can talk. But,' she added, seeing a frown appearing on Diane's face, 'Don't worry. I'll wake you in time to collect Emma if you sleep too long.'

An hour later Diane woke, disorientated, with that muggy feeling that comes with sleeping during the day. A clock on the wall, told her she hadn't been asleep long enough to make a difference to the exhaustion that had settled in for the long haul, but she did feel a little better.

Pushing the blanket away, she swung her feet to the ground and sat up, her eyes following the sound of soft clicks on a keyboard to where Anne was hunched over a computer on the other side of the room.

She stopped typing and turned suddenly, somehow sensing Diane's eyes on her. 'You're awake.'

She shook her groggy head. 'Yes,' she said, 'just about. You were concentrating so hard, I didn't want to disturb you.'

Anne waved a hand. 'I have to eat and drink,' she said reasonably. 'Sometimes I get so caught up that I forget but then I suffer the next day because I can't write at all. Take your time getting up. I'll make us something.'

Diane relaxed back and closed her eyes. The comforting sound of cupboard doors opening and closing, of plates clinking, the rustle of paper. She could stay here in this house. Never go home. Pick up Emma, and bring her here. In a house this big, there was sure to be a room to spare. Here there would be no stalker waiting outside, no room full of dread, no strange cries in the night.

Or would all her troubles follow her wherever she went? A tired smile flitted and faded.

Opening her eyes, she struggled to her feet and crossed the room to offer some help.

'No, I'm just done,' Anne said with a smile, nodding her head toward the table where she'd laid out cups and saucers, a pretty jug brimming with milk and a plate of sandwiches cut into triangles with the crusts cut off. 'Sit, relax. I'll bring a pot of tea in a sec.'

With a grateful smile, Diane pulled out a chair and sat. She didn't deserve the kindness the woman was giving her so freely, but she was relishing it. Anne put a fat red teapot down onto a wooden pot-stand, pulled out the chair opposite and sat. She picked up the pot again and held it out to Diane, who pushed the fine porcelain teacup and saucer toward her and waited while it was filled with strong, aromatic tea. Adding a drop of milk, she took a sip. 'Mmmm,' she said, 'this is lovely.'

'It's a special blend,' Anne explained. 'I discovered it years ago and got hooked. Now I can't drink anything else.' She pushed the plate of sandwiches toward her. 'Eat.'

'I'm not feeling very hungry,' she said, reaching for one. The bread was fresh, the ham and pickle salty and tangy. It was delicious. She reached for another, devouring it in a couple of bites and held her cup up for a refill when Anne held the tea pot out again.

When the plate was empty, Diane guessed she had eaten most. 'That was really good,' she said, putting her cup down on the saucer and pushing it away.

'You needed it,' Anne said simply.

'Yes.'

There was silence as both women waited for the other to speak. Finally, Diane met Anne's gaze. 'You were right, I really didn't want to believe that the man I married could be capable of planning all of this.' Her eyes swam with tears and her voice choked. 'But now, I have no choice.'

CHAPTER 30

Slowly, trying to sort it out in her head as she spoke, Diane told Anne about the wine bottles. 'I remembered when I brought the empty bottles to the bottle bank,' she said, 'it was the day I bumped into Red. Only last week. I've been drinking a lot recently but there's no way I'd have managed to get through all the bottles that were there since then.'

'How often do you finish a bottle?' Anne asked, holding a hand up quickly when she saw the look of annoyance on her face. 'I'm not judging, I'm just wondering when you last put a bottle in the cupboard?'

Diane tapped a finger on the arm of her chair. 'It's the bottom shelf of a low cupboard, I usually just plonk the bottle in without looking. I opened a new bottle last night, so it would have been the night before.' She shook her head. 'I don't remember having any problem.'

'Would he have had an opportunity?'

She thought for a moment. When could he have managed to fill the cupboard with empty bottles? To manage it quietly would have taken time. 'First thing in the morning,' she said, slowly, 'during the week, he is always down before me. I get myself ready and then get Emma up.'

'Every morning?'

She shrugged. 'He'd have known he had at least thirty minutes to get it organised. I think you're wrong, though,' she continued, her eyes bleak. 'I don't think he's trying to push me into killing myself. I don't think he'd go that far. I think he's trying to get me committed. To get full custody of Emma, it would be enough.'

'Maybe,' Anne said, the tone of her voice saying she wasn't convinced. 'But he'd never be sure you wouldn't recover, and the situation would then change.'

'You forget, he has this other woman waiting in the wings. While I was,' Diane made quotation marks in the air with her index fingers, 'recovering, he'd be showing the world the happy family life he'd made for Emma.' She threw up her hands in frustration. 'What court would rule against him?'

'Did something else happen last night?'

A long, shuddering breath was her only reply as Diane struggled to regain the feeling of calm she'd had earlier. She didn't want to talk about what happened outside the lounge, it was too raw; she wasn't sure she could talk about it without breaking down. 'I'm sorry,' she said finally, with a trace of a smile. 'I bet you regret agreeing to let me come here.'

Anne stretched a hand across the table and grasped her arm. 'I think you desperately need someone to talk to. I'm more than happy to be that someone.'

'You're right, thank you.' She took a deep breath. 'There was something else but I really don't want to talk about it, not yet anyway. Anyway, it wasn't why I wanted to come. You remember I told you about that strange cry I keep hearing?'

Anne nodded, releasing her arm and sitting back.

'I wondered if it was some kind of recording.'

'A recording,' Anne repeated, surprised, but to Diane's relief, not sceptical. Her eyes narrowed in thought. 'It's a possibility, not hard to do with an iPad, or iPhone. Hang on,' she said, getting up and crossing to her desk. She sat and, a few seconds later, called Diane over. 'A sound module. Have a look,' she said, pointing to the screen.

Looking over Anne's shoulder, she read it with a grim expression. 'One hundred seconds of recording that can be divided into four twenty-five-second segments,' she read aloud. 'And look,' she said, pointing to the next paragraph. 'A timer allows segments to be played at random times throughout the day.'

She moved away and paced the room. 'The bastard,' she said through gritted teeth. She turned and looked back at the other woman who was still reading the details on the computer screen. 'And that explains why he keeps his office locked. He must have it set up in there during the day. And at night he probably has it in his bedroom.'

Anne's eyebrows rose at this reference to Paul having a separate bedroom, but she said nothing. Diane was trying to remember if she'd seen any sort of sound module when she was in his office looking through his papers. She hadn't but that didn't mean it wasn't there. She had to go back and search again. When she found it, she'd leave it where it was, and photograph it for evidence.

'It's time you were leaving,' Anne said.

Diane blinked. She was being thrown out? Her face fell. 'Yes, of course,' she mumbled, averting her eyes; she'd overstayed her welcome. She didn't blame Anne for wanting her to leave.

Anne placed a gentle hand on her shoulder. 'I meant to pick up Emma, that's all. You're always concerned about being late.'

Diane looked at her watch in horror. 'Gosh,' she said, 'I'm so sorry. You're right, I'd better fly.' She turned to face her. 'You've been so kind to me, thank you, it is appreciated.'

Anne smiled briefly. 'You're welcome. But you can't keep going like this, you know. You'll have to do something, and soon. Whether your husband's aim is to have you committed or drive you to suicide, either way does not bode well for you.'

'I just need to get all the facts,' Diane said, nodding. 'Then…' She hesitated. 'If I needed a place to hide away, could I—'

'Yes,' Anne said, interrupting her, 'of course you could come here. For as long as you like.'

'Just let me get all the facts first. Enough to make sure he hasn't a hope in hell of getting custody of my daughter.' Diane looked at her for a moment. Maybe, she thought, a hug was the only thing appropriate. She stepped closer and put an arm around Anne's shoulder and held her for a moment. 'Thank you,' she said before stepping away. 'Now, I'd really better get going.'

At the door, she turned to say a final farewell. 'I'll keep in touch. I've nothing planned until Tuesday when I've an appointment to see the nursery manager, Susan Power. I want to know what Paul said to her that day.'

'You think it's connected in some way?' Anne asked, surprised.

Diane frowned. 'It was odd. Paul was speaking to her and she just looked over to me with a strange look on her face. Almost as if she pitied me.'

'Ah,' Anne said, 'so of course you're worrying about exactly what he said to her.'

Diane reached for the doorknob and opened the front door. Still frowning, she turned and looked at Anne. 'If, as I think, he's gathering information to use against me, and gathering witnesses he could, potentially call on to give a character statement, who better than the manager of the nursery Emma attends?'

With a glance at her watch, Diane shook her head, and headed to her car. She was still exhausted. Exhausted and worried. It all sounded so straightforward when she was with Anne. Everything seemed clear. But she hadn't told her about what had happened outside the lounge last night; the wave of sadness, the blackout. Diane wanted to believe her theory about the sound module, she really did, but after last night she wasn't sure that she wasn't imagining every single thing.

CHAPTER 31

Once again, there was no sign of her stalker outside the school and, once again, there was no relief, just a moment's surprise followed by intense, crippling anxiety. *Maybe she'd never been there.* Once Emma was strapped in, she looked for her again and when she didn't see her, walked to the gate and stared up and down the road for several minutes.

She was still standing there when Rose Metcalf stopped her car beside her and let down her window, scathing eyes raking her from head to foot. 'Diane,' she said, 'you do know your daughter is absolutely hysterical, don't you?'

Diane spun around and looked back to her car in horror. 'Emma,' she cried, sprinting back. Unfortunately, the cries had drawn the attention of a few other parents. Worse still, one had gone into the school and was returning at a run with a serious-faced Miss Rogers.

They all reached the car at the same time, Diane pulling open the door and engulfing the sobbing child in her arms, murmuring to her that she was sorry. She unsnapped the straps and pulled her out, holding her tightly as she cried. Over her head, several pairs of eyes were watching her, and she could hear the mutters of horrified onlookers before Miss Rogers chivvied them on to leave.

'Really, Mrs Andrews,' the young teacher said, in a tone Diane had never heard her use before, 'we can't have this.'

To make matters a million times worse, Emma, on hearing her beloved teacher's voice, turned from her mother's arms and reached out for her. Diane had no option but to allow her to be taken, feeling her departure as a physical blow. She stood on the sidelines watching her own daughter comforted and soothed by another woman feeling embarrassed, humiliated and, above all, guilty. It was only a few minutes, a small voice reasoned. She dismissed it. A few minutes to a three year old was a long time.

A few minutes, listening to Emma being comforted by someone else, was even longer. It was nearly five minutes before her sobs subsided into soft snuffles and another five before the teacher agreed to hand her back to Diane, the look on her face saying she wished she didn't have to. With Emma back in her seat, her tear-stained face looking calmer, she turned to the teacher. 'I'm sorry,' she said. 'You must think I'm a terrible mother.'

The teacher hesitated and looked into the car where an exhausted Emma had fallen asleep, damp eyelashes resting on soft pink cheeks. 'It's not for me to judge,' she said, looking back at her. 'But I will have to make a report about this incident to Mrs Power.'

Diane pressed her lips together tightly on words that had to remain unsaid if she wanted to keep sending Emma to the nursery. 'Fine,' was all she could manage without saying more.

Closing the car door gently so as not to wake Emma, she climbed into the driver's seat without another word or glance at the teacher. Emma was still asleep when they reached home. Diane opened the front door before returning to lift her out, envying her ability to sleep so soundly. Lowering her to the sofa, she draped a blanket over her and sighed. She'd had no lunch. Maybe she *was* a terrible mother. Continuing to berate herself, she trudged back to the car, slamming the doors shut and locking it before she returned to stand and stare at her sleeping child. What the future held in store for herself, she wasn't sure, but it had to be good for Emma. And that meant staying with Diane. Paul had shown what he was capable of, how manipulative, cruel and greedy he really was. She wasn't going to trust him with her precious daughter's future.

Putting the episode at the nursery out of her mind, she took her mobile phone from her bag and headed upstairs to search Paul's office for a sound module and end all this insanity. There was a moment's panic when she opened the drawer in her dresser and couldn't find the key, her hand rummaging among her underwear. And then the blessed relief as her fingers closed over it.

Back on the landing, she listened for a moment but there was no sound from downstairs. She didn't waste any time. Inserting the key in the lock, she turned it, pushed the office door open and began to search as she had done before, this time with a much clearer idea of what she was looking for. Nothing on the desk, or beside the computer, in the drawers or on the shelves. Nothing.

Maybe it was in his bedroom, hooked up to an iPad or something? Before leaving the office, she opened the middle drawer and took out the sheaf of papers she'd seen the last time. As fast as possible, she took a photo of each one and returned them to the drawer. With a quick look around to make sure everything was as she found it, she switched off the light, shut and locked the door.

The spare bedroom Paul had used since she came home from the clinic was at the back of the house. It was a bright room with windows on two sides and, like all the bedrooms, it was large with an original fireplace. It was smaller than the master bedroom, but probably the prettiest in the house.

She'd made the beds quickly that morning but obviously hadn't plumped up the pillow. Picking it up, she looked at the indent his head had made and put her face to it, breathing him in. Despite everything he'd done, her heart ached with the knowledge that he no longer wanted her, wondering, not for the first time, when he'd stopped loving her. Giving the pillow a quick shake, she put it back. She needed to get on with her search.

Ten minutes later, every piece of furniture in the room had been checked. She even looked on the windowsill behind the curtains. But there was nothing to prove he was tricking her. With a final look around the room, she left, closing the door behind her.

She should check on Emma but, instead, she returned to her room and sat on the bed, tapping the key to Paul's office against the palm of her hand. She'd heard the cry last night so perhaps he'd used it then, didn't have time to lock it in his office this morning, so took it with him. She bit her lip. That was a possibility. But so was the possibility that this was *all in her head*. She shook herself, she had to believe it was in his briefcase. It was her last hope. He usually kept it in the office, safe and secure behind his locked door. She'd have to look on Saturday morning when he took Emma out for the day.

Checking the time, she was startled to see it was five thirty. It had taken far longer than she'd expected. A frown creased her forehead. It wasn't like Emma to sleep for so long.

Her feet were light and fast on the stairs and she went through the open door to the family room with her heart racing and a feeling of dread in her chest. Emma was there just where she'd left her, curled up, unmoving, long eyelashes resting on porcelain-pale cheeks, rosebud mouth; a china doll.

Diane knew, if she touched her, she'd be so very, very cold. 'Oh God, no,' she said, the prayer coming on a desperate whisper even as she felt a familiar wave of nausea sweep through her body, legs weakening, a hand reaching out for support. She wanted to call out, scream her pain and loss, but words wouldn't come. She wanted to go and take Emma in her arms, shake her, make her wake up, but she knew it was no good. Somebody was sobbing, the sound deafeningly loud in her ears. It took a few seconds to realise it was her own cries she heard. The hand holding onto the door frame dropped away and she collapsed to the floor.

CHAPTER 32

She came to slowly, feeling the hard floor beneath her hip, a pain in the arm she lay on, a deep sense of dread and horror coursing through her, making her heave. It would be better to open her eyes, face the reality of her situation, life without her baby. But she couldn't do it. The darkness was better. If she couldn't see it, it hadn't happened. Stay hidden from the pain. Don't let it get you.

'Mummy?'

Her eyes snapped open. 'Emma?'

'You were asleep and you wouldn't wake up,' the little girl said, her lower lip quivering.

Diane reached a hand out and brushed the child's tear-stained face. 'Emma,' she breathed. She struggled to sit, waited for her head to stop spinning and stood, holding onto the door frame, legs shaking.

She looked down at her daughter, who looked back at her with such a serious look in her brown eyes. 'Poor darling,' she said, guilt lashing. She reached for her, holding her close, planting kisses on her head as she moved, slowly and carefully over to the sofa. A quick glance at the clock on the wall told her she'd been out for about ten minutes.

Ten minutes? The poor child. 'I'm so sorry, sweetheart,' she said, rocking her gently in her arms. When she started to get restless, to squirm to get free, Diane reached for her favourite book, which was never far away. 'I'll read you a story,' she said, relieved when Emma settled down. She wanted to keep her close, to feel her warmth, her breath on her face as she read the words she'd read so often before.

Despite the physical reassurance of the little body snuggled into hers, the ghost of her terror that Emma was dead still lingered. Reluctantly, she left her playing with toys while she prepared dinner but was unable to stop her eyes constantly darting in her direction to make sure that she was there, alive and well.

Dinner prepared, she returned to sit with her, giving in to her demands to read the book yet again. She didn't actually need to read the words; there weren't many and she'd read them so often she knew them by heart. She turned the pages, said the words and kept her eyes on Emma's face.

They were still sitting there when Paul arrived home, the rattle of his key in the front door making Emma squirm from her arms to run to greet him. For a second, she felt bereft, then she stood to set the table.

Paul had Emma in his arms as he came through, the affection on his face genuine. *About the only thing genuine about him*, she thought, turning to greet him. 'Hi,' she said, 'dinner's almost ready.'

'Good,' he replied, putting Emma on her feet. He watched as she toddled over to the sofa before turning to Diane. 'Did you have a good day?'

'Oh, just the usual,' she said, turning the heat down under one of the pots, concentrating on stirring the Bolognese in the hope that he'd ask no more questions.

Over dinner, the conversation was, as usual, desultory, neither of them making much effort. Even Emma, normally chatty, was quiet. Withdrawn, Diane thought, looking at her. It hadn't been an easy day for her; for a child who rarely cried to be in tears twice in one day was a huge leap. Guilt whipped through her. The one consolation was that the child hadn't yet mentioned either episode, so she didn't have to deal with Paul's criticism.

When they'd both gone, Emma to bed and Paul to do whatever it was he did in his office, she poured herself a glass of wine. Tomorrow she'd stop, but tonight she needed the crutch of alcoholic oblivion.

The glass was half empty when she heard the cry, her top lip rolling in a sneer as she convinced herself she'd been right. He'd brought the sound module to work with him, and now he was up there, playing it. Taunting her.

Her belief in his duplicity strengthened her. She took the remainder of the wine and threw it down the sink. Switching off the lights, she went up the stairs and stopped outside Emma's room where she stood for a long time, watching her slow, even breaths. The feeling of dread had almost gone, but the memory of it lingered. It had been so real.

As she stripped and got ready for bed, the same thought kept bouncing around her head. It had seemed so real, but it wasn't, the child sleeping quietly next door was proof of that. So maybe it was all in her head? Maybe there was no stalker outside the nursery today because there never had been? She'd thought talking to Anne had grounded her, making her believe in herself, in the truth of what she was seeing and hearing but, maybe, Red had been right to warn her about her relationship with a fantasist.

She slipped under the duvet with a heavy sigh. This exhausted, it was impossible to think clearly. She was just slipping into a deep sleep when a long, mournful cry broke the night's quiet. Just one, but it seemed to hang in the air for a long time before fading back to silence. With a lump in her throat, Diane realised it sounded just the same as poor Emma's heartbreaking cry outside the nursery. Perhaps it was her poor exhausted brain just replaying that awful memory, the sound of her cry, her woebegone, stricken face.

With tears running down her face, she fell into a restless sleep, waking numerous times to go next door to reassure herself that

Emma was alive and well. At five, she gave up and, throwing a robe on, padded barefoot down the stairs. She made a pot of tea and took it to the seat near the window again and sat drinking it as she watched the world wake; finding solace in one of the few remaining comforts she could depend on in her life.

CHAPTER 33

When, over the next couple of days, she saw no sign of the woman, heard no cries, and nothing out of the ordinary happened, she should have been happy. Instead, she felt more unsettled, constantly looking over her shoulder and shushing Emma to listen in the silence for…something, anything. The quiet was unnerving, and each time she would hug Emma to her and explain that Mummy was just being silly.

On Friday afternoon, she was bustling about in the kitchen when she glanced across to where Emma was sitting on the sofa, one of her toys dangling from her hands. She wasn't moving. And she hadn't sung in the car on the way home. In fact, she was unusually quiet. Diane had been so lost in her own anxieties she hadn't noticed.

Guilt stung. Sitting beside her, she brushed her hand over her curls. 'You okay, poppet?' she asked.

Emma turned to look at her with her serious brown eyes. 'Tommy doesn't want to play with me any more.'

Diane's heart leapt. The sins of the fathers, or in this case the mothers. How dare that bloody Metcalf woman take it out on a three year old? If she got an opportunity, she'd have a word with her. She put her arm around Emma and pulled her close, dropping a kiss on her head. 'Boys can be like that,' she said, 'don't worry, you'll find other boys and girls to play with, you'll see.'

A bowl of ice cream cheered her up a little and, for good measure, Diane switched on the TV and found a programme suitable for her to watch. She went back to the kitchen but kept a closer eye on her. Maybe she should have a word with Miss Rogers. The thought didn't appeal but, for Emma's sake, she'd do anything.

The day was followed by yet another restless night. When morning finally dawned, she lay until she heard Emma moving about before she swung her legs from the bed.

Today she'd planned to check out Paul's briefcase and find the sound module; it was going to be her only opportunity this week. She felt so weary; tired of playing charades and so very sad.

Strong coffee helped and she was smiling at something Emma was saying when Paul appeared down for breakfast. 'What are your plans for the morning?' she asked him, concentrating on pouring milk into Emma's cereal so he wouldn't see the unusual level of interest in her eyes. Before he answered, he peered out of the window, assessing the sky.

'I was going to take Emma to the park. The weather forecast is for a dry day, but those clouds look a bit ominous.'

Diane didn't turn around. *Please go, please go, please go.* The words danced in her head. Moving back to the kitchen, she put two slices of bread into the toaster and stood waiting for it to pop.

'But I think we'll risk it,' he said finally, returning to the table and tousling Emma's hair. 'What do you think, princess?'

Her mouth full of cereal, she nodded.

The toast popped up, startling Diane who had briefly shut her eyes. Carefully, keeping her face locked in neutral, she put it in the toast rack and brought it to the table. 'The coffee's fresh,' she said, sitting. 'Sorry, I missed what you said.'

'I was just saying that I think we'll risk it,' he repeated, pouring them both some coffee and reaching for the milk. He looked at the toast. 'Are you not having any?'

She shook her head. 'I had breakfast earlier.'

Accepting what she said without question, he continued with his breakfast, chatting to Emma about the park and the fun they were sure to have.

It was another hour before they went.

'You heading off to the supermarket?' he asked finally, grabbing his car keys.

She made a big deal of checking the time. 'I might leave it a bit,' she said, 'mid- morning is often the busiest time to go.' Afraid he'd suggest she go with them, she hurriedly added, 'I think I'll make a start on the ironing.'

He nodded. 'Oh good, I noticed I've only a couple of shirts left.'

Since Diane couldn't remember the last time she'd done any ironing, she wasn't surprised. A thought crossed her mind. The washing she'd done a few days before was still in the machine. 'I'll catch up with everything today. Have a nice morning."

'Bye, Mummy!' Emma waved.

She bent down, picked her up and gave her a noisy kiss on her neck, making her squeal with laughter.

'Let's go,' Paul said, suddenly impatient.

Diane dropped a kiss on her head and put her down. 'Have a good time,' she said, watching them go, Emma's hand clasped tightly in his.

She listened as the car doors opened and closed, the engine started and, finally, to the swish of tyres as the car pulled out onto the road. And then she waited five minutes. There was always the chance he'd have forgotten something and would return. But he didn't, and she headed up the stairs.

With the key in her hand, she looked out her bedroom window for a final check, and then headed to the office. Inside, the briefcase was sitting on the chair, waiting for her. Picking it up, she sat and put it on the desk in front of her.

She was lucky. The catch was a simple one, with no fancy combination coded lock; one flick of a finger opened it and she pushed the flap backward. Inside, there were the sheaves of company-branded documents she expected. She took them out, carefully placing them on the desk. There wasn't much else in the main body of the briefcase, just a few pens and some lose paperclips rattling around the bottom.

Along the back there was a zipped compartment. She opened it slowly, the sound loud in the quiet of the room, and then she slipped her hand inside. When her fingers located a small cold object, a smile of triumph lit her face, a feeling of relief rushing through her. It was real, she wasn't imagining it. 'I have you, Paul,' she said, pulling it out.

Then, with a grunt of annoyance, she shoved the calculator back inside the compartment and pulled the zip closed.

Locking the door, she returned the key to the drawer in her bedroom and sat on the bed. Unless he'd been very clever and hidden it somewhere she couldn't find, she had to face the truth; there was no sound module. The cries of a wailing child were all in her head.

Weary and frustrated, she headed downstairs. She needed to get the shopping done. Grabbing her purse and car keys, she opened the front door. She'd only taken a few steps before she looked up, startled to see the woman across the road, staring at her. Without thinking, she turned and hurried back into the house. Slamming the door, she leaned back against it and closed her eyes.

Why now?

Her eyes opened. She'd wanted to confront her, hadn't she? Well, why not now when, for a change, Emma wasn't with her. It didn't matter that she didn't know anything about her. She'd go over and demand to be told what was going on. She could do it.

Taking a deep breath, she opened the door. This was it. She stepped out, ready to do battle.

There was nobody there. She ran to the gate and looked up and down the street. Nobody.

Sudden nausea made her stomach heave, her hand covering her mouth as she dashed back inside. Making it as far as the kitchen sink, she vomited bile into the basin.

She waited a minute before she turned the taps on to wash her shame away. Staggering to the sofa before her legs gave way, she collapsed in a heap. The cries, the stalker; all her imagination. There was no way the woman could have vanished from sight that quickly.

Still feeling shaky, she sat up and swung her feet to the ground. A few minutes later, she stood, using the arm of the sofa for support. She had to go to the supermarket, there was no way she could face Paul's inquisition if he came home and found her like this. Her heart dropped as she realised that everything she did just gave him more ammunition. And what did she have to show for it, nothing but a calculator.

Grabbing her keys, she dragged herself upstairs for one final check from her bedroom window before she left.

There was no one there.

Of course, there was no one there.

CHAPTER 34

She felt weak and her head spun, but she made it to the car, started the engine and reversed out onto the road. At the intersection, she glanced in the rear-view mirror and saw Paul's car turning into the house. He wouldn't have seen her; his focus would have been on indicating and crossing the opposite lane to enter their driveway.

The shopping centre where she did her weekly shop was a ten-minute drive. It took her fifteen as she ignored flashing lights from irate drivers who objected to her twenty-mile speed in a thirty-limit area. Going faster wasn't an option for her, struggling as she was with the speed her world was spinning around her.

Somehow, she got the shopping done, loading everything she usually bought into her trolley, losing focus now and then and adding whatever happened to be in front of her. The trolley was full by the time she got to the last aisle and she headed to the checkout, desperate now to get out of the shop. Then she saw *her* again, at the other side of the tills, looking her way.

She wasn't really there. She knew that now but, despite that, she took a step backward and then another, pulling the heavy trolley.

'Excuse me!' an annoyed voice behind her, a man with a young boy in the child seat of his trolley. 'Could you watch where you're going?'

Diane looked at him but said nothing. She wrapped her arms around herself and stayed there, footsteps and voices swirling around her. A couple of customers shot her a curious glance but it was London and there were a lot of eccentric people about; nobody stopped to ask if she were okay.

Nor would she have thanked them if they had, lost as she was in her thoughts. She was imagining it all, wasn't she? But there was something bothering her. She thought back to seeing the woman outside her home. She was standing where she usually did, in front of the Prescott's garden wall.

Right next to their open gate.

If the woman wanted to hide, all she had to do was walk through the gate and stoop down a little. The Prescott's wall had to be almost five foot high.

Maybe she had a car parked nearby, saw Diane leave and followed her to the centre. Her face hardened; of course, she didn't have to. Paul would have told her where she did her weekly shop. Anger surged through her, giving her strength.

Back at home, she parked beside Paul's car. She took one bag in with her, opened the front door with her free hand, dumped the bag on the floor and turned back to get the rest. A glance across the road showed her that the Prescott's gate was still standing open. Leaving the car and the front door open, she crossed the road and, with a quick look around, stepped inside their garden. It was neat if unimaginative, a large grassed area surrounded on three sides by flower borders. Near the wall they'd chosen to plant low-growing bushes. Hydrangea and mahonia, neither of which she liked.

Her eyes scanned the ground, looking for footprints. Really, really wanting…no needing…to see them. And then she saw them. The distinct imprint of heels in the soft soil. It had to be *her*. She'd met Mrs Prescott and the elderly lady favoured flat lace-ups.

Pulling out her phone, she snapped the footprints, standing back to get the wall in the background. She was just about to move away when a quavering voice addressed her. 'Can I help you, Mrs Andrews?'

Diane looked innocently at the elderly lady who'd come through the gate, a newspaper under one arm. She pointed toward the shrubs.

'I was just admiring your garden,' she said, 'and these beautiful shrubs caught my eye. I took a photo so I can find out what they are.'

Mrs Prescott blushed, making Diane feel guilty for her deception. 'I can give you their names, my dear,' she said. Raising her hand, she pointed to the nearer shrub. 'That one is hydrangea macrophylla, Blushing Bride. The next along is mahonia aquifolium, Apollo. Then there's my favourite, hydrangea paniculate, Tardiva and, finally, mahonia media, Charity. The mahonia all have yellow blossoms, as you may already know, and the hydrangea I've chosen are all white.'

Diane struggled to keep the smile in place throughout, conscious of her open car and front door. 'That's so kind of you,' she said. 'Thank you.'

'I can write them down for you, if you'd like to come inside.'

'No, that's fine. I have a very good memory,' she said, hoping the woman wouldn't ask her to repeat them to ensure she had them right.

'Well, I wish you happy gardening,' the elderly woman said and walked slowly up the driveway to her front door.

Diane hurried back across the road, took the remaining bags from the car and carried them inside. There wasn't a sound. Checking her phone, she was horrified at the time. Emma was probably asleep. Paul, more than likely, in his office.

Closing the front door quietly, she left the shopping where it was for the moment and headed to the family room. The door was ajar, she pushed it open and moved inside, her eyes scanning the room. Expecting to see Emma asleep on the sofa, she was surprised to see Paul there too, his head resting on the back of the sofa, a soft snore coming with every exhale. Emma was curled up beside him like a dormouse.

Back in the hallway, she stepped over the bags and trudged up the stairs. Since they were both asleep, she'd lie down for a while, see if sleep would find her too.

It didn't.

CHAPTER 35

She couldn't lie there any longer. She came down the stairs and, picking up the first of the bags, went back to the kitchen, dropping them on the floor and heading back to pick up the rest.

Paul still hadn't stirred. She'd always envied him his ability to sleep through anything and, irritated, banged one cupboard door, and then another. Finally, in frustration, she slammed one shut, the contents of the cupboard rattling. Looking over, she saw she had succeeded in waking him.

'Hi,' he said, coming over. 'I didn't hear you come in, you should have given me a shout and I'd have helped.'

'I'm not in long,' the lie was automatic.

'You were gone a long time,' he said, 'was the supermarket busy?'

'Yes,' she said, 'and I got chatting to a few people so that delayed me too.' In case he saw the lie in her eyes, she looked across to where Emma still slept. 'Did you have a nice day?'

He gave a slight shrug. 'She enjoyed the park. It was busier than usual, she had to queue for the slide. One little tyke insisted on standing at the top of the ladder and refusing to move so that put everyone's backs up, especially since his mother kept insisting, he'd come down when he wanted to and we shouldn't be bullying him.'

Diane grinned in genuine amusement. She could just imagine the scene; irate parents, bored children and one rebel. 'How long did he stay there?'

'He'd probably still be there if one of the other parents hadn't walked up to him and said, 'Slide or get off!'

'What happened?'

'He wouldn't do either, so the man lifted him off. His mother started shouting at the man, calling him a bully, threatening to sue him for assault. It was crazy. But at least the rest of the children got to go down the slide.'

She looked at him curiously. 'You think he was right to do that?'

Paul's brow creased. 'We were letting a five year old hold us to ransom, so yes, I suppose he was right.'

Proving to the young boy that might always wins. A great lesson to teach him. 'You could have told everyone to go play on the other things, the swings, seesaws etc. and left him with the slide all to himself. He'd have got bored of being King of Nothing after a while. He'd have learnt a very valuable lesson too,' she added, meeting his eyes, her own hard, 'he'd have learnt that sometimes you win the battle but lose the war. Now all he's learnt is that the bigger man always wins.'

He laughed. 'He was five, it was a slide. I think you're seeing too much in this, Diane. Anyway,' he added, 'might *is* right.'

Still laughing, he went back to the sofa and switched on the television.

Unpacking the remaining groceries, weary from a day of mental cartwheels, she guessed he really believed that concept. The problem was, so did many others. And that's where he hoped to win. If might was right, then its opposite, weakness, had to be wrong. If he could convince the world that she was weak, in mind as well as in body, wouldn't it be wrong to give her even partial custody of Emma?

Of course, it would. So, she had to prove she wasn't weak. So far, she wasn't doing so well, wavering as she was between believing she was imagining everything, and that everything was real.

The photograph on her camera was the nearest she had to proof. Maybe it wouldn't convince anyone else, but she could look at it and know her stalker, at least, was real, that alone made her stronger. She just needed to stay this way.

She had to start believing in herself. After all, in the last few weeks she'd discovered her husband – who was having an affair – was trying to drive her crazy to get custody of their child. She'd run from the police, had been accused of theft, was being stalked and was terrified of going into a room she used to consider her retreat. Strong? Mentally, she was the bloody Incredible Hulk.

Physically, she didn't think she was doing so well. She'd never had a great appetite but these days, with all the stress, she didn't feel like eating at all. That was going to stop. Today.

Paul switched off the TV and stood.

'Are you coming back down?' she asked, guessing he was heading to his office.

'In a few minutes,' he said, his hand on the door knob. 'Did you want a hand with something?'

'No, I'm fine, thanks,' she said, keeping her voice casual. As soon as he'd gone, she grabbed her phone to look at the photograph. She swore softly. A better camera, or a better photographer, might have picked up the footprint but not her with her damn stupid low-tech phone. She zoomed in as far as she could. She couldn't see anything. *Or there was nothing there.*

She shut her eyes and took a deep breath. He was winning, wasn't he? Whatever way you looked at it.

After dinner, feeling guilty for how little time she'd spent with Emma that day, she spent longer getting her ready for bed, telling her stories of when she was young. 'My mummy used to help me get ready for bed, just like I help you,' she said. 'And, every night, she would tell me the same as I tell you. That you are the most precious little girl in the world, and I love you.'

'And did you tell her what I tell you, that I love you more?' Emma asked, loving to hear these stories.

'The very same words,' Diane said, kissing her daughter's soft cheek.

Opening the wide, deep drawer that held the child's pyjamas, she waved her toward it. 'Okay, madam,' she said, 'you get to choose which to wear.'

Emma took her time and eventually chose a yellow top covered in ducks and purple bottoms with a dinosaur motif.

Holding them up, Diane pursed her lips. 'You're sure the dinosaurs won't eat the ducks?'

The little girl sent blond hair flying. 'No, silly, they're best friends.'

There was no answer to that. Anyway, did it really matter if the top didn't match the bottom? She should be pleased her child was rebelling against convention instead of worrying that the three year old didn't realise that the little guy frequently got eaten by the big guy.

They returned to the family room, hand in hand, and Emma joined Paul on the sofa, cuddling in to him, his arm automatically opening for her. Diane sighed, remembering a time when it was like that for her. It didn't seem such a long time ago and yet so much had changed it felt like a lifetime.

He made no comment on the mismatched pyjamas. Concentrating on the programme he was watching, she doubted if he even noticed.

If she were imagining it all, she was wrong about Paul's role. That he was having an affair was probably a given, those damn earrings testified to that, but the rest no. But if she weren't imagining it, maybe she should expect it to get worse. She had to be ready for everything, anything. See-saw, see-saw, she was making herself dizzy, sick. See-saw, roller coasters, her life was off balance. She needed to take control. Today, she'd reacted. Tomorrow, she wouldn't. She'd ignore the woman, the cries, the increasing terror of the lounge. She'd be strong.

Wouldn't she?
She stared at Emma in her adorable mismatched pyjamas.
For her. She'd be strong for her.

CHAPTER 36

She considered taking a sleeping pill but, once again, discounted it. She needed a clear head. Today had been tough, tomorrow, she guessed, would be even tougher.

Moments later, exhaustion kicked her into a deep sleep.

When her eyes flicked open, she knew she hadn't been asleep long. Maybe only minutes. What had woken her? She listened, expecting to hear the cry, but there was nothing. With a frustrated groan, she closed her eyes again, willing herself to fall asleep. And then she heard it; just a few seconds, but enough to raise goosebumps on her arms and send a shiver down her spine. It didn't last long. Maybe ten seconds. She gritted her teeth.

Instead of trying to go back to sleep, she switched on her bedside light and picked up a book she'd started several days ago. She'd forgotten the story and flicked through the first few pages to reacquaint herself with the characters before getting back into it, but she'd only read a few pages when the cry came again, longer this time.

She got out of bed, threw on her robe and went downstairs to make some camomile tea. It might relax her. At least, she thought, switching on the kettle, it would pass the time. With a mug of it cupped between her hands, she sat at the window, reaching forward to pull back the curtain to look out at the night.

Her mug was empty before she heard the cry again. There was something about it tonight, a more piteous tone, the little hiccup at the end sounding more pathetic, needier. She bit her lip, waiting for it to stop, counting the seconds. But this time it went on, and on, until finally she put her hands over her ears and tried to shut it out.

Just when she thought she couldn't take it any longer, it stopped, leaving a silence that had no comfort in it, just a heavy anticipation. Her eyes were gritty from tiredness. She had to try and get some sleep. Leaving the mug on the table, she headed back to her room, slipped off her robe and slid back under the duvet.

The cry came at irregular intervals throughout the night. Occasionally she managed a few minutes sleep between them, but it wasn't enough. By the time the light of the new morning slipped around the edges of her curtains, she knew she was in for a nightmare of a day.

It had got worse. Did that mean Paul's plan was escalating? And did that mean she definitely wasn't imagining it all? Even if she weren't so tired her head ached; she wasn't sure she could work out that conundrum.

Slipping her robe back on, she grabbed her book and went downstairs. A pot of coffee and two slices of toast in front of her, she sat at the table and opened her book again. Determined to eat, she spread butter and marmalade on the toast and forced herself to eat both slices, washing them down with strong coffee.

She sat reading, forcing herself to concentrate until she heard movement from upstairs and then she went to get Emma ready. Sticking to routine was the only way she was going to get through the day.

In her bedroom, she pulled back the curtains. It was the usual grey, early spring day, heavier clouds than yesterday promising rain before long. It would take very heavy rain to put Paul off his Sunday afternoon golf. Crossing her fingers, she hoped the clouds lied.

Fixated on the sky, she almost missed the figure standing on the other side of the road. Enough was enough. Grabbing her phone from her bedside locker, she fumbled with the pin, put the phone in camera mode, and hastily took several photos of her before the woman noticed and scurried off down the road.

She stood staring down the now-empty road until she heard Emma calling several minutes later. Her finger hovered over the photo symbol on her phone to bring up the images she'd just taken, but something stopped her. What if she looked at the photos and there was no woman there at all?

'Mummy?' Emma appeared in the doorway.

'Coming, darling,' she said, slipping her phone into the back pocket of her jeans.

Paul was making coffee when she pushed open the door into the family room. 'You were up early,' he said.

'I woke early,' she said, pasting a cheery smile in place, hoping she wasn't overdoing it.

'You look a bit pale,' he commented, picking up the coffee pot from the table and rinsing it out before making a fresh pot.

Leaving Paul with Emma, she went back up to her room. She needed to talk to someone. And, sadly, there was only one person to talk to. She dialled Anne's number. It was answered almost immediately, and Diane felt herself relax. 'It's Diane,' she said, 'I really need to talk to you, are you free?'

'Has something happened?' Anne sounded anxious.

'To be honest, I'm not sure, it doesn't really make sense. But I'm so tired, I'm not sure I'm thinking straight. I thought—'

'That talking to me would help,' Anne interrupted her. 'Yes, of course, come whenever you want. I'll be here all day.'

'Isn't it your day for the charity shop?'

'Not any more,' she said, and there was a faint note of regret in her voice. 'Red rang me after your visit, she thought I should take a break.'

Diane squeezed her eyes shut remembering Red's phone call; something else she was to blame for. 'I'm so sorry,' she said.

The Housewife

'It means I'm here for you though, so come on over.'

'Thank you,' she said, 'I feel better already. I'll be over within the hour.' Ending the call, her finger, once more, hovered over the picture symbol, but she couldn't bring herself to look.

She went back down to the family room where a smiling Emma was now playing with her toys, Paul cross-legged on the floor beside her.

'What time are you going to play golf?' she asked, starting to clear away the breakfast dishes. She saw him frown. It wasn't a question she'd ever asked, he was looking for the reason.

'At two,' he said finally.

'Okay, good,' she said, loading the dishwasher. 'I've promised to call over to see Anne. I'll be back before that.'

'You never said,' he said turning to look at her, sounding aggrieved.

'Didn't I?' she said, her voice light and cool. 'I must have forgotten.' She offered no further explanation and he didn't ask. She bent to give Emma a kiss on her forehead. 'Bye, sweetie,' she said.

Traffic was Sunday morning light, so she made good time to Anne's house, pulling into her driveway and dashing from the car to the doorway in the soft rain that had started to fall. Not heavy enough to stop Paul's golf, she hoped it would stay that way.

She rang the bell, the door opening almost immediately as though the woman were waiting for her. 'Thanks so much for this,' Diane said with a warm smile, stepping inside and following Anne down the hall.

Walking into the room was like walking into a hug; instant comfort. She sighed and, without waiting for an invitation, sat into the sofa. 'Oh, Anne,' she said, 'I'm so exhausted, I can't even think straight.' She could hear the kettle humming, the clink of cups, a rustle of paper and, within seconds, she was asleep.

When she woke, there was silence. Not even the soft tapping of keys. She waited a moment, her eyes closed, enjoying the unusual feeling of complete relaxation. She opened her eyes and looked around. Anne was sitting at her desk, reading, her hair falling around her face.

'I fell asleep,' Diane said, blushing, getting to her feet and stretching. 'How long have I been out?'

'Just over an hour,' Anne said, closing her book and putting it down. She stood up and went to the kitchen to switch on the kettle. 'I guess you needed it. Sit, I'll make some tea.'

Moving to the table, Diane sat and watched as she bustled about. Soon there was tea and two types of cake on the table.

'Help yourself,' Anne said, pouring tea into a mug and handing it to her. 'And then tell me all about it.'

Helping herself to a slice of lemon drizzle cake, she broke a piece from it and popped it into her mouth. She broke off another piece. 'This is really good,' she said.

'I made it yesterday, it's a favourite of mine.'

'Mine too.' Finishing the slice, she took a sip of the tea and then looked across the table. 'I couldn't find the sound module,' she said. 'I searched everywhere.' She lifted the mug of tea, cradling it between her hands and continued, 'And yesterday, twice I saw the stalker, outside my home and in the supermarket. And then, last night,' she winced at the memory, exhausted tears forming, 'that cry came, all night long.'

'So, you got very little sleep?' Anne said, taking in the pallor, the dark circles under her eyes.

Diane ran a hand over her face. 'Hardly any. That's why I flaked out when I sat down.' She smiled gratefully. 'Your home is so relaxing. It's like a tonic.' She sipped her tea and put the mug down, keeping her hands wrapped around it. 'He's escalating.'

Anne's eyebrows rose. 'Escalating?'

'You write crime novels, isn't that what you'd call it when everything gets worse? Last night the cries were so much more heart-wrenching.'

Anne picked up the teapot and filled both mugs. 'I don't understand. I thought the sounds you heard were a recording?'

Diane shook her head in frustration. How could she explain? 'I'm not sure any more. They're…so real. They twist at something deep inside me, something terrifying and sad. It just makes me want to cry.'

She waited for a response, for Anne to say she understood. Then she remembered the photograph. 'I got the woman's photograph,' she said, standing to cross to the sofa and pick up her bag. 'At least,' she added, a quiver of apprehension running down her spine, 'I think I did.'

Returning to the table, she searched inside and took out her phone. 'I haven't looked at it yet,' she admitted, meeting her eyes with a worried look. 'I was afraid to, you know, because if there's nothing, I'll have to face the truth.'

'We won't know until you look,' Anne said reasonably.

Nodding, Diane keyed in her pin and then stared at the photos before passing it across with relief in her eyes.

A few seconds passed while Anne examined them. 'She's fairly ordinary-looking,' she said, handing back the phone, 'regular features, neat hair. She wouldn't stand out in a crowd.'

Diane shook her head. 'She does to me. But it's proof that I'm not imagining it, isn't it?' She ran a hand through her hair. 'It's such a relief to have something.'

There was silence for a moment and then Anne put down the mug she was holding in her other hand. 'I know we spoke the last time about Paul playing games with you. But I've been giving it a lot of thought, Diane. Remember I suggested that maybe something bad had happened in the lounge to account for the sensations you get there?'

Diane nodded.

'Paul couldn't be responsible for that.' She hesitated and then, with a shake of her head continued, 'maybe he *isn't* responsible for the cries you're hearing either.'

'You think I'm imagining it?' Diane said, her words coming out tight and quiet. Wasn't it what she was beginning to believe herself?

Anne held up her hands. 'No,' she said quickly, 'well, not exactly.' She indicated the mobile phone in Diane's hand. 'You've proven the woman exists, and I think you're probably right that someone, probably Paul, has arranged it. But the other bit, the unaccountable fear of that room and the cries.' She took a deep breath and lifted her chin as if she knew what she said next wasn't going to be liked. 'You said there were areas of your life prior to your admission to that clinic that are blank, yes?'

There was a distinct pause as Diane considered the question before she slowly nodded.

Anne chewed her lower lip. 'I'm wondering,' she said, hesitantly, 'you said you spent a lot of time in that room. That you considered it your sanctuary. Well,' she stopped again, looking across the table. 'I wonder if perhaps Emma wandered in, maybe made a mess and you overreacted and—'

'Hurt her,' Diane interrupted, her eyes wide. 'Oh my God, you think I hurt her? You think it's *her* cries I'm hearing?'

'You obviously love your daughter and would have felt so guilty that burying it was your only choice. Remember, the doctors said your memories would come back spontaneously, well, I think they are, the fear of the room is because of what you did there and the cries are part of that buried memory.'

Her eyes still wide, Diane held a hand over her mouth. Horrified and hurt, she stood. 'I think I need to go, Anne. Thanks for the tea and cake. Don't get up, I'll see myself out.'

Ignoring the woman's beseeching requests to wait, she ran from the house. The slam of the front door was still reverberating as she buckled herself into her car and locked the doors. In the safe cocoon of her Audi, anger melted away as fast as it had arrived, leaving her deflated. Anne was just trying to be helpful.

She should go back and apologise for storming out, explain to her that she was wrong, that she could never, ever hurt Emma.

But she couldn't because maybe, just maybe, Anne was right. Two nights ago, when she'd heard the cry, hadn't she thought it sounded just like poor Emma's heartbreaking cry outside the nursery? If it truly was a suppressed memory, she wasn't sure she could live with it.

CHAPTER 37

Starting the engine, she pulled out of the driveway and headed home. She'd just make it, she thought, checking the time. Paul would be anxiously waiting, afraid he'd miss his precious tee-off slot.

He was standing in the doorway when she pulled up, tapping his watch like a comic-strip cartoon figure. Did he realise how ridiculous he looked? Climbing out of the car, she gave an innocent smile. 'I'm not late, am I?'

The question seemed to throw him off stride. He clamped his mouth shut and stepped out, golf bag in one hand. 'I've given Emma her lunch,' he said, opening the boot of his car and swinging the bag inside.

'Good,' she replied, heading for the house. 'Enjoy your golf. See you later.'

She was inside, with the door closed, before he'd even started the engine. Dropping her coat and bag by the bottom stair, she headed to the family room hesitating a moment at the door to the lounge. It was easy to be brave away from the house, but here, standing right in front of the door, the familiar feeling of terror swept over her. She tried to brush it aside when Emma ran through to greet her.

'Mummy, you're back!'

Diane scooped her up. 'Hello, my little love,' she said, giving her a cuddle, burying her nose in her neck, smelling that delicious baby smell she still hadn't quite grown out of. No, Anne was wrong; there was no way she could ever have hurt Emma, it just wasn't in her to do such a thing.

The Housewife

'Silly Daddy left you in a right mess,' she said, a dart of irritation at seeing the remains of lunch spread across the child's mouth and hands, a second hitting her when she saw he'd left all the dirty plates on the table. Petty revenge for her being out all morning, she guessed.

She cleaned Emma's face and hands, then settled her on the sofa for her nap. 'When you wake up,' she said, giving the child a kiss on her cheek, 'I'll read you a story.'

Clearing the table, she thought about the lounge. It was just a room, she had to be imagining everything. She would go inside, prove there was nothing to be afraid of. She wiped suddenly damp palms on the side of her jeans and headed out to the hall, leaving the door open behind her. At the lounge door, she reached for the doorknob, stopping to wipe her hand again before turning it.

The terror that swept through her was like a living thing inside; uncurling and springing to life, ready to take over. She gulped, pushed the door open, and took a tentative step inside, keeping her hand on the door for balance. She could feel beads of perspiration gather on her forehead, and smell the acrid scent of body odour wafting from the open neck of her shirt.

It took several slow, tortuous steps before she reached the sofa. Gritting her teeth, she turned and sat on its edge, prepared to jump up and run at the slightest indication of anything unusual. It looked much as it always had, the only thing new was the fine layer of dust on the shelves and table, the only thing missing, one of the turquoise cushions from the sofa.

A trickle of perspiration ran down her back. She felt sick, her head spinning. It was time to get out. She'd proved she could do it, now she needed to leave. Her eyes flicked toward the door, it seemed so far away. She knew she was being stupid. It was only a few steps. Pushing herself up, she stood on trembling legs and, step after slow step, made it to the hallway, her hand dragging the door closed behind her. With a sense of relief, she stood there for several minutes. She'd done it. It wasn't easy, but she had survived. Tomorrow, she'd do it again.

Relieved to have had even this small success when everything else seemed to be so out of her control, she went back to the kitchen where Emma was still asleep on the sofa. She made a cup of tea and took it and a packet of biscuits to the window seat where she sat with a weary sigh.

It was impossible to put what Anne had said out of her head. She knew she couldn't have hurt Emma, but maybe her new friend had been on to something, maybe it wasn't that she'd hurt Emma, but rather that she'd failed to protect her. The guilt and the shame so overwhelming it triggered her breakdown? It was feasible. She chewed her lower lip. But it was pretty far-fetched. If Emma had been hurt that badly, wouldn't she remember? She pulled at her hair in frustration, she was driving herself crazy.

Just at that moment, an even crazier thought crossed her mind: Anne was the one who was so convinced that Paul was to blame and now it was she who was insinuating that she might have hurt Emma. Anne. Who was this woman with all her wild accusations? What was it Red had said about her? That she sometimes got confused between what was real, and what wasn't? A fantasist. Maybe. Or maybe she had a hidden agenda. Paul had contacted Red, so why not Anne, too? She knew she was sounding utterly paranoid and gave a silent, bitter laugh. What did they say: *just because you're paranoid doesn't mean they aren't after you.*

Standing, she crossed to the sofa, and curled up a couple of feet from her daughter, unwilling to disturb her sleep to pander to her mother's neediness. Maybe if she closed her eyes, clarity would come, and she could get some sleep.

She should have predicted it. Her eyes had barely closed, her lashes briefly touching her cheeks before they shot open again: the cry. She jumped to her feet, her eyes darting around the room. The sound suddenly coming from every direction at once, increasing in volume until it was a violent shriek in her ears.

When Emma woke with a start, Diane realised the scream was her own and stopped abruptly, scooping Emma up in her arms and holding her close. 'Sorry, darling,' she said, 'Shhhhhhhh. Mummy had a bad dream.'

'Poor Mummy,' Emma's hand reached up to pat her face, and then, 'I know what will make it better?'

'What?' Diane said, although she could guess.

'Ice cream,' she said seriously.

She was probably right.

After a bowl of ice cream, Emma was happy to sit playing with some wooden bricks, building towers, knocking them down and building them up again. Diane watched her for a moment, amused at her total dedication to what she was doing. Leaving her to play, she went up to her bedroom and changed into her slouchy pants and jumper. She so desperately needed sleep, could hardly keep her eyes open. Back downstairs, she pulled out a takeaway menu and rang through an order. With dinner sorted, she curled up on the couch again. She didn't think she'd sleep but within seconds she was drifting off.

She woke feeling groggy. Opening her eyes, she saw the bricks scattered about the floor and, with a smile, she sat up and looked around for Emma.

'Emma!' she called.

Getting no reply, she got to her feet and looked into the kitchen, the utility room and then the downstairs toilet. She wasn't there. Picking up speed and trying not to panic, she went into the hallway. 'Emma!' she called more loudly, stepping onto the first step of the stairway to listen. She couldn't hear anything. Jogging up the stairs, calling her name as she ran, she pushed open the door to her bedroom. She wasn't there.

Checking all the rooms, with no sign of her, she began to feel the first stirrings of panic. Continuing to call her name, she ran back downstairs. The only room she hadn't checked was the lounge. Taking a breath, she pushed open the door and stepped inside, almost relieved to find it empty. Almost. Where the hell was she?

Terror was beginning to take over. She dashed back into the family room, checked every corner again and then ran upstairs to do the same. Only then did she face the reality; if she wasn't in the house, she must be outside. Running through to the back door, she checked: not only shut, but locked. Charging through the house to the front door, she noticed for the first time that it wasn't completely shut; it was closed over, but the catch wasn't engaged.

A cold dread slipped through her and, with her heart in her mouth, she pulled the door open and looked out, her jaw dropping when she saw her three year old standing in the middle of the gateway only a couple of feet away from the stream of moving traffic. The footpath outside was a narrow one, if she stumbled…

'Emma!' she cried, racing forward, her heart beating as the child turned and then, perhaps startled by the look of fear on her face, took a step backward.

She grabbed her before she took another, holding her close even as Emma started to shriek loudly and continuously. Diane's attempts to soothe her were met with an increase in volume as she struggled to escape.

'It's Mummy,' she said, trying to turn the writhing girl in her arms. She was small, but strong, and Diane was bone weary.

And then, to make a bad situation absolutely hellish, Paul's car appeared in the road, his indicator signalling, his face a shocked look of concern. With Emma still in her arms, she managed to back up enough to allow him to bring the car into the driveway and then he was out, shaking his head, mouth a grim slash. The screaming child, seeing him, held her hands out and sobbed, 'Daddy!'

He almost snatched her from Diane's arms. 'What on earth is going on?'

'She got out of the house, somehow,' she tried to explain. 'She was standing in the gateway, probably waiting for you, and I was afraid she might run out onto the path. I called her, but I must have startled her because she took a step closer to the road. So, I grabbed her.'

'You grabbed her?' Paul was looking at her as if she'd lost her mind.

'I was trying to protect her.' Her hand went to her forehead. Was this what happened before?

He looked at the sobbing child in his arms. 'Well, it looks as if you failed miserably, doesn't it?' Without another word, he went into the house leaving her standing there, tears stinging.

She had no energy left to fight any more. It would be better to fall down there, fall down and let it be over with. Instead, she trudged back inside.

Paul was sitting on the sofa, a snuffling Emma on his lap, her head buried in the curve of his neck. His eyes followed her as she came in, critical, condemning. 'You mustn't have closed the door properly,' he said. 'She's too small to have been able to open it herself.'

Was that it? She couldn't remember shutting the front door at all, it being one of those things you did automatically. The catch was old and did occasionally stick. Was it as simple as that? Her fault.

The front doorbell announced the arrival of the takeaway. She got her purse and went to answer it, bringing the containers back moments later. 'We're having takeaway,' she said, redundantly.

'I don't think either of us are ready for food at the minute,' he said dismissively, gathering Emma even closer, cutting her out completely.

Just as he'd been planning to do all along.

In that moment, Diane knew he had won.

CHAPTER 38

It was over an hour before they ate, an uncomfortable silence around the table, Paul's face set, Emma's tear-stained, Diane's confused, exhausted, frustrated. She didn't argue when Paul insisted on getting Emma ready for bed, remaining at the table surrounded by half-eaten dishes, her wine glass empty, his barely touched. Reaching across, she pulled it toward her and took a sip. Alcohol, she knew, wouldn't help clear her thoughts, but it might ease the pain. There was no point in trying to think. Too tired, too hurt. Too alone.

A tear of self-pity trickled down her cheek. Brushing it away, she snuffled noisily. She'd take a sleeping tablet and get some sleep, maybe in the morning it would all make more sense. Her laugh was bitter. Who was she kidding?

Nothing made sense; and now she was putting Emma at risk. There was a lump in her throat when she thought about what the consequences of her carelessness could have been. She'd played right into Paul's hands, hadn't she? Painted a picture of a careless, incompetent, useless mother for him.

Pushing the glass to one side, she rested her head in her hands, as guilt hammered. Perhaps she should have agreed to speak to a counsellor on an ongoing basis, as the clinic had suggested. But she was so arrogantly sure, then, that she had everything under control. Paul had seemed so supportive. She frowned. How could she have been so blind?

Standing, she let her eyes linger a moment on the dirty dishes and half-empty containers before shrugging and taking herself upstairs where light peered from under Paul's office door. Hoping he wouldn't come out, she went into Emma's room, closing the door quietly behind her. She expected her to be asleep, so was surprised to see bright eyes shining at her.

'Mummy,' she said, reaching her hands up.

Diane sat on the side of the bed and gathered her in her arms, holding her and murmuring words of love and comfort into her ear. 'I'm sorry you were so sad, sweetheart,' she said eventually, lying her back down. 'It made me very sad too.'

'Sorry for going outside, won't do it again.'

Diane brushed a curl off her forehead. 'Mummy was silly not to have shut the door properly. She won't do *that* again.'

Emma's eyes fluttered closed and then opened again. 'It was the other lady who opened the door, Mummy. Not you.' Her eyes fluttered closed again and this time they stayed shut.

Diane was frozen to the spot. She'd like to have woken Emma, questioned her for the details but, looking down on the angelic face, she knew she couldn't do such a thing, not even for the proof she so desperately craved.

It was the other lady who opened the door. A look of horror crossed her face. Had she come inside her home and stood over her as she slept? She'd only slept heavily that one time, how on earth did she know to come in then?

The idea of hidden cameras flashed through her mind. She knew from watching crime shows that nowadays they could be tiny, but truth was, she wasn't even going to look for them. She'd had enough of playing the victim in Paul's mind games.

His games were now endangering their daughter.

Dropping a kiss on Emma's head, she left her room. On the landing, she heard the soft murmur of voices from Paul's office and felt twin darts of pain and anger. She wanted to bang on his door, to shout at him, to scream. Instead, she went to her room, took two sleeping tablets, dropped her clothes untidily onto a chair, slid under the duvet and waited for medicated sleep to claim her.

In the morning, Paul was, as usual, down before her. He'd ignored the mess on the table, eating his cereal standing in the kitchen. He gave a nod in her direction when she came into the room behind Emma. Helping her into her chair, she cleared a space on the table in front of her, filled a bowl with cereal, added milk and handed her a spoon. 'There you go,' she said.

She made coffee and took it back to sit beside her, pushing her half-empty plate from the night before out of her way, the unappetising smell making her stomach lurch.

'You're not going to clean up first?' She looked up at Paul, at his prissy face and condemnatory eyes. She refused to get annoyed, hell, she was too tired to waste the energy. 'No, I'm going to clean up second. First, I'm going to have my coffee.' She gave a half-hearted shrug. 'Feel free though.'

Everything took longer, and finally, rushing to the car, she strapped Emma in, started the engine and pulled out of her drive into the heavy rush-hour traffic. She looked in the rear-view mirror, lifting her hand in acknowledgement to the car behind who'd slowed to allow her out.

As it turned out, she made it just in time, the teacher still rounding up her charges as she pulled into the car park. She was last, possibly, but not late. Back home, she cleared the mess from the table, every movement heavy and slow. Then, she sat, crossed her arms on the table in front of her, lay her face down and sobbed like a child. On and on, she cried, until she was afraid she might not stop. She imagined Emma's little face, and tried to do what she knew Paul wanted to tell her so often, and pull herself together.

She lifted a face wet with tears and snot and carelessly wiped it with the arm of her dark blue shirt leaving snail-traces of mucus along the length of it.

Because she couldn't think what else to do, she picked up her mobile and looked at the photograph she had taken of the woman. Normal-looking. Nothing scary or cruel about her. She threw the phone across the table in frustration. Needing to be doing something, she decided to do what she'd promised to do yesterday and go back into the lounge.

With the door open, the distance to the sofa seemed immense and she had the strangest sensation that it was moving away from her as she inched closer. She swayed, a wave of nausea washing over her making her stumble and fall awkwardly onto the sofa, twisting her ankle. She lay there stunned, as much from the fall as from the crippling fear. And then, as if on cue, the sound of a child's gut-wrenching wail reverberated from the four walls of the room that imprisoned her.

'Stop. For pity's sake, stop!' she cried as she curled up, wrapping her arms around her knees and staying there until it stopped. With the last ounce of her energy, she rolled to the floor and crawled from the now-silent room, through the hall and into the family room, where she pulled herself up onto the sofa and dragged the throw over herself. And there, exhausted beyond belief, she finally slept.

CHAPTER 39

When she woke and opened her eyes, the darkness startled her. It took her a few seconds to realise the throw was over her head. She pushed it back, squinting against the sudden brightness. How long had she slept? Uncovering her watch, she struggled to focus on the numbers. About an hour.

Her foot hurt when she put it on the ground. Kicking off her shoe, she assessed the damage. It was swollen but just a little, she'd live. She put her shoe back on while she could.

She sat with her head in her hands for a moment. What was she going to do?

First, practicalities, she needed to see if she could walk. Gingerly, she stood on one foot and gently put the other to the ground, testing it. It ached, but it would be okay.

Her shirt, on the other hand, definitely wouldn't. With a quick look at the clock, she decided on a shower and change of clothes. It wouldn't solve anything, but it would make her feel better.

It certainly didn't make her look any better, she thought, looking at her reflection in her bedroom mirror fifteen minutes later and shaking her head at the half-hearted attempt at make-up. It would have to do; she had about thirty minutes before she needed to leave to collect Emma. More coffee was in order.

She was on the stairway, half-way down, when the doorbell chimed. The sound stopped her instantly. One foot on the step below, she stayed stock-still as she waited for the bell to sound again. When it didn't, it was several minutes before she managed to move again, gripping the bannisters with both hands as, step after step, she moved down to the hallway.

Silently, she pressed her ear to the door, listening for the sound of movement, of someone breathing. But the door was so solid, it was unlikely she could hear even if there were someone there. She bent down and, as quietly as she could, she pulled open the letterbox. She couldn't see anything, anyone.

Taking a deep breath, she unlocked the door and turned the latch to open it. There was nobody on the doorstep, nobody up or down the road. Was it the woman? Was she hiding behind Mrs Prescott's wall? The gate was open…

She put the thought out of her mind, slamming the door shut and marching into the kitchen. She would not be dragged into Paul's games. Not today. She flicked the kettle on to distract herself for a few minutes until it was time to go and collect Emma. At least she'd be spared that witch of a woman's presence at the nursery. If she was here, hiding behind Mrs Prescott's garden wall, she wouldn't be there. With that clear thought in her head, she dropped the mug into the sink, grabbed her jacket and phone and left.

Tiredness had become normal for her. She drove with extra care, indicated and overtook bicycles with exaggerated caution. Traffic was neither light nor heavy and she made it to the school with minutes to spare.

She stayed in the car. Waiting until the door opened saved her from the extra pain of having Rose Metcalf and the other parents pass judgement. She checked herself in the mirror; the eye-make up she'd put on had bled around her sunken eyes. She made a fruitless attempt to wipe it away.

It wasn't until she saw the children spill from the nursery that she opened the car door and got out, putting a bright smile on her face to greet her daughter. 'Hello, sweetie,' she said, swinging her into her arms. 'Did you have a good day?'

She headed back to the car with Emma still in her arms, strapped her in quickly and got into the driver's seat to start the engine. Waiting impatiently for her turn to exit the car park, beginning to move as the car in front did, she glanced across the road and was shocked to see her stalker waving at her.

The car in front stopped, waiting for a space to turn out on to the main road. Diane moved to hit the brake, but her shock at seeing the woman when she really didn't expect to, combined with the never-ending exhaustion, momentarily confused her and she hit the accelerator by mistake.

The bang was loud, the bonnet flew up and the airbag exploded with an extraordinarily loud hiss. Emma screamed. Children waiting in the car park screamed. Their parents screamed. For Diane, trapped behind the airbag, it seemed as if the whole world was screaming.

She twisted her head to see Emma who was now crying loudly. She didn't seem to be hurt. Desperate to get to her, her hand felt for the handle and she tried to pull the door open, but her fingers slipped. She tried again, managing to pull the handle, but with the air-bag pressed against her, she couldn't push the door open. By now, people were rushing to help and one of the other parents pulled open the door and helped Diane to squeeze out. She staggered a little, putting a hand on the roof of the car to steady herself as the ground rocked and rolled under her feet.

The driver of the car she'd hit had also got out and was looking at the damage to his car with wide eyes. His children in the back seat were crying loudly. 'What kind of idiot are you?' he asked, shouting at her, hand raised and finger pointing.

It was all just too much. 'It's her,' she shouted back at him, her head spinning. She jabbed a trembling finger across the road. 'It's all her fault.'

Other parents had rushed over to offer help but when they saw there was nobody injured, they stood back. There was silence as they all looked across the street to where Diane pointed.

'I'm telling you,' she said again, 'it's her fault.'

'There's nobody there,' said the driver of the other car.

Diane looked, her hand moving to cover her mouth. Of course, the woman was gone. She looked around at the gathered people, saw the closed, tight faces, the whispering behind hands and started to cry.

CHAPTER 40

Her shoulders heaved, as crying turned to sobs. The circle of closed faces around her suddenly looked embarrassed, sympathetic even at this display of emotion. They'd have handled rage or anger better, but tears, especially blisteringly heart-broken ones like these, made them all connect with their inner child and turn away.

Diane felt a hand on her elbow gently lead her away, but she resisted, turning back to the car as Emma's cries broke through the hubbub around her. Miss Rogers' hand closed more tightly over her arm. 'Someone is looking after Emma, don't worry, she's fine. You're in no fit state, Diane.'

Her voice was gentle and surprisingly motherly. Anger, even annoyance might have stopped the tears, instead this kind concern made Diane sob even louder. She went where she was led without further resistance, and when she stumbled, the guiding hand kept her from falling. When they stopped, she was pressed into a chair where she immediately leaned forward to rest her face in cupped hands.

She couldn't stop the tears, her sobs loud and heaving catching on a hiccup before rolling on and on. Somewhere in the background, she heard quiet whispering. She couldn't hear the words, but she guessed the content. A wad of tissues was pressed into her hand and she took it gratefully, rubbing her eyes, snuffling and gulping, trying to stem the tide of tears. She saw Miss Rogers look to Susan Power for guidance. They were in her office. The noise of the collision had been loud, she'd have dropped everything to rush and help. She would have seen her falling apart. They exchanged glances and shook their heads, obviously unable to decide what to do with her. She could have told them; there was nothing they could do.

'I've called your husband,' Susan told her. 'Unfortunately, and I hope you understand my responsibility to the school has to come first, I've had to call the police.' She leaned forward and rested a hand on Diane's shoulder. 'Is there anyone else you'd like me to call?'

Taking some deep breaths, Diane managed to regain some semblance of control. Raising her face, she wiped her eyes, blew her nose, gave one final, pathetic sob and dabbed at her cheeks with the soggy tissue. 'No, thank you,' she said, as more tears fell.

Miss Rogers picked up a rubbish bin and put it beside her before handing her another wad of tissues. 'Here you go,' she said gently, 'try to stop crying, Diane. You'll make yourself sick.'

She took the tissues, dropped the wet clump into the bin and nodded. Snuffling, she wiped her eyes again, but the tears didn't stop. 'I'm sorry,' she said, her voice thick. 'Everything is my fault.'

Susan poured a glass of water from the bottle she kept on her desk and handed it to her. Diane took a sip, dabbed her eyes some more, took another sip.

'I'm so sorry,' she said again. She couldn't think of another word to say.

A knock on the door startled them, all heads turning as one to look. 'Come in,' Susan said, moving to take her seat behind the desk. If it was the police, she wanted to be in a position of authority.

It wasn't the police, it was Paul, a harassed and furious look on his face. 'What the hell is going on?' he said, looking around the room. His expression changed to concern. 'Emma? Oh God, is she—'

Susan quickly interrupted him. 'Your daughter is fine, Mr Andrews, perfectly fine. She's being looked after by one of the other teachers. Please,' she waved to an empty chair, 'sit down.'

Instead of sitting, concern switching back to an anger that narrowed his eyes, flattened his lips and clenched his fists, he turned to look at Diane. 'What have you done now?' he spat.

Susan Power and Miss Rogers exchanged surreptitious glances and, without a word, Miss Rogers went to stand by Diane.

'Sit down, Mr Andrews,' Susan said, and this time her tone of voice made it clear it wasn't a request.

Diane saw Susan's eyes assess her and wondered what she was thinking. She knew she looked a mess. The eye make-up and mascara she'd applied earlier would be all over her face, she could see the signs in the damp tissue she clutched. But the manager's eyes were sympathetic rather than condemnatory and she took heart from that. She knew, too, that the younger teacher had moved closer to offer support. Their kindness was unexpected, she soaked it up.

Paul sat and crossed his arms. 'Well,' he said, this time addressing the manager, 'what has happened?'

Susan didn't waste words, giving a simple account of the crash and his wife's subsequent assertion that someone else was to blame.

A knock on the door stopped her explanation mid-flow. 'Come in,' she called.

This time it was the police. Two uniformed officers, their bulk filling the doorway, who responded immediately to her beckoning hand and entered the office. Diane, seeing their faces, felt herself shrink. They were the officers who'd stopped her outside Sophie Redmond's home.

The manager made quick introductions. 'I'm sorry to have had to call you,' she said, addressing the two officers with no hint of apology in her tone, 'especially since the accident was on school grounds but the car that was hit, according to the owner, suffered extensive damage.' She paused and did look slightly apologetic when she continued. 'We should, of course, have insisted the cars remain where they were but, to be honest, we needed to get the gate cleared to allow the parents to collect their children and leave.' She shrugged. 'The air-bag in Mrs Andrews' car was deployed so it will need to be taken away.' This last line was directed at Paul, who nodded curtly.

The manager paused a moment, looking down at her clasped hands before looking briefly at Diane and then at the two officers. 'Mrs Andrews maintains the crash wasn't her fault, that she was deliberately distracted by a woman who was standing across the road.'

One of the police officers was taking notes, he looked up. 'And this woman is?'

Susan looked at him calmly. 'Unfortunately, nobody saw her.'

'The driver of the car she crashed into must have,' the officer said, a frown between his eyes, 'he would have been closer.'

'He says he didn't see anyone,' she admitted.

The officer looked at his partner who leaned forward and said something to him that made his eyes widen. He looked closely at Diane. 'As it happens, we've made the acquaintance of Mrs Andrews before,' he said, causing manager's, teacher's and husband's eyes to suddenly look startled.

He continued. 'She was reported for harassing an elderly lady. Pretending she was looking for her friend.'

Paul looked totally bemused.

All eyes in the room were staring at Diane. She could feel them analysing, assessing, judging. They were waiting for her to say something, give some explanation, and all she felt was gratitude that they didn't know that other police had chased her through the streets. She blew her nose and took a deep breath. 'A woman has been following me; stalking me, I guess you could call it,' she said, avoiding their eyes, 'I've been trying to find out who she is.'

The officer looked at Paul. 'Were you aware of this?'

Paul rubbed a hand over his face. 'This is the first I've heard of it.'

'You've never seen anyone hanging around?'

'No, I haven't,' he said bluntly and then, slowly, he added, 'My wife hasn't been well. I thought she was in recovery, but she did spend a few weeks in a private clinic recently.'

Diane let their words swirl around her. They didn't believe her; what a surprise. Exhaustion took away any desire to care. Her eyelids drooped, she could easily fall asleep right here in this terribly uncomfortable chair. Drifting away, her eyes snapped open when Paul shouted. 'For goodness sake, wake up, Diane!'

'There's no need to shout, Mr Andrews,' Susan said firmly. She looked at the two officers. 'I needed the police to be involved in case the driver of the other car takes any action against the school. I don't know if you need to keep Mrs Andrews or her husband any longer?'

'The accident happened on private property, so we're unlikely to proceed further,' the officer said. He waited a moment, then looked at Diane, his face softening. 'I hope you seek the help you need, Mrs Andrews, before you do something that lands you in serious trouble.'

'Don't worry about that,' Paul said curtly, 'she'll be getting help.'

The officer looked him over. 'Perhaps a more sympathetic and supportive attitude on your part would help, Mr Andrews.'

Diane saw Susan exchange a glance with Miss Rogers, who gave a quick smile. Paul gave the officer a sharp look. 'We can leave?' At the officer's nod, he looked to the manager. 'Would you ring for a taxi to take Diane home please, I'll stay and sort out the car.'

'That won't be necessary,' one of the officers said. 'We could drop Mrs Andrews home and make sure she gets inside okay. Is there somebody who could be with her—'

Diane interrupted him. 'I don't need anyone, honestly, but I would like to get home.' She stood, holding onto the back of the chair for support. 'I do apologise to all of you for…' she shrugged, reluctant to put all her crimes into words, '…everything, I suppose.' Feeling herself well up again, she rubbed her eyes and turned for the door. She stopped and looked at her husband, 'You'll bring Emma?'

He nodded without saying a word.

Outside the school, the sun was shining, and the car park was empty. It was quiet. Normal. She stumbled, exhausted, as she walked toward the police car – grateful there was nobody to witness her shame. The thought of what Rose Metcalf would say made her cringe. She tried to remember if she were one of the faces that surrounded her earlier, but she couldn't remember. It didn't matter, if she wasn't there, she'd soon hear about it.

The police officers didn't speak as they drove her home. When they pulled into the driveway, one got out and helped her from the car. Seeing her sway alarmingly, he held her arm until she unlocked the door.

'Thank you,' she said, turning to hold out her hand. 'You've been kinder than I deserve.'

He tilted his head toward the door to the lounge. 'I'd prefer it if you were sitting down before I left you, Mrs Andrews. You look done in.'

She smiled at his gallantry and led the way into the family room. 'I'll probably fall asleep now,' she said, flopping onto the sofa.

'Are you sure there isn't someone we could call to come and be with you?' he said, clearly reluctant to leave her in such a state. She shook her head; that she had nobody a final, mortifying blow. 'Okay, well, is there anything I can do for you before I go?'

All she wanted was for him to go so she could rest and put this whole hideous day behind her. 'No,' she said, 'honestly, I'll be fine. But I am grateful.'

The officer, having to be satisfied with this, gave a final nod and left.

A moment later, she heard the front door shut. 'What a mess,' she muttered and then felt her cheeks flush with mortification. What must Susan Power and Miss Rogers think of her? She'd seen the look of shock on the manager's face when the police mentioned having had dealings with her. Miss Rogers's face, she was sure, held a similar look.

And poor Emma. She had a lot of making up to her to do. Ice cream every day for a start. And she'd read her favourite book as often as she wanted. Her eyes welled up again, but she was asleep before the first tear could fall.

CHAPTER 41

She wasn't sure how long she'd slept but, when she opened her eyes, the light had faded. A few hours, she guessed, because she felt better.

The house was quiet. Paul was later than she'd expected. Poor Emma would be exhausted. Hopefully, she thought, she'd have been able to have a nap somewhere. When she came home, Diane wanted to hold her close. Squinting at her watch, she was surprised to see it was later than she'd thought. Six. She'd slept for around three hours. But where were Paul and Emma?

Getting the car sorted must have taken a long time. He'd be furious. She went into the kitchen and opened the fridge. Furious, and hungry. There wasn't much to choose from, but she found a couple of frozen chicken breasts in the freezer. Half an hour later, she had a casserole cooking in the oven.

An hour later, she turned the oven down low to keep it warm. Where were they? Her brow furrowed; he hadn't said anything about going elsewhere, had he? A lot of the conversation was a blur. She smiled weakly, wishing more of it were.

It was another ten minutes before she heard the front door opening. She rushed into the hallway, eager to hug Emma to her, coming to an abrupt halt when she saw he was alone.

'Where have you been?' she asked, 'and where's Emma?'

He took off his jacket, threw it on the banisters, then opened the drawer of the hall table and dropped the car keys inside before slamming it shut. Every movement was angry, mirroring the expression on his face. 'She's fine,' he said, passing her by and going into the family room. He switched on the TV and sat into the sofa.

Diane stayed in the hallway for a moment, feeling as if her insides had been ripped out. She wanted her daughter. Shaky steps brought her to face him. 'Where is she?'

He ignored her until she grabbed the remote and switched off the TV. 'Where is she!' she screamed. 'What have you done with her?'

Standing, he grabbed her arm, holding it tight enough to make her wince before snatching the remote from her hand. 'I told you,' he said, 'she's fine, she's safe.' And then, he shook his head and sat. 'She's with Emily,' he said. 'Happy?'

He said the name as though it should mean something. Frustrated, she shook her head. 'Who is Emily?'

The TV came on again. Paul switched to the news channel before looking up at her with a look of scorn. 'Emily. Emma's teacher. For goodness sake, don't tell me you can't remember who she is?'

'I've only ever heard her referred to as Miss Rogers,' she said, trying to keep her voice calm even as she wanted to scream at him. 'Why has she got Emma?'

'Because the child has been through enough,' he said, turning the volume down. 'I wasn't sure what kind of state you'd be in when I got home, so she volunteered to keep her for a few days. Emma was quite happy to go with her.'

Diane's eyes rounded in horror. A few *days*? 'No, I'll go and collect her now. I'm fine, I just hadn't slept well. It's better for her to be here with me.'

His look said it all but he didn't leave it there, his eyes raking her. 'You really think so?'

It was time she started taking the offensive. 'You lied to the police, Paul,' she said, her voice tight, 'you know everything about this woman I've been seeing. It's part of your plan to get custody of Emma. I know all about it.'

He lifted the remote control. For a moment, she thought he was going to throw it at her but he flung it across the sofa before standing to glare at her. 'What are you talking about?' He ran a hand through his hair and took a few steps away, turning to look at her with a slow shake of his head. 'I thought you were getting better, Diane, I really did. But bloody hell, you sound like you've gone absolutely crazy.'

'You're lying,' she said.

'I'm not listening to any more of this,' he said, 'tomorrow, I'll take a day off work and drive you to the clinic. You'll have to stay there until they're sure you're better this time. Maybe,' he said, coming back to stand in front of her, 'if you'd taken the damn pills they prescribed, none of this would have happened.'

'You're lying,' she said again, but there was less conviction in her words. Had she got it all wrong? 'No, I know you're lying,' she insisted. 'I have her photograph.' She reached for her handbag and took out her mobile. A few taps brought the woman's photograph to the screen. 'See,' she said, holding it toward him, 'this is her.'

When he didn't take the phone from her, she held it in front of his face. 'Look at her,' she yelled. 'Don't tell me you don't know who she is.' She watched as his eyes flickered over the picture. She wanted to see recognition, to hear him admit it, and for a moment she thought she had him; for a nanosecond she thought she saw surprise, shock flit across his face but then he just shrugged.

'You could have taken that anywhere; she could be anyone.' He jammed his hands into his pockets and turned away. 'I've had enough of this nonsense, Diane, we've all had enough of it.' He grabbed the remote and sat. Moments later, the room was filled with the sound of shouting and gunfire.

Diane turned the phone around and looked at it. He was right, of course. *She* knew it was taken from their bedroom, but it could have been taken anywhere. And, at the distance it was taken, the woman's always very ordinary features looked even more ordinary. In fact, the only thing Diane recognised was her sleek bobbed hair. Tears were close. She was damned if she was going to cry in front of him, give him more reason to think he was right to leave Emma with Miss Rogers. Emily.

She left the room and used the banisters to pull her weary body up the stairs, her feet heavy and unsteady. Emma's bedroom door was ajar, she pushed it open and went inside. She wouldn't have her funny pyjamas to wear. Her toothbrush with the dinosaur handle. The soft hairbrush for her silky curls. And yet, because of her, she was better off with strangers and without these things.

She sat on the bed holding one of Emma's soft toys against her heart. Her eyes stung, her head ached. She'd eaten nothing all day, but the thought of food now made her feel ill. Her heart sank as it dawned on her that she'd left the damn chicken in the oven. She had to go back down.

Kicking off her shoes, she stepped back onto the landing and started her quiet descent, hoping to slip in and out of the kitchen without him noticing. She'd left the door open and, at first, she thought it was the television she heard, then she realised it was Paul speaking. He was on the phone. It wasn't hard to hear, he was making no attempt to keep his voice down.

Then she heard him say words he hadn't said to her in a long time. 'I love you. Remember that. Emma will be fine, don't worry, I'll pick her up in a couple of days. It will all be over soon.'

She held a hand to her mouth to prevent the gasp escaping. Stepping back as quietly as she'd arrived, she flew up the stairs on suddenly sure feet. Emily. No wonder he knew her damn name. And, of course, that was why he'd wanted her to go to that particular nursery. She and Emma would get to know one another. She bit her lip. Emma adored her. When it went to a custody hearing, what a united front they would be able to show.

Over her dead body.

Picking up her shoes, she headed back downstairs, eased the hall table drawer open and took out his car keys. Leaving the drawer open, she moved to the front door. Hopefully, Paul wouldn't have locked it yet. It was usually the last thing he did. She turned the catch and pulled, relieved when the door opened smoothly. Slipping on her shoes, she stepped out, pulling the door closed behind her. It made a soft clunk that she hoped would be lost in other sounds and went to his car, opened the door and climbed in.

Seconds later, she was pulling out onto the road. He wouldn't know where she'd gone, never guessing she'd know where the teacher lived. She owed a debt of gratitude to Rose Metcalf for that nugget of information. *Around the corner from her, next to an ugly church.*

It should be easy to find.

And it was. The road was a short one of only about twenty houses. It was a cul-de-sac, ending in a plain, dull building, the only indicator that it was a church being the huge and imposing sign that said so. Rose had been correct; it was quite unattractive.

Unfortunately, there was a house on either side of the road. It was a toss-up. Going to the closest one, she rang the doorbell. Moments later, a light switched on and she could hear the sound of a lock being turned. The door was opened widely as if she were expected, the elderly woman with her hand on the door smiling a welcome, unfocused eyes staring at her.

'Sally,' a voice called from further within the house, and footsteps came rushing forward. A man, probably a few years older than the woman, with grey hair and sad eyes, took her hand from the door and gave her a gentle push. 'Go and make me a cuppa,' he said, his voice gentle.

Once she'd gone, the man closed the door over slightly and asked, 'Can I help you?'

Diane smiled. 'I'm looking for Emily Rogers.'

He indicated the house across the street with a jerk of his chin. 'Over there, love,' he said.

'Thank you,' she said. 'I'm sorry for disturbing you and your wife.'

He shook his head. 'Sally thinks every knock on the door is our Tom coming home.'

Diane was about to reply that she hoped that their son would be home soon, but quickly stopped herself when she saw in his sad eyes that that wasn't going to happen. 'I'm sorry,' she said again and stepped away.

Crossing over the road, she walked up the neatly kept driveway. There was a knocker, but no doorbell. She rapped it smartly three times and stood back.

It was answered by a tall, handsome smiling man. 'Hello, can I help you? he asked with a pronounced Scottish burr.

'Oh, hi,' she said, taken aback. *Who was he?* 'I was looking for an Emily Rogers, perhaps this isn't the right house.' She looked down the road toward the next house. Maybe she hadn't meant right next door.

'No,' the smile was friendly, 'you've the right place. Come in, I'll tell her you're here.'

She stepped inside just as a door opened behind him and Miss Rogers came out, a look of surprise tinged with concern on her face when she saw her.

'This lady wants to see you,' the man said, turning toward her, a puzzled look on his face when he saw her expression. 'Is everything okay?' His eyes flicked from one to the other.

'It's fine, darling,' Emily said, placing a reassuring hand on his chest, looking at him with a look that told Diane, as clearly as if it were written in stone, she'd got it wrong, this woman wasn't having an affair with anybody. 'Head on in, I'll just have a word with her.'

He put his hand over hers, before nodding. 'Shout if you need me,' he said, with a final glance at Diane.

Emily waited until he'd closed the door behind him before saying, 'Sorry, he's very protective of me.'

'He's your partner?'

The teacher smiled. 'My husband, actually, it should be Mrs Rogers, but I was *miss* when I started, so…' She shrugged and her smile faded. 'Why don't we sit down,' she said, 'and you can tell me why you're here.' She waited until Diane nodded before opening a door into a small room they obviously used as a home office. It would be a claustrophobic place to work, filing cabinets stood on either side of a battered wooden desk. The remaining available walls were lined with bookshelves. Emily took a pile of books from a chair and offered it to Diane, taking the swivel chair at the desk for herself. 'You look calmer,' she said quietly.

'I managed to get a few hours' sleep,' Diane said with a quick smile, 'it helped.' She brushed her hair behind her ears. 'When Paul came home without Emma, I was upset,' she explained. 'I wouldn't be able to sleep tonight until I was sure she was okay.'

Emily's eyes were warm, her smile kind and reassuring. 'She's fine, honestly. My daughter, Ivy, is two, they got on like a house on fire. There's a spare bed in Ivy's room so she's asleep in there.'

'It was kind of you to help out.'

'It isn't the first time I've brought a child home. Emergencies occur. It isn't a service the nursery advertises, but it's one it is happy to provide. Ross and I have had all the required checks to allow us to accommodate a child in need.' The teacher's smile faded. 'Actually, it was my idea, this time. Your husband wanted to take Emma home, but he was still so angry, I was worried for her.' She didn't add that she was also worried for her mother. She leaned forward and rested a gentle hand on Diane's arm. 'I thought if you two had a chance to talk, alone, you might be able to sort things out.'

Diane gave a bitter, brittle laugh. 'I'm afraid we've gone way past that.' She sighed heavily. 'I know you all thought I was crazy today when I told you I was being stalked.' She took her phone from her pocket. 'This is her,' she said, bringing up the picture and holding the phone out.

'It's just—'

'Yes, I know,' she interrupted, frustrated, 'it's just a picture of a woman. But I see her outside my house, outside the school, in the supermarket. And, every time, she's staring at me. I'm not imagining it.'

Emily shrugged, looking a little out of her depth. 'I don't know what to think,' she said. She indicated the computer on the desk. 'Send it to me, let's blow it up and see what she's like in detail.'

A few minutes later, they both stared at the photograph of the woman on the twenty-one-inch computer screen. 'See,' Diane said, pointing, 'it was taken from my bedroom window. That's our front railing, that's the Prescott's house behind her.

Emily pressed a key to zoom in on the woman's face. 'She's pretty average,' she said, peering closely. 'Attractive, but not enough so you'd remember her face.'

Diane nodded in agreement. She was just about to move away when she stopped, eyes widening. 'Can you zoom in closer?' she asked, pointing to the screen. 'This part?'

Nodding, Emily tapped a few keys and the section appeared large on the screen.

'I don't believe it,' Diane said in a faint voice.

Emily stared at the screen. 'Nice earrings,' she said.

'They're nice all right. Three grand's-worth of diamonds and emeralds, according to the receipt I found in Paul's office.'

CHAPTER 42

Diane sat back on her chair with a look of disbelief on her face. 'I suspected Paul was having an affair but it never entered my head that he'd use his…' she hesitated, looking for an appropriate word, '…mistress in his sordid little game.' She gave a quick humourless chuckle at the expression on the teacher's face as she desperately tried to make sense of it all.

'Sordid little game?' Emily asked, bewildered.

'I think Paul is trying to discredit me so he can get full custody of Emma when we divorce.'

Emily thought a moment and then her eyes narrowed. 'Ah,' she said, 'that makes sense.'

It was Diane's turn to look puzzled. It wasn't the reaction she was expecting. 'What do you mean?'

'Would you like a coffee or tea or something?' Emily said. 'I think I need a drink.' She stood, waiting for a reply.

A glass of wine would have been perfect, but Diane wasn't going to dull senses that had finally sharpened. 'Coffee would be great,' she said, 'milk, no sugar.' She was suddenly ravenous. 'And something to eat, if you have it,' she shrugged. 'I haven't eaten all day.'

Emily grinned. 'I'll see what I can do.'

Several minutes passed before she returned. Diane sat thinking about what she'd learned, shaking her head again at her blindness. Just when she'd thought he couldn't stoop any lower, he had reached new depths.

The door opened to reveal Emily carrying an overflowing tray. 'Just shove that pile of papers onto the floor,' she said, using her chin to indicate the pile that sat next to the computer and, when it was cleared, set the tray down.

A pot of coffee, a plate of sandwiches, a plate of cake and a glass of wine. Diane looked at it all and was suddenly starving. 'This is great,' she said, 'thank you.' She reached for a sandwich and wolfed it down in three bites while Emily poured coffee for them both.

Emily, watching her eat, waited until she was on her third sandwich before she explained. 'When I offered to look after Emma for a day or two, your husband said something that made no sense at the time. I can't remember his exact words,' she said, frowning, 'something about making his case stronger. I assumed he was referring to trying to persuade you to go for counselling but his tone was off.'

The silence was only broken by the sound of Emily's mug as she put it back on the tray and picked up her glass. 'He's a bit of a prick, your husband, isn't he?'

Diane's laugh was genuine amusement. It wasn't the kind of thing she expected to hear from the teacher's mouth. But she'd hit the nail firmly on the head. 'Yes,' she said, 'he is that all right.'

'What are you going to do?' Emily looked at her. 'If you don't mind me saying so, you looked a bit of a mess earlier, lost and hopeless but, now, you look better, stronger.'

Diane nodded. 'Strong enough to put an end to his games. I showed him the photo earlier and he denied any knowledge of her. I'm going to go home and confront him again.' She smiled slightly when she saw the concern on the teacher's face. 'Don't worry, I'm ready for him this time.'

Emily didn't look convinced. 'He's a big man, and he has a nasty temper. Are you sure you shouldn't just go to the police?'

Diane sighed, and reached for another sandwich. 'I've not made myself the most believable of witnesses, and I've no proof of any wrongdoing. I don't think going to the police is an option. Unfortunately, adultery isn't a crime.'

'Would you like me to come with you? Or, even better,' she added, 'I'll send Ross with you.'

Diane was touched by her kindness. 'You've been so kind to me, I'm sure I don't deserve it.' She hesitated and then rushed on, 'Actually, I didn't think you liked me.'

Emily looked taken aback. 'What gave you that idea?'

Maybe she'd got it wrong. It seemed to be her forte, after all. 'You pulled me up for leaving Emma crying in the car,' she said.

A puzzled look crossed the teacher's face. 'I honestly can't remember,' she said, 'but that happens all the time, so I think I can be forgiven. Mrs Power's office faces the car park and she doesn't like disruptions.' She gave a tight smile. 'She doesn't have children, you know, everything she knows she's learned from books. Sometimes theory is just that.'

Diane felt foolish. 'I'm sorry,' she said, wondering how many times she'd said that today. Putting her mug down, she stood up. 'I should go. Thank you for your offer, but I think I'll be okay.'

'Do me a favour then,' the teacher said and, reaching behind her for a pen and a scrap of paper, she scribbled down a number. 'Text me, let me know you're okay. If you don't, I'll ring the police.'

Taking the number, Diane folded it and put it in her jeans pocket. 'Thank you,' she said, 'I won't forget.'

Emily stood. 'You'll want to see Emma before you go.' She led the way from the room and up the stairs. The landing light had been left on. She stopped outside a half-open door and nodded for Diane to look inside. 'She's wearing a nightie of Ivy's, it's a little tight but she didn't complain. She's a very sweet child,' she said quietly.

Diane felt the lump in her throat that had been there since Paul had come home without Emma melt away. She was safe and well. Miss Rogers could be trusted to make sure she stayed that way. Reaching down, she brushed a curl gently back from Emma's forehead. Then she straightened and joined Emily on the landing.

'Thank you,' she said, 'seeing her safe makes me more determined than ever to stop Paul.'

'I'll be waiting to hear from you,' Emily reminded her. Stepping closer, she enveloped her in a quick hug. 'Stay strong,' she said, 'and remember you're not alone.'

CHAPTER 43

Diane was surprised at how empowered those simple words made her feel. As she pulled into her driveway, she looked up at the house. She'd come here for the first time all wrapped in love, full of happiness at the prospect of spending the rest of her life with the man she adored. It seemed like only yesterday; but it was a lifetime ago.

The night was chilly, the skies clear; looking up, she could see the plough clearly. It was the only constellation she could recognise and she'd pointed it out to Paul on one of their first dates. 'See the curve at the bottom of it,' she'd said, 'you can hang your dreams on that. It helps them come true.'

He'd laughed, she remembered, and wanted to know who'd told her such nonsense. She should have known then they weren't suited. Looking up at the plough now, she hung her dreams on the curve of the stars before turning to open the front door.

He appeared immediately, standing in the open doorway to the family room, his arms crossed, mouth a narrow slash. 'Where the hell have you been?'

She heard the contained anger in his voice and closed the door slowly behind her without answering.

'I asked you a question.'

The anger in his voice sizzled. Perhaps she should have been scared; he was taller, bigger, stronger than she. But he was real; flesh and blood, not her imagination and, as long as she could touch it and feel it, she could deal with it. Reality no longer had any power to frighten her. He covered the distance between them with long, quick steps and snapped the keys roughly from her hands.

'I went to check that Emma was all right.'

'I don't believe you,' he sneered, refusing to back away. 'You don't know where her teacher lives.'

She was so close to him, she could smell garlic on his breath. 'I know a lot more than you think,' she said, 'including where Emily Rogers lives.'

That took the wind out of his sails; he turned and moved away. She followed, a grim expression on her face. 'I know everything, Paul. I'm not sure if you were trying to drive me crazy or just make me believe I was. It doesn't really matter; either way, you've failed. I know exactly what's going on now.'

He walked across the floor before turning to glare at her. 'I've no idea what you're talking about.'

Her laugh was bitter. 'And no idea who the woman on my phone is either? The woman wearing the earrings you splashed out so much money on.' She saw the look of surprise that crossed his face before he could hide it. 'You see, Paul,' she said, stepping closer to him, watching as his eyes darted from side to side as if looking for an escape, 'I know all about it.' She reached out and jabbed him hard in the chest with every word. 'All about your rotten plan to get custody of Emma.'

He grabbed her hand and held it tightly before pushing it and her away.

She staggered backward, wincing as she twisted her damaged ankle. 'Stop lying, Paul,' she shouted at him, clawing her hands into fists and shaking them at him. All the weeks of pain and grief he'd caused her. 'It's over,' she shouted louder, 'it's all—'

'I didn't know,' he yelled, stopping her in her tracks, her mouth hanging open. 'I didn't bloody well know about any of it, okay?' He shook his head, turned away and then turned back holding a hand out to her, eyes narrowing as she backed away. 'I swear to you,' he said quietly, 'I didn't know.'

'I don't believe you,' she said, watching as he went to the sofa and sat heavily, dropping his face into his hands. 'You know the woman who's been following me, the damn earrings you bought are a giveaway.'

'I didn't know,' he mumbled into his hands.

I didn't know. Not, I don't know her. Diane sat on the coffee table, her knees almost brushing his. 'But you do know her?'

He sighed heavily. 'Pam. Her name is Pam.' He lifted his face, his eyes dull. 'I didn't know what she was doing. I swear,' he added when he saw her look of disbelief. 'Not until I saw the photograph on your phone today. I rang her.' He shrugged. 'She meant well.'

'She meant well,' Diane's voice went up several octaves. 'Are you serious?'

'She knows how much I love Emma,' he said quietly.

She couldn't sit still. Standing, she glared down at him. 'Are you saying all of this was her idea?' She watched, appalled, as he nodded, and took a few steps back shaking her head in disbelief. 'It was *her* idea to try to drive me crazy so you'd get custody of Emma?' She didn't believe him; he was just trying to confuse her. 'No, I don't believe you.' She had to concentrate, remember the proof she had. The papers! 'You want to have me sectioned,' she yelled at him. 'I saw the damn papers in a drawer in your desk. I could go and get them now…proof!'

'Papers?' he said puzzled. Then his face cleared. 'The GP who came the night you were taken away left some papers behind. Just leaflets and stuff. They weren't important so I dumped them on my desk and then shoved them into a drawer and forgot about them.' He frowned. 'You've been going through my desk?'

Ignoring him, she frowned. 'Why didn't you just throw them out, why keep them unless you were going to use them?'

He threw up his hands. 'I didn't even know what they were. I just wanted them safely out of the way. Where did you find them?'

Was it a trick question? 'Under a folder in the bottom drawer.'

'Well, there you go,' he shouted. 'I shoved them in and forgot about them.'

Diane looked at him, trying to see if she could believe him. 'So, you weren't trying to drive me crazy and get me sectioned, it was all her idea?'

'I told her you were doing much better, but I never mentioned you had gone to work in the charity shop. She stopped at the shopping centre on the way to visit her aunt and popped in to look at the books. There's a photograph of you in my office, so she recognised you immediately. You gave her quite a shock, she said.' He ran a hand over his face. 'She was worried if you were doing so well that you'd fight for custody, so she thought she'd weigh the scales in my favour by unbalancing you a bit.' He looked up at her, his brown eyes pleading. 'She didn't tell me because she knew I wouldn't have approved.'

Diane shook her head. 'Nobody in their right mind would have approved, Paul! It's deranged! And if you seriously think you're going to have Emma staying with you and that…that psycho… then *you're* deranged.' Clasping her hand to her head, she turned away. 'I can't believe this.' She paced the length of the room and then stopped. 'Sophie Redmond? I did see her going into her house, didn't I? I wasn't imagining that.'

He looked confused for a moment. 'I don't know. Sophie is Pam's aunt, she was taking time off work to visit her. What has she got to do with anything?'

Feeling her head was going to explode, she whirled to face him again. 'The police mentioned Sophie Redmond that day in the manager's office. You have to have known then that she was involved.'

He shook his head. 'They didn't,' he said firmly. 'They said you'd been harassing a vulnerable old woman, but they never said who or where. And, anyway, you had to admit you were doing a pretty good job of making everyone believe you were crazy without help.'

She shook her head, it was all just too unbelievable. Then she gave a short laugh, her eyes narrowing as she looked at him. 'You had to have been in on it,' she said, 'what about the wine bottles?' He lifted his head and looked at her, puzzled. 'Don't play games with me, Paul. You know damn well what I'm talking about.' She waved a hand toward the cupboard. 'I emptied the cupboard of bottles and then suddenly *hey, presto*, it was full again.'

His face cleared. 'Believe it or not, that was supposed to help.' Seeing her disbelieving face, he continued. 'You thought I didn't notice how much you were drinking, but I did. For goodness sake, Diane,' he said, his lips curling in a sneer, 'do you think I'm stupid? That I wouldn't guess why your breath often had a minty smell, that I didn't hear you opening the fridge door as soon as I'd left the damn room. When I filled the cupboard with the empties, I thought you'd know that it was me, that I knew about your drinking and maybe,' he shrugged, 'slow down or give up.'

Her sceptical look continued. 'You didn't think that maybe speaking to me about it would be easier than playing damn stupid games?'

Paul held his hands up. 'We haven't talked for a long time, Diane.'

She opened her mouth to argue and closed it again. He was right, of course, they hadn't. He was also right, putting the empty bottles in the cupboard had been a stupid idea, but it had worked. She pushed on. 'What about the crying?'

He was rubbing his eyes, he stopped and looked at her. 'What crying?'

Pulling out a chair, she sat heavily. He really didn't know anything about it, he'd no reason to lie now. 'It doesn't matter.' She was wrong about so many things, it seemed she was wrong about this too. He looked sad, weary. She supposed it hadn't been easy on him since her breakdown. 'How long?' she asked.

He didn't insult her by asking what she meant. 'Over a year,' he admitted. 'She's a marketing analyst, she works in the same building. I saw her in the lift a few times, and then one day I asked her if she were free for coffee. And that's all it was for a month or so, just coffee. We talked about work, problems we were having with staff, things like that. It was good to talk. We'd been meeting for a couple of months before it became anything more.' He took a deep breath, 'I knew then I wanted to be with her. I was going to tell you, ask you for a divorce, but—' He broke off and shook his head.

Diane was still trying to deal with the idea he'd been seeing another woman for a year. She blinked away tears and looked at him in disgust. 'Did I know? Was that what made me have a breakdown?' She hated the thought of being so weak.

He shook his head quickly. 'No, you didn't know anything about it. We were careful.'

Careful. She looked at him. Was she supposed to be grateful? 'You were going to ask me for a divorce? When?'

'Several months ago,' he said, hanging his head.

Several months ago! She frowned, trying to unlock some of the memories that were still hidden. 'But something happened, and you didn't?' She stared at him, trying to read his expression. 'Why don't you just tell me, Paul?' she said quietly.

His eyes were bleak and there was a crack in his voice. 'I… can't, I just can't, Diane.'

A memory flashed into her head: her waiting for Paul, bursting with news, expecting to see a look of delight on his face when she told him, stunned by the sight of a quick flash of dismay that he'd struggled to cover. A memory; it faded before she could get a grip on it.

Lost in her reflections, it took a while to realise that Paul was speaking. 'Sorry,' she said. 'I missed what you said.'

His groan was part frustration, part irritation. 'I said Emma will be better off with us. Me and Pam. We can offer her stability, a calm family environment. I think you still need more help than we realised.' Then he added, reassuringly, 'You'll be able to visit, of course. Maybe, have her for a weekend now and then, once you're doing better.'

He was wearing his most sincere expression. She shot him a sharp look. He was good; she'd almost been fooled, almost convinced she wasn't well enough. With a twist of her lips, she thought of the other papers she'd found in his desk drawers, the ones she'd so carefully photographed.

'Does the CEO know you're creaming money off some of the company accounts?' she asked, watching as his face changed from eager and sincere to confused and then worried. She gave a quiet laugh. She stood, walked to the sofa, crossed her arms and looked down her nose at him. 'You're a cheat and a thief, and you will *never* get custody of *my* daughter.'

He stood, his face reddening with rage, spittle gathering at the corners of his mouth. Grabbing her by her arms, he shook her. 'You stupid cow! You think any judge in his right mind would hand Emma into your care, with your history and your recent antics.'

She felt his fingers bruise, refusing to let him see he was hurting her. 'I'm a good mother,' she almost snarled, lifting her eyes to meet his.

'Really?' he said, dragging out the single word in a sneer as he increased the pressure on her arms. 'Not such a great mother to Emma's sister, though, were you?'

CHAPTER 44

Diane's eyes widened, and she stepped back as his hands fell away. 'What?' She watched as a fleeting look of regret crossed his face.

'I'm sorry,' he said, reaching for her again.

Holding her hands up, she took a step away. The memory that had slipped away came back, with perfect clarity. *I'm pregnant,* she'd said, bubbling with joy, expecting to see it reflected on his face.

'That's why you didn't ask me for a divorce,' she said, staring at him, with shock-widened eyes. 'I was pregnant.' She saw the truth in his eyes, the depth of his betrayal twisting her gut as her hands clasped her belly.

The colour drained from her face as a wave of weakness swept over her. It sent her staggering backward into the wall. She leaned against it, eyes unfocused as she tried to make sense of it all; ragged glimpses of half-buried memories flickering like worn-out film tape.

Then, on a sob, she closed her eyes and saw her, that first time when the midwife handed her over. With slicked-down hair and a crumpled baby face, Diane had taken one look and her heart had sung. 'Jane,' she said, the name bittersweet on her lips. 'You told Emma she was an angel in heaven,' she whispered. 'I didn't understand.'

'That's what the doctors advised me to say,' he said wearily, sitting on the side of the coffee table. 'I didn't know what to do. You were in the clinic, I had to do the best I could. Pam wanted to help, but I didn't want to confuse Emma by bringing another woman into the house. I just kept repeating that Jane was happy as an angel in heaven and then I spent a lot of money on new toys to try to distract her. After a couple of weeks, she didn't ask about her any more.' He frowned and looked at her. 'You remember everything?' She slid down the wall and wrapped her arms around her knees, her mouth opening to make a long, low keening cry that came from somewhere deep in her soul.

She'd been so very tired. When Emma settled down for her afternoon nap, she'd brought Jane into the lounge, fed her and laid her on the sofa beside her. The way she always did. She remembered the sun was shining, and it was warm and cosy. She'd looked at her sleeping baby, smiled and rested her head back, closing tired eyes.

Her body, exhausted, sought comfort, her head drifting to rest on one of the big turquoise cushions, her hand reaching to pull it into place. She'd slept until she heard the front door open, listening without opening her eyes as footsteps went into the family room and then returned. Paul had come home early. She opened her eyes to greet him as he came in.

'Hello, darling,' she'd said.

'Hi,' he'd said, but his voice was puzzled. 'Where's Jane?'

She remembered laughing, thinking he was joking, because she was right there, safe, beside her. She pushed up from her awkward position, shaking the last of the sleepiness away as she heard him ask again, his voice sounding worried.

'Diane, where's Jane?'

She'd seen the look of horror on his face before she'd looked down. The cushion. Somewhere in her exhausted sleep, it had fallen, or she had pulled it down. From the side of it, tiny bluish fingers curled onto a minute mottled palm.

She remembered the sound of loud, agonised screams. And then a blank.

Ragged-edged memories, some clearer than others, came trickling back as if his words had been the key she'd been searching for. The months of pregnancy, the easy labour, the beautiful baby. Jane. Her second child.

'I fell asleep,' she said, her voice low and trembling. 'I remember.'

Chewing his lower lip, he nodded reluctantly. 'I'd been away overnight. A conference. You were only home from the hospital a few days, but you said you could manage. But I felt a little guilty so came home early the next day.' He gulped and took a steadying breath. 'I pushed you out of the way,' he said, dropping his face into his hands as his voice broke. After a pause, he took his hands away. Tears were running down his face. 'She was lying there, like a little doll, but when I touched her…' He held his hands out. 'Sometimes I can still feel her, that icy coldness that said there was nothing I could do.' He wiped his face with his shirt sleeve. 'You started to scream,' he said, 'and you didn't stop, not even when the doctor came and gave you a sedative.' He looked at her, shaking his head. 'I've never heard such an awful sound. The doctor rang someone and very quickly an ambulance came and took you away. The consultant told me later that they had to give you an extraordinarily high dose of drugs to stop you screaming. You were hysterical, inconsolable.' He paused again, taking a deep breath to steady himself. 'When you eventually woke up, you'd blocked it all out. The pregnancy, Jane, the last day. Everything.' He shrugged. 'They said it was a coping mechanism. That your memories would eventually return.'

'And they have been coming back for a while,' she said. 'I just didn't realise what they were.'

'It was so easy for you,' he said, his voice bitter. 'You were tucked away from all the grief and trauma. The police, the social workers, the endless questions I had to deal with on my own. And my own grief, and Emma's. You left me with all of it. And,' he shook his head, anger in his eyes, 'I just couldn't forgive you for Jane. I was just waiting until she was a little older to tell you

I wanted a divorce. After her…' he gulped, '…death. I wanted to tell you but when I mentioned it to the therapist in the clinic, he said it would jeopardise your recovery if I subjected you to more trauma. So…'

She gave a sad smile. 'But you got tired waiting, didn't you?'

He closed his eyes briefly. 'Not me, it was Pam. I swear, I didn't know anything about what she was doing until today. She won't bother you again.' Meeting her eyes, he bit his lip and said, 'I love her, Diane.' He stood. 'I'll move out, it's not fair keeping her waiting any longer. She wants children of her own. We can come to some kind of amicable arrangement about custody of Emma.' He looked away. 'I'll just pack a few things to take with me and arrange to get everything else in a few days.'

She stayed seated while he went upstairs, listening to his heavy footsteps overhead as he packed to leave her. It was the end of their marriage; the sad thing was she didn't care. All she could think of now, was Jane. There had to be pictures of her somewhere, the photograph of the scan. She remembered the excitement of seeing it. So many questions still to be answered. Had she been cremated? Buried?

Grief curled inside her and the deep shock of loss and guilt at what she'd done. No wonder she had blacked it all out. How was she going to cope with the knowledge that she'd been responsible for Jane's death? The shock was a jolt that seemed to reset her brain and the memories, those ragtag memories, started to form and firm. She gave a sad smile at the memory of Jane's baby-soft skin and shook her head when she remembered frightening Emma. She'd been right, it hadn't been that long ago.

There were bits of that awful night that she would probably never remember. Trauma too horrendous for her brain to deal with. But other parts were coming back.

She felt an uncontrollable anger bubble inside her. When the door opened, Paul stood there with a holdall in his hand and a conciliatory smile on his face. She stood and spat fire. 'Pam rang me, Paul. The night before, did you know that? You'd said you were going to a conference,' she laughed, the sound edging toward hysteria. 'I remember reassuring you that we'd be fine and encouraging you to go.' She stepped closer, raised a hand and, before he could move away, she slapped him across the face, hard enough to make him stagger from the force of it.

'She rang me from the hotel where you'd gone for your sordid little tryst and told me you were just waiting until Jane was a few weeks older and then you were going to leave me for her.'

He tried to step away as she took a step closer, but the wall was behind him. She grabbed his jacket in her two hands. 'I didn't sleep that night, Paul. I was devastated by your betrayal. Babies pick up on moods, did you know that? Jane cried all morning, nothing I did settled her.' She clutched his jacket. 'Her cry, it was piteous and pathetic. It's that cry I've been hearing the last couple of weeks. A memory trying to break through. Do you know what it's like to have that as one of the last memories I have of her?

'It wasn't until after lunch that she cried herself into an exhausted sleep.' Still clutching his jacket, she dropped her head and wept. 'I put her down on the sofa beside me, and I fell asleep too.' The words came thickly through the tears. 'So, don't you ever dare say again that you can't forgive me, Paul, because some of the blame lies with you.'

He looked down at her for a moment, then pulled her hands from his jacket, grabbed his keys from the counter and left without another word. She heard his footsteps on the stairs and, minutes later, the front door slamming.

Long after the sound had faded into the silence of the night, she stood staring out into the hallway. Then, with slow steps, she moved to the lounge, opened the door and went inside.

There was no terror now, just an ineffable sadness. Switching on the light, she looked at the sofa. That explained the missing cushion. Anne had been right. Something awful had happened in here.

Sitting, she felt calmer than she had in a long time. Under the scab of the memory blackout, her mind had learned to cope. Now, laying her hand on the spot where she would have placed her baby, although sorrow and guilt still twisted her heart and she felt a deep, bottomless sense of loss, she knew she would get through it. She cried then, piteous, sad tears for Jane, for her marriage, for herself.

After a few minutes, she snuffled and stood. She took a final look around, switched off the light and shut the door. What was it Paul had said? *We can come to some kind of amicable arrangement about custody of Emma.* He was lying, she could see it in his eyes. He'd present the court with all the ammunition she'd kindly provided him with. It was enough to cast doubts on her sanity, certainly enough to damage her credibility as a mother. She had lost one child, she'd no intention of losing another.

She hadn't looked at the documents she'd photographed in detail. She did now, her brow furrowing. He'd managed to embezzle a large amount of money. Over a million pounds. A thought struck her. Wouldn't keeping such a vast amount of money in a UK bank account give rise to questions he wouldn't want to answer? He'd have had to transfer it abroad somehow. He was an accountant; he'd know how to do this.

Abroad. With a gasp, she dropped the phone and flew up the stairs, almost falling over her feet in haste. The office door was ajar. Inside, it looked as tidy as usual. She dashed to the desk and yanked out the top drawer. Their passports. They were gone. All three of them. He wasn't going to risk her following. She stood a moment, wide-eyed, and then ran back downstairs, grabbing her phone and dialling.

It was answered immediately. 'Emily!' she said, trying to control the panic in her voice. 'Paul has taken Emma's passport. I think he's going to take her and run.'

'He rang a few minutes ago, Diane. He's coming to pick her up in twenty minutes. I wanted him to wait until the morning, but he insisted that the best place for her was with her parents.'

The bastard. 'I'm on my way. Will you have her ready to go? I'll need to get away quickly.' There was a heavy silence. 'Please, Emily, I can't lose her.'

'Get here as fast as you can.'

Diane hung up and redialled. It wasn't answered for a few tense minutes and then a sleepy voice, 'Hello?'

'It's me. Everything has come to a head. I need your help; can you get here as soon as you can?' Her grip on the phone eased when Anne responded immediately.

'On my way.'

Waiting out on the road, she bit her lip as the minutes passed, breathing a sigh of gratitude when Anne's car careened around the corner and screeched to a halt just inches away. 'Quick!' she said, jumping inside. 'Just drive, I'll give you directions.'

She checked the time as Anne shot through a junction against the lights, a flash telling them they'd have to answer for it later. Without wasting words, she filled her in. 'Emma is staying with her teacher, Paul has taken her passport. He's heading there. We have to get there first.'

With a nod, Anne increased speed. Diane checked the time again. Another minute and they'd be there.

As they approached the teacher's house, Diane looked behind them. They needed to have left the cul-de-sac before Paul arrived. If he saw them, he could block the car. Heart beating, she jumped out of the car as it was still moving, stumbling before righting herself and dashing up the pathway to the front door.

It was opened before she got there, a grim-faced Ross standing sentinel. 'You sure we shouldn't just ring the police?' he asked. Emily appeared with a sleeping Emma in her arms. She offered Diane a shaky smile before handing her over, her eyes glistening.

Diane took her daughter gently, pressing her face into her curly hair for just a moment. 'Thank you so much,' she said and, without another word, turned and ran back to the car. She climbed into the back seat with Emma still in her arms.

With a screech of tyres, Anne did a three-point turn and headed back out onto the main road. Diane looked back as they sped away, breathing raggedly and clutching Emma to her. They'd made it.

Once they were a reasonable distance away, Anne slowed to a normal speed. 'You'll be safe in Parkside Gardens,' she said.

They would be. Paul didn't know where Anne lived. She doubted if he even remembered her name. Tomorrow, she'd employ a solicitor and start divorce proceedings. If he agreed to let her have full custody of Emma, to keep the house until she decided what she wanted to do and, of course, maintenance, she'd keep quiet about those dodgy accounts.

She looked down at Emma, still asleep in her arms, felt her warmth and, at the same time, the deep, enduring, sorrowful memory of the other daughter she'd held; her darling, precious Jane. There had been so much pain, so much sorrow. Lifting her head, she met Anne's eyes in the rear-view mirror. So much kindness too. 'I owe you so much,' she said quietly, 'thank you.'

Anne nodded but said nothing.

Diane reached forward and laid a hand on her shoulder. 'You were right, you know, something terrible did happen in that room. When we get home, I'll tell you all about it.'

EPILOGUE

It was a cold night. Diane had wrapped up well, a scarf around her head providing warmth and disguise. She'd found a good place to stand unobserved and she watched as Pam strode along the path to her house, looking as if she hadn't a care in the world.

Sometimes, like tonight, when she went inside, she didn't pull the curtains for a long time. Diane crossed the street to stand in the shadow of a tree and watch as Pam moved across the room to switch on a lamp. Her gut twisted as Paul entered the room, twisted tighter when she saw them kiss. She clutched a branch of the tree for support as she saw Pam throw back her head and laugh, her hand caressing his cheek. *That* woman and *her* husband.

Paul had said he could never forgive her for what happened to Jane, and it seemed they shared the same unforgiving streak. Because Diane would never forgive the woman who had stolen her husband and whose phone call had resulted in the death of her precious baby.

Her grip on the branch tightened as she saw her move to the curtains and stand staring out for a moment before slowly shutting them. She wouldn't have seen her, Diane had become very good at hiding in the shadows.

'Don't worry, Jane,' she whispered into the night. 'I'll make sure she pays for what she's done.' She listened for a moment and a strange smile flickered as, drifting on the slight breeze, she heard the soft gurgle of a child's laughter.

A LETTER FROM VALERIE

Dear Reader,

I'm so pleased you chose to read *The Housewife* and hope you enjoyed how the story unfurled. If you'd like to be among the first to know about future novels, please sign up here:

www.bookouture.com/valerie-keogh

The Housewife was a challenging, and at times, difficult book to write. I cannot begin to understand what it must be like to lose a child, so I hope I managed to convey the intense sorrow that Diane felt, a sorrow so deep and devastating as to rob her of her memory for a while.

If you enjoyed *The Housewife*, it would be much appreciated if you could write an online review. I also love to hear from readers, as it is one of the most enjoyable parts of being a writer, and feedback – both positive and negative – guides my writing. You can join me on Facebook or Twitter – the details are below.

Love,
Valerie

valeriekeoghnovels
@ValerieKeogh1

ACKNOWLEDGEMENTS

There are many people to whom I owe a debt of gratitude, so I'd like to take the opportunity to thank the following:

My readers, for reading, reviewing and commenting. It makes it all worthwhile.

The wonderful Bookouture team who produce my great covers and the amazing marketing graphics. My amazing and always-enthusiastic editor, Jessie Botterill, who makes me a better writer, and the dynamic duo of publicity, Kim Nash and Noelle Holton.

The support and encouragement of my writing friends has, as usual, been constant. I'd especially like to thank Leslie Bratspis for keeping me sane, and Jenny O'Brien whose novel, *The Stepsister*, kept me hugely entertained while I battled with edits.

My family, to whom this book is dedicated.

Printed in Great Britain
by Amazon